MEMORIES FOR SALE

GIACOMO GIAMMATTEO

INFERNO PUBLISHING COMPANY

Print ISBN 978-1-940313-36-8

Electronic ISBN 978-1-940313-35-1

This book is a work of fiction. Names, characters, places, and events herein are either the product of the author's imagination or are used fictitiously. Any resemblance to actual persons, living or dead, is entirely coincidental.

ISBN: 978-1-940313-35-1

❀ Created with Vellum

AUTHOR'S NOTE

I normally write my mysteries in both first and third person point of view (POV), and I distinguish which POV it is by using chapter headings that have images of a gun for third person and a badge or bullet for first person.

This novel was written entirely in third person; however, there are different timelines involved, so the badge represents the timeline featuring the detective and the investigative part of the novel, and the gun represents the other (most of it in the past).

Please note also that the story goes back and forth in time, so please pay attention to the dates at the beginning of chapters.

INTRODUCTION

The future is only as bright as the light that technology bestows on it.

DREAMS REMEMBERED

Washington, D.C., February, 2030

Ellis Piersol spread the morning paper on the table just to the left of his coffee. He hoped it would be refreshing news, but he wasn't expecting it.

Violent Crime Up 37 percent in Nation's Capital

He sighed and went on to read, but saw that other major cities fared no better. Violent crimes were up by 17 percent in New York, 22 percent in Chicago, and 43 percent in Los Angeles.

What the hell was the world coming to?

He finished the article, drained his coffee, then called for a car. He needed to get to the hospital.

Twenty-five minutes later he sat in a chair opposite Megan's bed. An oxygen mask covered her face, and tubes were sticking out of her nose and throat, but at least she was still breathing. That was one thing to be thankful for.

They had brought her in, unresponsive, promising not much of anything. At one point they had even pronounced her dead, but miraculously, she had survived.

She had been in a coma-like state for almost two months, and she hadn't spoken a word, but the prognosis was better than it had been. It still wasn't good, but it was better. At least he had something to pray for. Ellis had been through a lot of shit in his life, including the nasty business of politics, but nothing had prepared him for this. Nothing was worse than seeing his child in a position like this while he sat helpless.

He scooted his chair closer to the bed, then reached out and held her hand. He squeezed in gently. "I'm here for you, baby. Daddy's here. And I'll be here every day until you don't need me to be, although I hope that day never comes. Try to remember the good times, the times we spent together with Mom. She loved you as much as I do. Remember that. Don't forget."

He patted the back of her hand, bent down and kissed her forehead, then whispered goodbye. "Be back tonight, babe."

Four of the best bodyguards in the world waited for Ellis in the hallway. He left the room and joined them, walking down the corridor. A man turned the corner, heading their way.

Dennis Markum, the lead guard, drew his gun and moved forward to intercept the man. "Stop. Who are you? Why are you here?"

The guy held up his hands. "Whoa! I'm reaching for my badge, nothing else. My name is Detective Grant Langley."

Dennis had his gun pointed at Langley. "State your business."

"I'm here to look into the Megan Piersol attack." He then nodded toward Ellis. "Mr. President."

"Are you armed?" Dennis asked.

"Yes. A gun in my holster, nothing else."

Dennis held out his free hand, palm up. "I'll hold it."

Langley opened his coat, exposing the gun, and let Dennis grab it. Afterward, he took a cautious step toward the president. "Mr. President, I'm here about your daughter."

"My men are looking into it," the president said.

"I'm sure they are, sir. But that doesn't let me off the hook. I drew the case, and I have a few questions."

Ellis sighed. "Go ahead."

"How did you learn of the attack, sir?"

"We were notified by one of our agents and by the hospital, shortly afterward. Apparently, someone found her in the bushes not far from Nordstrom, and then they called an ambulance. That's all I know."

"The Nordstrom's entrance to the mall?" Langley asked.

The president nodded.

"Where were her guards?" Langley asked and cast a casual, but accusatory, glance toward Dennis.

"They...let her go into the mall by herself," the president said. "But it wasn't their fault. I okayed it. I'll wish I hadn't for the rest of my life, but I did. And there is no going back."

Langley was busy writing notes when the president started moving. "Listen, Detective. Not much is more important than finding out who did this to my daughter, but I've got a meeting in less than a half an hour. It might qualify."

Langley stepped aside. "Of course, sir. My apologies. And don't worry, we'll find out who did this. I swear."

Dennis handed Langley's gun to one of his men, who lingered behind until the president was out of sight. Then he handed the gun to the detective and ran to catch up.

Ellis got to the Capitol Building a few minutes early. Despite that he hurried in, surrounded by his Secret Service protection. Rich McCabe was in the hall talking when the president entered.

"How is she?" McCabe asked.

"The same. Nothing different."

"Goddamn sin is what it is. Don't worry, sir. They'll get the son of a bitch who did this."

"I'll be happy if they get him," Ellis said, "but I'll be happier if she just comes out of this okay."

"Of course, sir. I'm sorry."

Ellis laid a hand on McCabe's shoulder. "No harm done, Rich. And thanks for asking."

After the normal ceremonial activities, the president stood to speak. "Have you all seen the papers? I hope so. Violent crime is up in almost every major city. And not just by a little bit. We're talking double digits in every location. Some places it was up over 40 percent. Forty percent!"

He let the mumblings roll around the room before continuing. "And I think you *know* what's to blame—these new visors."

"We can't blame a product for what other people do," a representative from Colorado said.

"Really? That's easy for you to say." Ellis looked through his notes. "Denver only had a 10 percent increase in crime. Not nearly as much as other big cities."

"That's not fair to say, Mr. President."

"It might not be fair, but it's true. You people sound like those NRA lobbyists who say guns don't kill, people do."

"It's true," someone shouted from the back of the room.

"Yes. I know it's true. I know that people are the ones who aim the gun and pull the trigger. But it's the gun that holds the bullet."

Ellis took a drink from his glass of water, then placed his hands on the podium. "I'm proposing a ban on the new visors. And I'd like your support."

"A ban? We can't ban that product."

Rich McCabe stood. "Mr. President, we all know of the terrible misfortune that befell your daughter, and we all feel for you, but I have to agree with my esteemed colleague from Colorado. On what basis could we request a ban on the product? Give me one, and I'm with you."

"On the basis that it's evil," Ellis said. "On the basis that it drives men to do things they wouldn't ordinarily do."

"Mr. President, I empathize, but I still don't see how we can do this. The Constitution—"

"To hell with the Constitution," the president said. "Who cares about the Constitution? What is the Constitution anyway? A bunch of words written by ordinary men two hundred-plus years ago." He scanned the room. "Ordinary men. Two hundred years ago."

"You can't say that about the Constitution," one man said.

"I can and I did. These people lived in the eighteenth century. They couldn't possibly have foreseen what's happening now, and they wouldn't have any idea what to do if they could have foreseen it. And I can't imagine they'd approve of it. Imagine yourself trying to write legislation for the year 2230."

Senator McCabe stood again. "As I said, I empathize with you, Mr.

President. But I want to do what's right. We need to protect these people who make the product, no matter who they are. I say we put it to a vote. See who is in favor and who isn't."

Piersol nodded. He knew this was as good as he was going to get. "Show of hands," he said. "All in favor of banning all visors, raise your hand."

Besides the president, only half a dozen others raised their hand, McCabe included.

Afterward, McCabe approached the president and shook his head. "I'm sorry, Mr. President, but it doesn't look good. Perhaps we could increase the police protection? Maybe that would help with statistics?"

Piersol stared at the floor. "We've already done that, Rich. And the cities where we approved increased protection, it did no good. I'm afraid that short of calling out the National Guard in every city, we're not going to do any good. As far as I'm concerned, it's a lost cause."

"Don't despair, sir. We'll think of something."

"We can think all we want, but until we get rid of these damn glasses, we won't make any progress. But thanks for your support. I appreciate it."

McCabe patted his shoulder. "Of course, sir. No problem."

TEENAGE LOVE

Washington, D.C., December 2027

Megan stretched up and gave Justin a peck on the cheek. Then she grabbed his hand and pulled him toward the front door.

"And where do you think you're going?" Her father's voice rang out from near the bottom of the steps.

She turned, face all smiles. Her father was standing at the bottom of the steps with his hand on the railing. "To the mall, Dad. Pentagon City."

"What's so important at the mall? What's wrong with Union Station or Georgetown?"

"Nothing that a few hundred dollars wouldn't cure," Megan said.

Her father laughed. "I guess so, but you're not getting a few hundred dollars; in fact, you're not getting fifty dollars. You've already received your allowance for the month, and you'll get nothing more until Christmas."

"That's why we're going to the mall," she said, then grabbed hold of

Justin again and turned back toward the door. "How did I know that would be your answer?"

"Because you're smart," her father said. "What time are you coming home?"

She sighed, an exasperated sound. "Eleven," she said. "And yes, I know the rules: don't talk to strangers and don't tell anyone who I am."

"You're correct. Those *are* the rules."

"I know I'm correct. I *know* the rules."

"Good, then you know to take Dustyn or Dennis with you."

"No way, Dad. I'm fine. I don't need a bodyguard."

"You need what I say you need," he said, and pulled a phone out of his pocket and dialed.

"Dustyn, it's Ellis. Megan and Justin are going out. She'll need to be accompanied."

"Yes, sir," Dustyn said. "Right on it."

"They're leaving now for the Pentagon City Mall. Make sure someone goes with them and make sure she doesn't lose you. It doesn't have to be you, but someone."

Dustyn raised his voice while he gestured to Dennis, a signal to get moving. "Yes, sir. Megan and Justin, Pentagon City Mall. Yes, sir. Dennis is leaving now."

"And why am I leaving now?" Dennis asked, after Dustyn had hung up the phone.

"Because it's your turn," Dustyn said, then laughed. "Have fun."

Dennis checked that his gun was secure in the holster, then headed for the door."

Dennis tailed Justin closely, turning when Justin did and keeping pace when he sped up. He made no attempt to hide the fact that he was following him. *They could have taken the metro.*

"He's right behind us," Justin said, and laid his hand on her thigh.

Megan turned in her seat and looked behind her. Sure enough, there was Dennis in his black SUV, not a hundred feet behind them. "Son of a bitch, he makes me mad," she said.

"Who? Dennis or your father?"

"Both of them, I guess. They should respect my privacy."

Justin laughed. "You can forget privacy, girl. You're not getting any of that. At least not anytime soon. Not for three more years at least."

"And it's getting worse," Megan said. "We can't even make out without *somebody* peeking over our shoulders."

Justin shrugged. "I know. That part really sucks. I almost shit that night we were at Rock Creek and Dustyn knocked on the window just as I pulled your top down."

Megan laughed. "*You* almost shit. What do you think I did? I wonder if he ever told Dad?"

"Your dad never said anything?"

Megan shook her head. "Not a word. Maybe Dustyn is more discreet than we thought."

"I hope so," Justin said. He let his hand creep upward. "Because I intend to push the limits."

Megan grabbed hold of his wrist and tossed his arm aside. "Keep your hands on the steering wheel," she said. "You don't know how bad my dad can be about stuff like this."

"Point made," Justin said. "I know I don't want to get on the bad side of your dad."

"Come on," Megan said. "You know I'm kidding. He's a pussycat. You don't know him like I do."

"If you say so. But if that's the case, then why the brush-off?"

"Maybe I'm not ready? Did you ever think of that?"

"I thought about it, but I dismissed it as nonsense. You want to do it as much as I do. I can tell."

Megan laughed. "You think so, huh? Well, get your mind out of the gutter and see if you can ditch them," Megan said.

"No way. I might risk copping a feel, but I'm not risking ditching them. It'll be my ass if I try and both of our asses if I succeed."

"Just as well," Megan said. "I doubt if you'd have lost them anyway. They're used to following people."

"Why does your dad send them? He's got to know it pisses you off."

"Because he's the goddamn president," Megan said. "And he's used to people doing what he says. That's why."

SENATOR RICHARD MCCABE

Washington, D.C., December 2027

The trip to Pentagon City went as expected, with Justin and Megan traipsing all over the place and Dennis following not twenty feet behind.

Sometime around eight-thirty Dennis was joined by another agent that Megan didn't know, but he was easy to spot as an agent—at least for her he was. Maybe she'd gotten used to them—their stiff demeanor, almost-identical dress mode, and slight, but noticeable gun bulge under the upper-right or left-hand side of their jacket.

"Don't look now," Megan whispered, "But Dennis now has company. We've got two sets of eyes on us."

"Are you saying that even the call of nature won't let me steal a kiss?" Justin asked.

Megan laughed. "I'm afraid not. I guess you'll have to behave."

Justin sighed. "I guess so," he said. "Another night of frustration."

Megan playfully tapped his arm. "Get used to it, Buster. You've got another few years, minimum."

Pentagon City mall

Justin and Megan shopped in a few clothing stores geared toward teenagers then, as they were heading to the third floor, the loudspeaker announced the closing of the mall in a few minutes.

Justin turned to face Megan. "We might as well be going," he said. "I need to get back anyway."

Megan looked at her watch. "We've got fifteen minutes. Let's wait."

"Fifteen minutes isn't enough time to do anything. And like I said, I have to get home."

Megan exhaled sharply. "Fine. Just take me home."

Not long afterward, the guards opened the gates to allow Justin access. He drove through, dropped Megan off—making sure to walk her inside—then got back into his car and drove home. It was a half-hour trip, but he didn't mind; it gave him time to think by himself. In fact, he usually turned his cell phone off during the drive so he wouldn't be disturbed.

Things with Megan were moving too fast yet not fast enough, and he didn't like it. He wanted in her pants, no doubt about that. Who wouldn't? She was a fox.

And he *did* like her, just not in the way she wanted him to. But because of who she was—or more accurately, who her father was—the relationship was more complex than most. He didn't dare do anything to upset her, or it would cause a scene, and he couldn't do anything physical with the Secret Service always following them. He was even afraid to talk about it on the phone, fearing that someone might be listening. It made the prospect of getting laid a far-off dream, and he didn't know if he wanted to wait that long.

It took Justin five minutes longer than expected to get home, but that was all right, it was still an acceptable time. His phone began ringing as soon as he turned it on. He answered just before opening the door. "Hello?"

"Where have you been? I've been calling."

"I was driving home. Christ, I just dropped you off."

"Justin, is that you?" came a voice from the other room.

"Hang on, Megan. My dad's calling." He put Megan on hold by hitting the mute button. "Yeah, it's me, Dad. I just got here. And I'm on the phone with Megan," he added.

"Well hang up, for God's sake. You've been with her all day. I need to talk to you about something."

"All right," Justin said, frustration in his voice. He hit the button to take the call off mute. "Megan, I'll have to call you later. My dad wants to see me about something."

"All right, but don't forget. No matter how late it is. I'll be up."

"Okay. See ya."

Justin popped into the kitchen full of smiles. "What do you need, Dad?"

"I just wanted to remind you of what day it is tomorrow."

Justin raised his head and sighed. "I *know*, Dad. You don't have to remind me every year."

"Really? I don't have to remind you? I don't see any flowers. No wreaths for the graves. When did you plan on getting those? Or didn't you plan on it?"

"I planned on picking mine up about the same time as you, from the *same* flower shop." Justin saw the surprised expression on his father's face. "Yeah. I *did* get the flowers; in fact, according to Matt, who works there, I got them *before* you did. And for your information, I've already made plans to take Megan to the cemetery at lunchtime. I'm actually *going* there, not sending a driver to place the flowers in front of the headstone."

"I'm sorry," McCabe said. "I didn't mean—"

"Yes, you did mean it. And no, I won't forgive you." Justin ran from the kitchen and headed for the stairs. "Goodnight."

He slammed the door to his bedroom, flopped on the king-sized bed, and dialed Megan using the phone on the nightstand.

She picked up immediately. "Yes, this is Megan. Who is this?"

"Cut the shit, Megan. It's me."

"About time," she said. "I've been waiting half the night."

"Bullshit. It's been fifteen minutes."

"Then maybe I should change my attitude. Justin! Thanks for calling. I was sitting here doing nothing. What are you doing?"

"I'm talking to some snotty bitch that I spoke to a few minutes ago. And she's acting like it's been a week."

Megan laughed. "You sound a little grumpy. Anything wrong?"

Justin presumed she was going to ignore his comment about how short a time it had been since they spoke. "Nothing's wrong. Just my dad. He's a pain in the ass. He was already giving me shit about the cemetery, and he didn't even ask if I was going."

"Did you tell him we're going tomorrow?"

"Yeah, I told him, but it was an after-the-fact type tell. I had to use that to shut him up. He jumped in on me, assuming I wasn't going. Then, when I told him I had already planned it, he had nothing to say. No apologies either."

"God, parents are a pain in the ass," she said.

"You're right. If I didn't think we'd end up living with one of them, I'd suggest we get married."

"Maybe we should," Megan said. "Get married, I mean."

"We will. But not yet. It's not the right time."

"When is the right time? You've been saying that for months."

"I know, but it's *not* the right time. Neither one of us has a decent job. We're not even out of school. And I don't want to rely on either of our fathers for support. Besides, I don't think I'm ready yet."

Megan laughed. "You're right about relying on them. But at least your father gives you money. And what do you mean, "you're not ready yet?" How can you say that?"

"Megan, we're not even out of high school. If we don't want to live with our parents, what are we going to do? And as far as my father giving me money, he only does it so he doesn't have to spend time with me. I look at it in a different light. At least your father spends time with you."

"I'll take the money," Megan said.

"And I'll take the time," Justin said. "And another thing, we don't yet know if we're sexually compatible. We *should* try that out."

Megan laughed. "Dream about it. In the meantime, I'll see you tomorrow. Luv ya."

"Me too," Justin said. "See ya tomorrow. And don't forget we're going to the cemetery."

CLINICAL RESULTS

Washington, D.C., December 2027

Ginesh scanned the results on his computer screen then glanced at Nancy. "Three point one percent," he said.

Nancy sighed. "I got three point six. Not much different."

"What was it last time?" Ginesh asked.

Nancy tapped a few keys on the keyboard, then squinted as a new screen appeared. "Three point four."

"So nothing significant," Ginesh said.

"Not enough to matter. We needed a big jump. Something over 12 percent."

"And we knew that wasn't happening. We haven't seen more than a 1-percent deviation since we started."

"And that was a looooong time ago," Nancy said.

"Tell me about it. Raji wasn't even pregnant when we started."

The door to the lab opened and Barney Franklin, the vice president of RA (regulatory affairs) and clinical, walked in. "Anything new, Ginesh?"

Ginesh lowered his head, as if staring at the floor, then shook it slowly from side to side. "Not a thing."

"It's the next to the last week of the trial. We need *something.*" Barney said.

"I know that, but there's nothing new. I can't fabricate numbers. This trial produced almost identical results as the last time."

"So another failure," Barney said, and slammed his fist on the corner of Nancy's desk. "What the hell is it going to take to get something to work?"

"Sometimes things just don't work," Nancy said. "The brain is complex."

"I'll tell you what's *not* complex," Barney said. "The goddamn stock market. And if we don't get something going soon, that IPO isn't going to be worth shit, which means your stock won't be worth shit. And most importantly, *my* stock won't be worth shit. So get something going. Now!"

Barney walked around the lab, shoving things aside and kicking at anything in his way. "If we don't do something soon, then we're all going to be looking for new jobs. I don't know about you, but I don't want to go through that turmoil. There's a snowball's chance in hell that I'd find a suitable job in D.C., and I don't want to move."

"Me neither," Ginesh said. "Don't worry. We'll get something."

"I don't know how. You've only got a week and a half left."

"Like I said. We'll get it."

Barney headed for the door. "Then you better get busy. Let me know if anything breaks."

The door slammed behind Barney as he left. Nancy turned to Ginesh. "What the hell did you say that for? We're not going to find anything in a week and a half. You know that."

"Then we turn the tables in our favor."

"What? How?"

"I don't know. Maybe we increase the dosage and see what happens."

"Are you nuts? We can't indiscriminately increase the dosage. There are guidelines."

"Screw the guidelines. I'm not moving. And it's like Barney said, it's doubtful if any of us would find another job here. This isn't a biotech haven."

Nancy thought about her roommate and all of her local ties. "I don't want to move either, but what choice do we have?"

"We do what I said—increase the dosage of the drug and see if it affects anything. What do we have to lose?"

"Somebody could die. That's what we've got to lose. We have no idea what a dosage increase will do—how it will affect people, what adverse effects might happen."

Ginesh scoffed. "Have you looked at the people in the trial? They're old. They've had strokes. If they die, they die. It's not our fault."

Nancy shook her head. "Are you kidding me? It *will* be our fault if one of them dies because of the drug. Doesn't that bother you?"

Ginesh could see he was getting nowhere with his argument. "Okay, forget I said anything, but I hope you like living in California or New Jersey, because that's likely where we'll end up."

"I don't want to move, but I can live anywhere as long as my conscience is clear."

"I guess you're right," Ginesh said. "But let's give it the best we can. We'll work like hell until it's over. Who knows, maybe we'll get lucky."

"Maybe," Nancy said, and she started back in on her number crunching.

At the end of the day, Ginesh and Nancy left, walking out together. "See you tomorrow," Ginesh said.

"Yeah, see ya'," Nancy said, and got into her car and drove off.

Ginesh waited for Nancy to leave, then he waited another fifteen minutes. When he was certain that no one was around, he surreptitiously re-entered the lab and replaced the normal dosage with one of a higher quantity.

I'm not about to move to California.

∼

The bell rang signaling lunchtime, and the kids poured out of their classes. Megan rushed toward the parking lot and found Justin waiting. He was leaning against a light pole about fifty feet from the building.

"You been here long?" she asked as she ran across the parking lot.

Justin stepped toward his car and opened the door for her. "Only a minute. Hurry up, though. We don't have much time."

Megan slid in the passenger-side seat and buckled up. Justin jumped behind the wheel. "We need to pick up the flowers first," he said. "Then we'll drop them off and scoot back here."

Justin drove to the flower shop, got his flowers, and then sped to the cemetery. He passed his father's limo driver on the way. "There goes my dad's show of love and dedication."

"He means well," Megan said.

"Like hell, he does. If he meant well, he'd deliver the flowers himself. Not send a driver."

"Isn't it better than not getting flowers at all?"

"No," Justin said. "At least if he didn't get them he'd be showing his honesty. He just gets the flowers so he can take a picture of them sitting in front of the headstone. Then he can display it in his office to look good." Justin looked at Megan. "He does that, you know. He has the driver take a picture of the flowers in front of the grave, then he gets it framed and sets it on his desk."

"Okay. I have to admit, that's pretty bad," Megan said.

Justin parked, then he and Megan walked through the cemetery to the plot where his mother was buried.

"I don't mean to be rude, but how was it she died?" Megan asked.

"That's not rude. At least you cared enough to ask. She was hit by a drunk driver on her way home from shopping."

"That's terrible," Megan said.

Justin laid the flowers in front of the gravestone next to the ones his father had sent. Then he knelt and said a prayer. Megan did likewise.

When they finished, they stood and started walking back to the car. "We can't take too long," Justin said. "If I miss geometry class one more time, I think it'll affect my grades."

Megan bent and picked up a handful of snow. She formed it into a snowball and threw it at Justin. It smashed on the back of his coat. "What? Your average will drop from a ninety-five to a ninety-four?"

He laughed. "Smart ass," he said, then he ran for the car. Megan followed suit.

THE MEETING AFTER THE MEETING

Washington, D.C., January 2028

Barney hung around after the monthly board meeting, hoping to talk to Keith. When Susan, the vice president of marketing, left, Barney addressed Keith in a voice not much more than a whisper.

"Keith, you got a minute?"

Keith looked to the door, wondering what the secretive tone was about. "Sure, what do you need?"

"Trial results are not good. It's not over yet, but it's only a week and a half, and I doubt anything will change."

"Not good, how?"

"I mean not good, as in they are no better than the previous drug. In some respects, it's even worse."

Keith slapped the palm of his hand on the conference table. "Shit! I was hoping for more."

"We all were," Barney said. "Even a minor improvement…"

"We needed a hell of a lot more than a minor improvement. We needed a home run."

Keith glanced around again. "Who's running the trial?"

"Ginesh and Nancy," Barney said.

"Tell them we need to see results, and I mean *good* results."

"I already told them. I made it as clear as I could."

"Then make it clearer. Do whatever you have to, but get me results that I can take to the board meeting next month. If you don't, there will likely not be another board meeting."

"Yes, sir. You got it," Barney said, and he walked out of the conference room, closing the door behind him.

Keith sat in one of the chairs, wondering what to do. There was no way results would come in fast enough, even if Barney played with the numbers. And the company needed money badly.

Rich McCabe came to mind, bringing some of their earlier conversations to the forefront. McCabe always had interest in neurological research. Maybe he could provide some funding?

Keith pulled out his phone and looked up McCabe's number, then pushed the button to dial him. A few seconds later, McCabe answered.

"Keith? Is that you, you old fox?"

"Obviously you know. How are you?"

"I'm doing fine. The question is how are you, and what do you want?"

"Just called to say hi," Keith said.

"Bullshit. You've never called anyone just to say hi. You want something, and it must be important for you to call in the middle of the day."

Keith laughed. "Okay, you caught me. I called because I thought we could help each other."

"How so?"

"You've told me in the past that you had some interest in neurological research. We just might have common ground."

"In what way?"

Keith paused, took a sip of water from a half-full bottle left on the table by someone. "I need money. You need...something. Maybe I could provide what you need and you could provide what I need."

"In other words, I give you money in exchange for you trying to solve my neurological problems?"

"In essence, yes."

There was a long silence while McCabe apparently thought. "How much?"

Keith got excited, but he knew he dared not show his emotions. "I don't know, maybe ten million."

"That's a lot of money, Ratcliff."

"That depends on how you look at it and who's looking."

McCabe laughed. "Let me think about it. I'll call you."

"Don't wait too long," Keith said. "There are other people with money."

McCabe laughed. "Don't try to mess with me, Ratcliff. If you could have gotten that money from someone else, you'd have already called them."

Keith laughed. "Okay, McCabe. How about we meet for coffee? You name the place."

"You know where the Starbucks is on Pennsylvania Avenue? I think it's in the two hundred block."

"Yeah, I know it. By the bank. How about seven-thirty tomorrow morning?"

"Make it eight. I like to sleep a little."

"Okay," Keith said. "See you tomorrow."

Keith sat at a table near the door. He had arrived ten minutes early and was already on his second cup of coffee when McCabe pulled up.

The senator parked about halfway down the block, then got out, wrapped a scarf around his neck and walked briskly to the coffee shop.

"About time," Keith said when McCabe walked in. Then he stood to shake hands. "Good to see you again, Rich. It's been too long."

"I'd imagine when you're looking for ten million dollars, an hour is too long."

Both of them laughed, then Keith asked, "What are you drinking? I'll get it."

"Tall latte, but with a double shot. I need the jolt today."

Keith returned a couple of minutes later with the drink for McCabe and another one for himself. He handed McCabe his drink then sat in the chair across from him. "Last time we met, you said you might need some things done. Things of a neurological nature."

"What did you have in mind?" McCabe asked.

"That's what I'm asking you. You know what we do—neurological research. If you've got an interest, I'm listening. Tell me what you want, and if it's something I think we can do, I'll tell you. If we can't, I'll tell you that, too."

McCabe nodded. "You know I'm the head of the committee that funds military research."

Keith nodded as he sipped his coffee, but he kept his eyes focused on McCabe. "I remember."

"We've been searching for a drug that would allow us to "persuade" or "suggest" things to people, like foreign diplomats. We need to be able to implant ideas in their heads, so to speak."

"Pretty radical stuff," Keith said.

McCabe nodded. "We have some pretty amazing nanotechnology that can do far-fetched things, but so far, we haven't been able to crack this problem. I think we're missing the chemical aspect. Ideally, it would be fast acting, something that would work within hours. We might be able to work with it took a little longer, but nothing major."

"What makes you think we could do that?" Keith asked.

"I'm not saying you can, but you could try. If successful, it will make you rich. Which I would hope means that it would make me rich as well."

Keith laughed as he took another sip of his coffee, then bit into his bagel. "Same old McCabe. I *knew* there had to be something in it for you."

"It wouldn't be fair if the split wasn't even."

"In addition to the funding, you'd have to cover the cost of the trial," Keith said. "I can't afford the upfront money."

"Don't worry about that," McCabe said. "That's what I'm here for. I'll send the forms over to your office. Once you get them, fill them out, wait a week or two and you'll have your money."

"What about the FDA?" Keith asked. "Are we going to have trouble there?"

McCabe shook his head. "You remember Porter Kelley?"

"From back in college? Yeah."

"His little brother is head of the FDA."

"No way! Little Teddy?"

"That's him," McCabe said. "But he goes by Theodore now. So if you meet him, make sure to address him properly."

"Sounds easy enough," Keith said.

"As easy as taking money from the government," McCabe said, and laughed.

THE RESULTS ARE IN

Washington, D.C., January 2028

Everyone was in attendance when Barney entered the meeting. "Good morning," he said as he made his way toward the front of the room. "It's Tuesday. Time to update your résumés."

"What's that supposed to mean?" the scientist next to Ginesh asked.

"It means that if we don't have positive news by the end of next week, we'll be out of money in a month."

Murmurs rolled around the room, disrupting the silence. "Any chance of funding?" Nancy asked.

"None that are realistic," Barney said. He seemed to give it more thought, then said, "Maybe one. Keith told me about a possibility dealing with neurological research. But it seems like a long shot."

"If we're going to be looking for job, can we count on you for recommendations?" a scientist next to Nancy asked.

"Of course. Pick up one of my cards on your way out. It has my email and cell phone number on it. You can use that for references. And we'll have an outplacement advisor working with HR next week, starting on Wednesday."

"What's the possibility Mr. Ratcliff was talking about?" Ginesh asked.

"Something to do with making a person receptive to suggestions. I'm sure it's government related; Keith has a lot of ties there. And besides, the government is always looking for a way to get people to do things that they don't want to do."

"Despite the sinister implications, tell us more of what he wants," Ginesh said. "None of us want to leave the city." Ginesh looked around at the other scientists. "At least, I don't think we do."

Barney waited until it got quiet in the room, then he said, "We need a drug to make people susceptible to suggestions, like before they go to bed or something. I think the government wants to have a way of extracting secrets from foreign diplomats. It's cold-war spy stuff, but it still happens today. It's a fact of life."

"So nothing's changed?" Nancy said.

Barney shook his head. "Nothing—including our test results. Now get to work and find me *something* I can take to Mr. Ratcliff."

 week had gone by, and Ginesh and Nancy were once again busy crunching numbers, doing the final results of the clinical trial for stroke patients.

Ginesh was busy entering data when Nancy interrupted. "I'm halfway done and not much has changed. I don't see any improvement."

"I don't see any either, but there *is* one difference. I've run across notes on twenty-one patients who reported having vivid dreams—"

"What's the big deal with vivid dreams? I have them all of the time."

Ginesh sighed. "If you had let me finish...They were having vivid dreams that were identical to what they were thinking about right before going to bed. That's similar to what Barney said they were looking for."

Nancy stopped what she was doing and turned to face Ginesh. "What? Let me see the reports."

Ginesh handed her the papers. She leaned back in the chair and began reading. "Twenty-one is a pretty significant number. I wouldn't have raised an eyebrow if it had only been a few, but twenty-one..."

"Is a lot," Ginesh said. "My thoughts exactly. Especially since this hasn't happened before."

"But what's different? Why now?" Nancy said. "If you look at these results, you have to wonder why. Why did something change now? Same people, same circumstances, same..."

She set the papers on the desk and glared at Ginesh. "You upped the dosage, didn't you? You did it without telling me." She stood, walked over, and poked him in the chest. "You son of a bitch. If somebody dies, it's on your ass."

Ginesh held up his hands, as if in surrender. "Nobody's going to die. Besides, it's like I said, they're old anyway."

"They have a goddamn life," Nancy said. "Some of them have fun. They laugh. They read. They joke and play games. It's not your call as to who lives and who dies. It's your job to keep them as safe as you can."

"Okay. We'll worry about safety if something happens. If not, we'll reap the rewards."

"What rewards? We haven't gotten anything. All we've got are some people having dreams, for Christ's sake. What good is that? We don't even know what caused the dreams to start, although we might presume it was your increased dosage."

Ginesh threw up his hands. "It's not that they're having dreams, Nancy. It's what they're having dreams *about*. They're dreaming about their thoughts just prior to going to sleep. I know that some people do that and it's not that uncommon, but if you read the notes, these people didn't do that before, which means *something* changed. And that something might be the drug. And if it's because of the increased dosage, great. If it's not that, we'll find out what it is."

"Okay, even if I buy into your theory, so what? What good does that do us?"

"Think. You heard Barney at the meeting. Keith is working on a new research contract, and I think we can safely assume it's for the government. They're looking at neurological *suggestion*. This might tie in somehow. If these people are dreaming about things they were thinking about just prior to bed, isn't that a form of suggestion? Maybe we're only a few tweaks away from something that works."

"Yeah, and we might be a few years away, too. Let's not get ahead of ourselves."

"How are we going to test this further without knowing exactly what they want?"

"I don't know yet, but we need to tell Barney about it; he'll know what to do. I'm sure that once he knows what is involved, he'll tell us what we need to know."

Ginesh caught up with Barney in the parking lot after work. He explained the data results, and he added his interpretation. "If these people are dreaming about what they were just thinking prior to bedtime, that's a form of *suggestion* isn't it?"

Barney leaned back against the car and folded his hands across his chest. "That's a good question, Ginesh. I'll mention it to Keith. At this point anything is worth exploring."

Ginesh smiled. "Good. I don't want to update my résumé."

"Me neither," Barney said. "I'll get back to you in a few days. Have a good night."

"You too, Mr. Franklin. And thanks for listening."

"Nonsense. Thank *you* for thinking."

SHE'S AWAKE

Washington, D.C., February 2030

Ellis sat in the back seat, wringing his hands. Dennis was driving. This was one of those times—one of many times—when he wished things were different. If he were driving, he'd be going eighty miles per hour, not sixty. Sure, he might get arrested, but that's a chance he'd take. His daughter was awake after two months in a coma. *And Dennis is driving sixty?*

"Can't you go any faster, Dennis?"

"Yes, sir, we could, but I'm afraid we might lose the cars following us. I'd rather be safe, sir."

Ellis sighed. *Rather be safe. A practice he'd preached all of his life, now he was proposing to ignore it.* "You're right, Dennis. I'm sorry for suggesting otherwise."

"No problem, sir. I understand."

"Maybe I should call that detective, the one who met us in the hospital?"

"I don't know if it will do any good, sir, but it can't hurt."

Ellis looked in his wallet for the man's card. He couldn't even remember his name.

"Langley, sir, his name was Grant Langley."

Ellis smiled. "I don't know how you remembered that, Dennis. I forget someone's name the moment I leave them."

Dennis smiled. "It was easy sir. Grant, as in President Grant, and Langley, as in Langley, Virginia, where the CIA headquarters are."

"Ah, I see," said Ellis, but his mind was elsewhere. He located the card then dialed the number.

"Langley."

"Detective Langley, this is Ellis Piersol."

"Mr. President! I never expected to hear from you."

"I thought I should call. The hospital said that Megan is awake. She's not talking *much*, but she *is* talking."

"I'll be there in twenty minutes, sir. Thank you for calling."

L angley walked at a brisk pace, but slowed as he turned each corner. The last thing he wanted was to startle one of the Secret Service and have them fire on him.

As he rounded the last corner, he saw two of them standing in front of Megan's door. He slowed, then called out to them. "Detective Grant Langley," he said. "The president asked me to come."

One of the guards stepped forward. "Keep coming, Detective. Just don't make any unusual moves."

Langley nodded. He kept his hands at his sides until he reached the room, then he knocked on the door before entering. "Detective Langley," he said, to announce his presence.

"Come in," Dennis said.

When Langley entered, two more Secret Service agents had guns pointed at him. Langley had his hands at his sides still. "I left my gun in the car," he said. "I'm unarmed."

Dennis looked to one of his men, then gestured to Langley with a sideways twist of his head. "Check him."

The man frisked Langley, then gave a thumbs-up signal to Dennis, who then put his gun away.

Ellis reached out his hand to shake. "Sorry for all of this."

"I understand, sir," Langley said. "Can't be too careful."

"She hasn't spoken since I've been here," the president said. "She seems to have had a few waking moments, but drifted back. Since then, nothing else."

"I'm sorry to hear that, sir. I know how high your hopes must have been."

The president sat, but Langley continued to stand. "Sir, if you don't mind, I had a few questions."

"Go ahead."

"Do you know why Megan was at the mall that night?"

"Just shopping," he said. "I think it was a little last-minute Christmas shopping combined with an early start on spring and summer shopping."

"Did she go there often?" Langley asked.

"Yes, though usually not alone, and usually with an agent. As I said the last time, it was my doing that no agent was with her."

"And if she went with someone, who would it be?"

"Her boyfriend, Justin McCabe, Senator McCabe's son."

"I see," Langley said. He then looked to Dennis. "Were there any witnesses or surveillance cameras?"

"No witnesses. And we've already pulled surveillance," Dennis said, "as I'm sure you have. But the spot where Megan was attacked was a blind spot. Cameras didn't see anything."

Langley nodded. "You're right about that. I checked every one of the store's cameras and got nothing. I also checked video in the subway after the fact and ran down those leads in case the person who did this escaped using the metro. We're still working on a few, but so far we haven't gotten anything of value."

Langley made a move toward his jacket, then must have thought better. "I'm reaching for a notebook," he said.

Dennis nodded. "Go on."

Langley pulled out a notebook and a pencil. "I appreciate the cooperation, sir, and I know you said she went alone, but do you know if she was supposed to meet anyone there? It's my experience that teenagers seldom go to the mall themselves; they're usually with someone."

Dennis started to answer, but the president held up his hand. "You're right. I agree with that. And if anyone would know, it would be her boyfriend, Justin. He wasn't with her, but he might know if she planned to meet anyone."

Langley started writing. "Justin McCabe?"

"Yes, as I mentioned earlier, he's Senator McCabe's son. He's a nice boy. He and Megan have been seeing each other for more than a year now."

"Do you have his contact information, sir?"

"I'm sure Dennis can get that for you."

"I'll get it to you tomorrow," Dennis said. "We have your card."

"Great," Langley said. "Do you know why he wasn't with your daughter that night? From my own experience, teenagers who are seeing each other are seldom apart."

"Dennis?" the president said.

"I don't remember, sir," Dennis said to the president. Then he turned to Langley. "I'll check the files before I call you tomorrow, Detective. I remember asking, and I recall being satisfied with the answer, but I don't remember what that answer was."

"It would be a big help if you could share whatever you have," Langley said. "That way I won't have to keep asking."

Dennis fidgeted and shifted his weight from one foot to the other. "I don't know—"

"Give him what he needs," the president said. "Anything that might help to find this person."

"Yes, sir," Dennis said, then he stared at Langley. "I'll send the files over by courier tomorrow. You'll have *everything*."

"Thanks," Langley said. "I'll do the same. You never know, there might be something in mine you could use."

Ellis looked to Megan, then back to Langley and Dennis. He lowered his voice. "I've been sitting here listening to both of you talk about leads and surveillance and such, but neither of you have mentioned anything solid. Am I to infer that we have nothing more than when we started? We know the spot she was found, but nothing else."

Dennis lowered his head. "I hate to say it, but I'm afraid so, sir."

Ellis punched the drawer of the nightstand next to him. "How is it you people can solve complex plots to blow something up but you can't find a goddamn mugger?"

"Sir, the more complex a plot is, the more evidence there is left to trace. The trail is more visible. A mugging is just that—a mugging. It might be an act of random violence or it could be planned. We won't know until we catch the guy. And we *will* catch the guy, sir. I promise."

"I add my promise to Dennis', Mr. President. I'm not going to stop until we find out who did this."

"I'd like to think we'll find him," Ellis said. "It's a sorry state of affairs when something like this happens, and we can't find out what caused it or who did it."

Langley looked at his watch, then up to the president. "Sir, it's been almost an hour and she hasn't woken yet. I've got to get going soon, if—"

"Go on. Do what you have to do. We'll call you if she wakes again."

Langley smiled, then shook hands with Dennis. "Thank you for bringing me in on this. You won't regret it."

Dennis stared at him without smiling. "I'm counting on that, Langley. Let's keep each other posted."

As Langley headed for the door, Dennis said, "Detective, tell me one thing. How come a DC detective is investigating a crime that happened at Pentagon City?"

Langley turned to face Dennis. "Easy enough. My lieutenant said since Megan lived here, we weren't going to let her attacker go free. He assigned me to the case with orders to get it solved."

Dennis nodded. "Okay. Just asking."

After Langley left, Ellis walked over to Dennis. "I know your guys can handle this. I'm counting on it. But there's no sense in refusing his help. Work with him. See if he can contribute."

"Yes, sir," Dennis said.

∼

The next day, just before noon, a special courier delivered a package to Detective Langley.

One of the secretaries walked it back to him, wide eyed. "Stitch my britches, Detective, it's a delivery from the goddamn White House."

"What?" the lieutenant asked.

"The White House," she repeated. "Sixteen hundred Pennsylvania Avenue."

"What the hell are you getting from the White House?" the lieutenant asked. "You making headway on that case?"

Langley took the package from the secretary's hands, then turned to his boss. "No disrespect, sir, but it's none of your business. You gave *me* the case. Remember?"

Everybody laughed, then Langley took the package to his office and closed the door. *Looks like Dennis did what he said.*

Langley started unpacking the files and setting them on his desk. As he did, he realized how much he didn't want to be on this case. Forget that she was the president's daughter—she was a teenage girl who'd been brutally beaten and was lying in a coma.

It hit too close to home. His own son had been about her age when he was brutally attacked and put into a coma. Langley vividly remembers spending every night at the hospital, sitting on the bed holding his son's hand, or sitting in a nearby chair and praying. That was back when he still prayed. Back when he still believed God cared about people. That all changed when He took Eric away.

Rhonda, his wife, thought he should take the case and work it hard. "Maybe it will do some good" she said. Langley doubted it, and he was leery of doing it. He didn't want to be reminded of Eric every day. He was reminded too often already.

The phone rang and Langley answered. "Hello?"

"Langley, it's Dennis Markum. Did you get the package?"

"Yeah, I just got it," Langley said. "I'm going through it now."

"Call me when you get done. We need to get on this."

Langley didn't know if he should share his doubts or not, but at that point something inside him changed. He recalled the look on the president's face, the sorrow and sadness. "I'll go over this tonight," Langley said. "Let's get this son of a bitch."

"All for that," Dennis said. "Glad to have you on board."

DETECTIVE GRANT LANGLEY

Washington, D.C., February 2030

Rhonda Langley walked through the house, looking for her husband. "Grant. Grant, where are you?"

She looked in the living room, then the kitchen, and finally the garage. He wasn't in any of those places. Rhonda got a sick feeling in her gut. She went back in the house and made her way to the stairs. It had been a while since he'd done this, and Rhonda had thought he was finally over it.

When she got to the top of the stairs, she saw the light shining underneath the door of what used to be Eric's room.

She knew she should open the door and talk to him, but she wasn't ready. She went back down the stairs and into the kitchen to fix tea.

G rant sat slumped in a chair in the corner of the room. He held an iPad Mini in his hands that had belonged to Eric. It had been his favorite thing.

He thought about hacking into it; instead, he stared at the walls. A picture of The Flash, a superhero hung on one; a picture of one of the Victoria Secret models hung on the other. It was an old poster of the model. It reminded Langley that he used to have one on his own bedroom wall.

Grant shook his head and smiled. Eric had always been a mystery.

On the one hand, he obsessed about The Flash, reading comics and watching TV shows; on the other, he fantasized about the near-naked poster of the model that was positioned on the wall to allow him a perfect view from his bed. Langley couldn't blame him; he hadn't been much different in his youth.

Langley wiped tears away with his handkerchief. He would never forget the phone call, when they told him Eric had been almost killed, beaten, and shot down like he was a piece of dirt, like his life meant nothing. And he'd never forget the endless nights he and Rhonda had spent in the hospital, praying for an outcome he felt certain wouldn't happen.

Tears rolled down Grant's cheeks, and his knuckles got white streaks in them from gripping the arm of the chair so tightly. And for the millionth time he asked God how it had happened. How God had allowed Eric to die. Eric wasn't perfect, but certainly other people deserved to die more than him. *Why hadn't He taken one of those others instead?* Eric had faults, but there were hundreds of kids who deserved to die more than he did.

Grant's life had been empty since then ten years of emptiness. He and Rhonda were still married, but it seemed to be in name only. She had managed to put Eric's memory aside, to go on with life, but it wasn't so easy for Grant. Everything Grant did reminded him of Eric.

Every place he went reminded him that Eric went there, too. It was a nightmare that wouldn't go away—the worst kind of nightmare.

He heard Rhonda calling his name. His gut tightened. *What the hell does she want now?* He knew he should go, unless he wanted to start another argument, and he didn't want that. He was sick of the arguments. He wanted his family back. The one he used to have. The one when he used to be happy.

He said goodnight to Eric, got up slowly and opened the door. Then he made his way down to the kitchen.

$\sim$

While nursing a second cup of tea, Rhonda heard the all-too-familiar creak of the old wooden steps. Even if she hadn't known, it was obvious from Grant's appearance what he'd been doing. His eyes were reddened, and when he finally spoke, his voice had a nasally tone.

"Where have you been?" Rhonda asked.

"Nowhere."

"Nowhere? I've been calling you for twenty or thirty minutes. I've looked everywhere, and now you come down here from upstairs and say *nowhere*'?"

"Like I said, *nowhere*."

She moved her teacup to the sink and almost dropped it. The clattering of glass upon stainless steel was nerve-wracking. "Grant, this has got to stop. I know what he meant to you, but he meant a lot to me also. I miss him just as much. I loved him just as much. Every day my heart aches, but you can't let it get to you."

She wiped tears from her eyes and went to Grant to hug him. "My God, baby, don't let it ruin what we have left of our lives. We've still got each other. A long time ago we said 'for better or worse'. This might be some of the *worse*, but we've been through a lot and it *can* get better. It *will* get better if we try."

Grant held her tightly and squeezed. She was right. He *did* need to move on, let the good memories remain and the bad ones go away. He held her for a moment, then whispered. "All right. All right. Let's give it a try. But we're not touching his room. Not yet."

Rhonda stepped back from the embrace and looked up into his eyes. "If you promise to stop going in there and bringing yourself down, I'll leave it like that forever. Maybe once in a while we can visit it together."

Grant pulled her back to him and hugged. "Deal," he said. "I love you."

They held each other for what seemed like the longest time. When he broke off, Rhonda had tears in her eyes. "That's the first time you've said that in years."

Grant looked stunned. "Really?"

She nodded. "Really."

"I'm sorry," he said. "It won't happen again. I *do* love you, and, from now on, I'm going to show it. We'll get back to where we used to be."

"I'd like that, Grant. Let's give it a try."

A NEW DIRECTION

Washington, D. C., February 2028

The door to Keith's office opened, and Barney stuck his head in. "You wanted to see me, sir?"

"I'm just responding to your voicemail. You said you had something that might be of interest."

Barney finished entering the office and took a seat. "Ah, yeah. We finished the trial on the neurological drug to treat spasms, and while it showed no improvement over current treatments, something did come up."

Keith raised his eyebrows. "I'm waiting, but if the trials showed no improvement, then the *something* that did come up better be damn good."

Barney cleared his throat, then continued. "Several—actually more than several—I think it was twenty-one of the patients reported extremely vivid dreams that were exactly what they had been thinking of before going to bed."

Keith focused on the wall behind Barney, then back at him. "And you're thinking this is significant why?"

Barney leaned forward. "It might indicate that the drug has a *suggestive* quality. It might be useful in the research you mentioned last week. If what they dreamed about is what they were thinking before they went to bed, then perhaps we could implant a suggestion and produce dreams based on our own suggestions."

"But what good is a dream?"

"I don't know," Barney said. "I don't know the specifics of what you were looking for."

Keith rested his chin in the palm of his left hand. He thought for a moment of the implications, then nodded. "You're right, Barney. It just might be important. Have your people interview everyone who reported these dreams. Find out the details—what the dreams were about, how often they dreamed about such things before, anything. When you get it done, report back to me. But it has to be quick."

Barney stood, wearing a satisfied grin. "Yes, sir. I'll get on it right away."

~

Ginesh met with the outplacement counselor, who did his best to sound optimistic, but Ginesh saw through the lies. As he expected, there would be no job in D.C. That meant he was probably going to have to move to California or New Jersey, neither one of which were high on his wish list for places to live. *Or to grow a family.* That was a foreign thought to him, but now that Raji was with child, he had to start thinking about it. Besides, he felt certain that New Jersey and California were nowhere near as high on Raji's list of nice places to live.

When he got back to his desk, he saw a note from Barney.

Urgent! See me right away.

A glimmer of hope surged in Ginesh. Perhaps Barney had something for him to do, something besides looking for a job.

Ten minutes later, Ginesh knocked on the door of Barney Franklin's office, waited for an invitation, then entered. "You wanted to see me?"

"Have a seat," Barney said, gesturing to one of the chairs. "I spoke to Keith about what we discussed. He seemed excited."

"Really? How excited? Is it going to help us get money?"

"I don't know any of that," Barney said, "but Keith did say he wanted us to look into it." Barney picked up a note he had scribbled onto a piece of paper and read from it. "Let's see. Keith said, and I quote, 'Find out the details—what the dreams were about, how often they dreamed about such things, anything.'" Barney looked up and met Ginesh's stare. "How's that for interest?"

"I'll take it," Ginesh said. "Nancy and I will get right on it."

Two days later, Ginesh leaned against the wall in the corridor outside of Barney's door. He straightened when he saw Barney coming. "Mr. Franklin, I've got what you need. You know, what you asked for?"

Barney looked at his watch. "I have a meeting I'm late for, but let's talk at lunch. Meet me in the cafeteria at 11:45."

Ginesh smiled. "See you then."

Barney was already seated when Ginesh arrived. Ginesh took a seat across the table from him, looked around to make sure they wouldn't be overheard, then started talking. "I spoke with every one of the people who reported having the vivid dreams. I even spoke to some of the ones who didn't, just to make sure."

"And?"

"And it's better than I imagined. In every case, the people had been doing something just prior to bed that seemed to have triggered the dreams. I don't know how they triggered the dreams, but it seems probable that they did."

"How can you be certain?"

"I can't be certain, but they all said that they hadn't dreamed about things like that in years. Hadn't even thought about them."

"Give me an example," Barney said.

Ginesh looked through his notes and pulled one out to read. "Here's a report from an older man—eighty-two-years old— who had just watched a movie on baseball, and he ended up dreaming about his days spent as a youth playing in the little league."

"That doesn't seem so odd," Barney said.

"No, but he swears he hadn't dreamed about Little League in ten or twenty years, even though he watches baseball all the time."

"Interesting," Barney said, as he bit into a cinnamon twist.

"Here's another report about a person who dreamed about surfing as a youth, and this was after seeing a blip on the TV showing results of the surfing championships in Hawaii."

"Still not convinced," Barney said. "Any one of them could be explained by reactions to everyday events."

Ginesh leaned closer. "That's it! Any *one* of them could, but it's difficult to attribute *twenty-one* of them to those same everyday events." Ginesh turned his notebook around so that it was facing Barney. "Look at the list: weight lifting, horse racing, boxing, a Miss World competition—and I'm sure you can guess what *those* dreams were about."

"And you're sure these aren't recurring dreams?"

Ginesh shook his head. "They're not. I checked. All of them swore that they hadn't had dreams about this subject or dreams that were so vivid, in years, many years."

"Okay," Barney said. "You've convinced me. Now I have to convince Keith, who has to convince the investors, so it's still a long shot."

"But it's a shot?" Ginesh asked.

Barney nodded slowly. "Yes, Ginesh, it's a shot. I would still keep my résumé polished up, but it *is* a shot." Barney got up from his seat and grabbed the empty tray. "Now let's see if we can hit the target."

The earliest appointment Barney could get with Keith was four o'clock. He made sure to be on time. At four on the dot, Keith walked out of his office. He glanced at his watch when he noticed Barney sitting in a chair next to his secretary's desk. "Shit! Is it four already? All right, give me a minute, Barney. I've got one call to make."

About five minutes later, Keith made another appearance. "Sorry, Barney. That took longer than I expected." He gestured with his right hand, and said, "Come on in."

Barney sat down and repeated the results as Ginesh had related to him. "As far as I'm concerned, there's something to be had by pursuing this," Barney said. "It can't be a coincidence, not with twenty-one people."

Keith nodded. "All right. I agree. I'll meet with the investors and discuss how we can proceed—*if* we can proceed."

Barney smiled. "Does this mean—"

Keith returned the smile. "I'll let you know Barney. In fact, you'll be the first to know after me. I'm as eager as you to learn."

When Barney was gone, Keith picked up the phone and dialed.

The senator answered right away. "McCabe."

"Rich, this is Keith. Feel like coffee?"

"Why? Do you have something?"

"Just might at that. Something to interest your friends."

"Then I'll meet you at eight. Same place."

"Sounds good," Keith said. "I'll have a latte waiting."

LET'S LOOK AT THE LAB

Washington, D. C., February 2028

Keith found a table in the corner of Starbucks and took a seat, spreading the morning Post on the table before him. One of the reasons he liked coming here was access to a printed paper; besides, he might as well catch up on the news while he waited for McCabe to join him.

McCabe was twenty minutes late, but Keith didn't say anything. For a few million dollars, he could afford to wait. Besides, he'd have been reading at the office anyway.

He stood to greet McCabe when he arrived. "Rich, how are you?"

McCabe took off his coat and draped it over the back of a chair. "Late, as usual. I apologize."

"No problem. Hang on and I'll get a hot latte. This one must be cold by now."

"Thanks, that would be great," McCabe said. "I need one."

Keith got the latte and sat back down, then filled McCabe in on what he knew. "It looks promising," Keith said. "As promising as anything can look at this stage."

coffee shop

"Did you try anything with just voice, no visuals?" McCabe asked.

"Meaning what?"

"I mean just *suggesting* topics via conversation or a microphone in their room. No TV or anything real."

Keith lost the smile that had been on his face all morning. "No. I hadn't thought of that. But it wouldn't be hard to put into practice."

"In the scenarios I picture, we probably won't have the opportunity to present visuals. I need to see if we get results using audio only."

McCabe sipped on his latte, then said, "And we'll need some way of finding out what our targets dreamed about. This isn't like a clinical trial. The real targets sure as hell aren't going to wake up and tell us."

Keith gave a fake laugh. "No. I guess not. But like I said, this is *promising*. I didn't expect it to be just right."

"All right," McCabe said. "But I want to visit. I want to talk to your scientists, see the lab. If we're putting this much money into your place, I've got to know what I'm getting. Kick the tires, so to speak."

"Of course," Keith said. "When would you like to do this?"

McCabe pulled out his phone and brought up his calendar. "How about four o'clock. I'm free for almost two hours."

"Today?" Keith asked.

"Yes, today. Is something wrong with that?"

"No. Not at all. I just want the lab to look good. I'll tell the scientists, and they'll be ready for you at four."

McCabe drained his cup, then stood. "All right. See you then. And I won't be late," McCabe said.

Keith walked at a controlled pace up the block then across the street. All the while, he wanted to run, race back to the office and get prepared. A lot was depending on this meeting—a hell of a lot.

He opened the car door and got in, then looked around to make sure McCabe was gone. When he saw the taillights of McCabe's Audi almost a block ahead, he grabbed his phone and pushed the number for Barney Franklin.

"Franklin."

"Barney, it's Keith. We've got visitors coming to the lab today. Big visitors. Important visitors. And they want to meet Ginesh and Nancy, so make sure everything is ready."

"What? What time?"

"Luckily, not until four. Still, that's not a lot of time to prepare. Get it done, Barney. Everything depends on how this goes, and I mean *everything*."

"You've got it, sir. I'll go down there myself, right now."

"Okay, good. I'm on my way in. I should be there shortly."

❧

Barney prepped Ginesh and Nancy, then helped them clean up and get organized. "We can't have it look like we're operating on a shoestring budget," Barney said.

"But we are," Nancy said.

Barney shot her a glare. "*I* know that. You know that. Ginesh knows that. But this investor *doesn't*, and it won't be good if he suspects."

"Who is it?" Ginesh asked.

"No idea," Barney said. "I presume he'll introduce himself when he gets here, but then again, he might not. Either way, it doesn't matter. What matters is he's got the money and we don't. So for now, just think of him as Mr. Moneybags."

"But we must have something he wants, or he wouldn't be coming here," Ginesh said.

"Keep thinking that way and you'll be spending the rest of the night polishing up your résumé."

"Yes, sir," Ginesh said. "Sorry."

Ginesh spent the rest of the day organizing the lab and straightening his workstation, as did Nancy.

"You think this could pay off?" Nancy asked.

"Who knows?" Ginesh said. "The people who have money are all weird. You never know what gets them excited, or what turns them off."

Chaz, the rat, began chirping from his cage, and the ruckus was getting louder. Ginesh sighed and threw his hands up in the air. "Just what I need today, a freaked-out rat."

He walked slowly to the cages where he kept the trial rats and opened Chaz's. Chaz was a large gray-and-white rat with a button-like pink nose.

Ginesh picked him up, held him against his shoulder and petted him. Then he whispered, "Come on, Chaz. This is an important meeting we've got. You can't be acting up and making noise. Be on your best behavior. Be good and Daddy will give you some treats. Maybe some sharp cheese?"

Nancy let out a loud huff. "I can't believe the way you talk to that rat. You're sweeter to him than you are to Raji."

"Chaz doesn't give me shit," Ginesh said, and laughed. "And besides, he's been a star. He's been in five trials now and survived them all, *and* he's shown positive results three of the five times."

"And I guess you're going to say it had something to do with Chaz?"

"Of course it did. It wasn't coincidence."

Nancy shook her head and went back to cleaning her desk. "I don't know about Chaz, but what I do know is if you don't get busy, it will *not* be a coincidence that you'll be sleeping with Chaz after those investors leave."

Ginesh kissed Chaz on the side of the face, then set him back in his cage. "I've got to go to work now, buddy. You be good."

Nancy shook her head again. "I swear. You people worship cows, play with cobras, and kiss rats. I have no idea how your population is so huge."

Ginesh laughed. "It's our natural charm. It can't be denied."

At five minutes after four, Keith walked in followed by three men in suits. He approached Ginesh with his hand outstretched. "Ginesh, this is Senator Richard McCabe, and these are two of his top scientists."

Ginesh shook hands, staring all the time. Keith introduced Nancy next. Then Mr. McCabe introduced the men with him.

"This is Bob Dancer, chief neuroscientist for the government's military weapon's division, and this," he said, pointing to the other gentleman, "is Christoper Reilly, head of electrical engineering for the same division. I felt it would be good to have their input."

Ginesh smiled as he shook Christopher's hand, but his stomach was in knots.

What was a neuroscientist doing with the government's weapon's division? And why bring him here?

"I understand you're interested in our work," Nancy said, stepping up to fill the gap left by Ginesh's silence.

"Yes, we are," McCabe said. "Why don't you tell us about it? And feel free to speak technically. I won't be able to understand you, but I'm sure Bob and Chris will."

Nancy smiled. "No need. I can tell you about it using lay terms."

Nancy went on to tell him about the patients who had the vivid—and apparently *suggested*—dreams. Bob interrupted a few times with questions, but nothing she couldn't handle. The bigger problem was Chaz, who kept squealing from the cage.

"Will somebody shut that thing up?" McCabe said. "Feed it to a cat or a snake or something. Just shut it up."

"Excuse me," Ginesh said, and got up to tend to Chaz. He opened the cage door, cupped Chaz in his right hand, and walked him to the back of the room, which must have been fifty feet away. Once there, he set him in another cage and locked the door. "Be good, Chaz," Ginesh said, in a firm and commanding tone.

"I'm sorry, Mr. McCabe," Ginesh said when he returned. He tends to get noisy when a lot of people are around."

McCabe waved his hand in the air as if it were nothing, but the look on his face said otherwise. "What brought on these dreams? From the data you've shown us, nothing changed in six months, then all of a sudden—wham."

Ginesh looked to the side at Barney, then to the other side at Keith. Keith nodded and said, "Tell him. It's all right."

"Tell me what?" McCabe said.

"I increased the dosage shortly before the dreams began," Ginesh said.

"Increased the dosage by how much?" Bob asked.

Ginesh lowered his head, ashamed. "I doubled it."

"Doubled it!" Bob said. "That was pretty dangerous."

"Any deaths?" McCabe asked. "Or serious side effects?"

Ginesh shook his head. "Thank God, no. Nothing."

"Then increase it again," McCabe said. "We need to see where this will take us."

"Increase it again? We can't. We don't know what it will do."

"Then use it on the rats first," McCabe said. "Use it on that mouthy one. What do we care if a few rats die?"

"How much of an increase?" Ginesh asked Keith.

"Double it again," McCabe said. "I'm in a hurry and you need money."

"Double it? I can't. It might kill them."

"That's what the rats are for," McCabe said. "If they die, they did their country a service."

Chaz could be heard throwing a fit from his cage in the back of the room. He was squealing and screeching and rattling the cage. Ginesh got nervous. He knew the noise bothered McCabe, but Ginesh couldn't do anything about it at the time.

McCabe stepped closer to Ginesh and Nancy. "We need to find a way to make audio suggestion work. More importantly, we need to find a way to extract the data *without* the person knowing."

"I don't know how that could be done," Ginesh said.

"Well, it won't be done using your goddamn rats," McCabe said. "We need to test this on real people."

"Audio suggestion is one thing," Ginesh said. "I think I could make that work, but I have no idea how to extract the data."

Bob moved forward, inching between them. "I've been giving that a lot of thought. You're familiar with the research that's been going on in Norway dealing with chemical neural transmitters and electronic ones?"

"I've read a little about it, but not extensively" Ginesh said. "All that I know is that it focuses on sending signals from the chemical transmitters to the electronic ones, which are located outside the body."

"Correct," Bob said. "So imagine if we could use nano technology to insert electronic transmitters *into* the brain, then use the transmitters to send electronic signals that would be picked up by electronic neural-type receptors."

Ginesh was still giving it thought, when Nancy shouted. "Oh my God. It could work. It just might work. If we could have the drug enhance the nanobots so that they only attached to the transmitters for dreams then it might work."

Ginesh was now caught up in the excitement. "You'd have to have the right drug, one that would affect the transmitters enough so that the electronic receptors would pick up the signals, and you'd have to make sure the signal was strong enough, or that the receptors were close enough—but yes, I agree, it could work."

McCabe stood up from where he was half-sitting on the edge of the desk. "Then let's get moving, people. I need this yesterday." He looked at his guys and said, "Chris, Bob, give them your cards and get theirs. I want you to coordinate working on this."

McCabe said goodbye to Ginesh and Nancy, then walked to the door, trailed by Bob and Chris, with Keith bringing up the rear.

As they approached the exit, Keith reached out his hand to shake. "So we've got a deal?"

McCabe nodded. "I'll have five million for you next week."

"Five? We talked about ten."

"I know what we talked about, Keith. But that was before I knew how much you needed money."

"You son of a bitch."

"Yeah, I'm that and more. Now get busy on this, and you just might get your ten million; in fact, if your people are successful, you'll have a hell of a lot more than ten million. But I need it done quickly."

"It can't be too quick," Keith said. We have to have trials with rats first, then—"

"Forget all of that," McCabe said. "This is a national emergency, for God's sake. We're dealing with terrorists, and they're beating the hell out of us." McCabe placed his hand against the door jamb and leaned close. "They're winning. Do you understand that?"

He downed the last sip of a latte that Nancy had given him, then said, "We captured a terrorist a few months ago in Munich. We knew he had something going on, but we couldn't break him, and that was *with* us using unconventional techniques in conjunction with the normal. Two days later, the terrorist cell he was with set off a bomb in a train station in Germany, killing fourteen people. That's fourteen *real* people."

"If we had something to let us 'see' inside their brains, we'd be able to stop them."

McCabe straightened. "That's what we're working for, Keith. That's why I don't care about a few rats or even a few old men." He looked down the hall, making sure no one was around, and said. "I'd kill a few people myself if I thought it would do any good."

He started to leave, then turned, "By the way, do you know PJ Connor over at Spring Meadows?"

Keith shook his head. "No."

"He's chief of psychiatry there. It's a nursing home for people who have had strokes. It's perfect for what we want. They're located over in Silver Spring. Meet me on Thursday morning and we'll drive up there. Don't worry about having to use rats. I'll get your patients. PJ will play along."

"There's no way he's going to let you do that," Keith said. "Providing clinical trial patients is a little more than *playing along.*"

"He'll let me. He owes me."

Keith says. "If that's the case, then good. We'll get some patients."

On the long drive home that night, Keith worried about what he was doing. He'd never done anything like this before, he'd always stuck to the rules. Maybe in the past he had bent the rules now and then, but this wouldn't be just bending the rules, he'd be snapping them into pieces. And he was putting people's lives in danger.

Hours later, as he stared at his daughter while she was sleeping, he thought, *but it is for a good cause.* It was to help the government stop terrorism—and besides, without the payoff he expected to get from his stock he'd be living in a damn shack on the wrong side of town.

Later, Keith lay awake, unable to sleep, thinking of what to do from a moral standpoint, but also what to do from a research standpoint. *There has to be a way to make this work.*

THE RESEARCH CONTINUES

Washington, D. C., April 2028

As instructed by Barney, Ginesh and Nancy increased the doses of the drug, but they were careful to do it in small increments, no more than 5 percent at any one time. They tried out the dose increases on the rats first; when no adverse effects were observed, they switched the increased dose to humans.

At the end of eight weeks, they had upped the dosage by 40 percent but kept it to once a day. So far they had noted no side effects; however, this was on rats only. At this point, they had increased human doses by only 10 percent.

After reporting this to Barney, he wanted them to begin human trials but Nancy fought hard to stall that, wanting to stick to animal testing for the present.

Barney insisted on moving ahead. No doubt he was acting on orders from Keith and McCabe. "You need to move faster," Barney said. "We can't afford to be so cautious."

"What we can't afford is to have someone die," Nancy said.

Barney shook his head. "Then jump the dose up so that it doubles the original amount, and test it on the rats. Give them more drug or give it to them more frequently. I don't care what you do, but do it. We *need* this drug. If it works on the rats, we'll shift to human trials without delay."

Ginesh seemed as apprehensive about testing the rats as he did humans. Despite Senator McCabe's feelings about rats, Ginesh liked them, especially Chaz. Chaz had personality.

After Barney left, Nancy looked to Ginesh and said, "I know you don't want to, but it looks as if Chaz and his buddies are in for a ride."

Ginesh sighed. "All right, but we need to document this well. I don't want them hurt if we can help it."

fter seven days of testing at the new levels, Chaz and his compatriots seemed fine. It looked as if it was time for humans to take the tests.

Ginesh informed Barney of the results, telling him they had seen no adverse effects but warning him that it hadn't been enough time. Barney nodded, then he informed Keith, who relayed the messages to McCabe.

"We're ready, McCabe. We need your contact in Silver Spring," Keith said. "If you want to get moving on this, now is the time. I need patients."

"Consider it done," McCabe said. "I'll make the call today."

Within one week, Keith had all the patients he needed, and all of them eager to participate.

Keith started things off with a slow introduction of the drug, building it up to the level the rats had been subjected to. Before another week passed, Bob and Christopher dropped by with naanochips they said were ready to test.

"I don't know if they work," Chris said, "but it's worth a try."

Each of the patients was fed naanochips with their meals. According to Christopher, the chips would make their way into the bloodstream, then, due to a pre-designed affinity for neural transmitters, specifically, the ones associated with memory compression, the nanochips would find their way to the brain at just the right spot.

"How do they make their way to the bloodstream?" Keith asked.

"I'm not positive. All I know is that Bob worked night and day with a scientist who had extensive experience with transdermal patches, so I'm presuming the chips are absorbed somehow."

"But this isn't transdermal," Keith said.

"I know that, but according to Bob, while they were working on absorption through the skin, they stumbled upon this. They said it works better."

"And how do they find their way to the brain?"

Christopher sighed. "You're asking me for details that I'm not familiar with, but I'll do my best to explain." He grabbed a piece of paper and started drawing a map of the brain. "As I mentioned, Bob pre-designed these nanochips with an affinity for neural transmitters, and specifically for the transmitters that work with memory compression, which is associated with dreams. So once the chips enter the bloodstream, they target those cells—like a magnet would—then they *swim* to wherever they are and attach. This makes it—or *should* make it—easy to transfer the information from the neural cell to the nano cell, presuming the drug does its job."

Keith nodded. "And these naanochips are electronic transmitters?"

"Both transmitters and a receivers. Mr. McCabe said he wanted to be able to send audio signals to nanochips and see if they pick the signals up."

"Interesting," Keith said. "We'll have to see if it works."

"One other thing," Christopher said, and handed Keith a USB drive. "There's an audio file on here. It is recorded in a frequency that the human ear can't hear, but it *will* be picked up by the receivers. Mr. McCabe wants you to broadcast this message every night right before the patients retire."

"What's on the file?" Keith asked.

"I'm assuming it's none of our business, or McCabe would have told me. I learned long ago that if I'm not told, I don't ask."

"Fine by me," Keith said. "We'll do it."

Another week passed and there were still no results—at least none that showed positive. Barney Franklin waited outside of Keith's office. He was a few minutes early for a one o'clock appointment.

At precisely one o'clock, Keith came out of the office. "Barney, come on in. I hope you have good news."

"It depends on how you look at things," Barney said. "No one has died. That's good."

Keith frowned. "Not good enough. Time is running out, and we need money."

"I'm working on it," Barney said.

"How do we know if we're getting results?"

Barney pulled a notebook from his briefcase. "I have a monitor assigned to each patient, including the rats. We even have monitors assigned to Ginesh and Nancy, and all of them special made by McCabe's man, Chris. If we get an image or signal of any kind, an alarm goes off on the monitor and a message is flashed on the screen every five minutes until someone manually dismisses it."

Keith nodded. "Sounds good. Let's hope we get something soon. McCabe is not a patient man."

"Yes, sir," Barney said, then he got up to leave.

Barney returned to the lab and had a talk with Nancy and Ginesh. "We have to get something going," Barney said. "If we don't show results soon, Keith is convinced that McCabe will pull the funding. If he does that, we're sunk."

"I don't know what else to do," Ginesh said. "We're already cutting all the corners."

"Then cut some more, but get me something. And I mean fast."

Barney left, and when the door closed, Ginesh moved to a chair alongside Nancy's. "What should we do?"

"You mean besides look for a job?" she said. "I'm going back through all of the data. I want to see if we missed anything."

"I can't imagine what we might have missed." Ginesh said.

"If you help me, we'll find out if we did miss something twice as fast."

Ginesh sighed. "Let me call Raji and tell her I'll be late."

"How's little Ramesh doing?" Nancy asked.

"If womb activity is any indication, he's doing fine. Kicking all the time and causing Raji endless turmoil about what she eats."

"Sounds like he's going to take after his father," Nancy said, and walked back to her desk. "By the way, I'll take A through M."

"I guess that leaves me N through Z," said Ginesh.

About 11:00, as Nancy was poring over data from the initial trial, she noticed something strange.

"Ginesh, look at this," she said.

Ginesh walked to her desk and looked over her shoulder at the data displayed on the screen. "What am I looking at?" he asked.

"Check it out. Six of the twenty-one patients who reported the dreams had been taking melatonin at the time."

"Six of twenty-one is not a lot," Ginesh said.

"But *no one* else was taking melatonin," Nancy said. "That means that 100 percent of those taking it had the vivid dreams."

Ginesh thought for a minute. "And maybe the other fifteen people naturally produced melatonin in greater quantity."

"Measure it," Nancy said. "It's easy enough, a simple urine test will suffice. See if they produced more melatonin than the other trial patients."

Two days later, Ginesh walked into the lab wearing a smile like it was the beginning of Diwali. "Every one of them," he said. "Every one of the patients who had the dreams produced significantly more melatonin than the others."

For the following three days, they combined high doses of melatonin with the neurological drug, seeing if it had any effect on the rats. Chaz was the *lead* patient, the one who got the treatment first, and the protocol was that if he fared well, the others followed.

When nothing happened to Chaz, Ginesh and Nancy told Barney about their findings.

"Fantastic! Then add melatonin to the patient mix. Twenty milligrams. What are you waiting for?"

Nancy raised her eyebrows. "Sir, we haven't tested that much yet, not even with the rats."

"And we don't have time to," Barney said. "The melatonin didn't hurt them at the original dosage, so it shouldn't do anything here. It's not a drug with a lot of adverse reactions."

"Excuse me, sir," Ginesh said. "But we don't know that. We've never tested it before with this drug. We should be certain before proceeding."

"Certain? You want certain?" Barney said. "I'll tell you what's certain. If we don't get something soon, it's *certain* that McCabe will pull the funding. Then it won't make a damn bit of difference what happens, will it?"

"No, sir," Ginesh said. "We'll add the melatonin."

The next morning Ginesh and Nancy added twenty milligrams of melatonin to the drug dosage for the patients, fingers crossed that nothing would happen.

For four more days, things were normal, then on the fifth day Ginesh was greeted by a message on the screen of monitor one.

Image received...

...was all it said. But as he frantically searched for the image, he noticed that there were messages flashing on monitors two, three, four, and others. As he cursed Nancy for leaving too many apps open at once, he finally located what he wanted—a picture of a bunch of young men playing baseball. Further searching of the data revealed that it came from patient number one, Salvatore Marino.

He ran to the next monitor and repeated his search, finding the picture much faster. It was of two men water skiing on one foot behind a speed boat. This was from the transmitter that had been ingested by patient number two.

As Ginesh went to the third monitor, Nancy came in. "What's going on?" she asked.

"It worked!" Ginesh said. "We've got images. Lots of images."

Nancy tossed her coat aside and sat at the first monitor. A moment later, she said. "Ginesh, these aren't just images, they're videos. It's like watching a damn movie."

"What?" Ginesh said, and ran to sit beside her. She hit *play* and the video started again, showing a group of young men playing baseball.

"Oh my God," Ginesh said. "Oh my God. Do you know what this means?"

"Hopefully that we won't have to look for jobs," Nancy said.

"It means it works. It means something is happening."

"Now we have to find out what, because this still isn't what McCabe said he wanted—and besides, the videos are a little fuzzy."

"It may not be what he wanted," Ginesh said, "but it's showing that the transmitters work. That's something."

"We need to get more detail from the patients," Nancy said. "Let's talk to them."

Ginesh and Nancy interviewed patient number one and asked if he remembered what he dreamed about.

"Baseball," he said. "I can remember it as if it really happened. A bunch of guys from work and I were playing major-league ball, *and,* we were winning." He laughed. "Felt just like it was real."

Patient number two recited his dream about water skiing with his brother. "And on one foot," he said. "I felt as if I were a damn pro."

The same answers were given by the rest. Each patient told their dreams, which matched the videos received, and they were able to provide all of the details.

"This is incredible," Nancy said. "I've never heard of people that recalled this much detail."

"And I've never heard of so many people who even remembered their dreams," Ginesh said. "A lot of people forget what they dreamed."

t the four o'clock meeting that day, they relayed the information to Barney.

"Do you know how this is working? What's causing it?"

Ginesh shook his head. "I can't be certain, but I'm assuming that the drug is altering the chemical signals sent by the neurotransmitters, and it's doing it in a way that those signals are then picked up by Christopher's nanochips. Those same signals are then transmitted to our receivers in the monitors."

Barney wore a smile that seemed a mile wide. "Good job," he said. "But don't quit now. We have a lot more to do."

WHAT NOW?

Washington, D. C., May, 2028

Keith met McCabe at the same coffee shop and sat at the same table as the last time. They both had the same drink.

coffee shop

"I hope you have some news, Ratcliff. My people are getting antsy."

Keith told him what they had. "It's not what you were looking for. The audio seems to be doing nothing so far, but it's a start."

McCabe leaned over the table. "Clarify something for me. You mean you can actually *see* the dreams?"

"Yes. The images are a little fuzzy, but the videos are recognizable. And it's worked on every patient we've tried it on."

"And why is that significant?"

"Because trials almost never work on all the patients."

McCabe sipped his coffee, not talking.

"I know it's not what you wanted, Senator, but—"

"Forget about what I wanted. This has commercial potential."

"What?"

"Think about it. What husband wouldn't want to *see* what his wife was dreaming. Is she dreaming of other men? Of doing certain things? And what parent wouldn't want to *see* what their teenage son or daughter is dreaming of?"

Keith nodded. "Maybe so."

"No maybes about it," McCabe said. "It would sell millions. Hell, tens of millions."

"We'd need to have something to view the images with," Keith said. "We can't expect people to have their loved ones hooked up to monitors."

"No. You're right. It would have to be something portable. A device that would be easy to mistake as something else."

Keith snapped his fingers. "Like a pair of glasses," he said.

McCabe thought for a moment, then smiled. "Exactly. Like a pair of glasses. Dream Visors."

"We could even call them that—Dream Visors."

"I'll get my people at the nano center working on this. Christoper should be in touch by the end of the week with questions regarding collaboration with Ginesh."

"What do you think we could charge for them?" Keith asked.

"I don't know. It depends on what they cost to manufacture. At a minimum, I'd say $299."

"We're talking tens of millions in sales," Keith said.

"Bullshit. If Apple can sell fifty million iPhones a year, we can sell fifty million of these. We're talking billions."

"And just so you know, I haven't forgotten the original plan," Keith said.

"I have," McCabe said. "This is money in the bank. Which reminds me, when can I see the videos?"

"Any time you want. We'll drive over after coffee if you feel like it."

"Sounds good. I want to see this myself."

Forty minutes later, Keith had Ginesh show McCabe what they had captured on video from patients one and two.

"Keep playing," McCabe said, and he proceeded to watch all the videos. Afterward, he turned to Ginesh and Nancy. "This is good. Really good. But the image is a little fuzzy. Anything we can do about that?"

"That part is beyond my skills," Ginesh said. "Maybe Christopher would know. He's the electronics expert."

McCabe called Christopher on his cell and asked him to join them. While waiting, Chaz was busy making noise. "Will somebody kill that goddamn rodent?" McCabe said. "How the hell do you put up with him all day?"

"He doesn't cause trouble, except when you're here, sir."

McCabe turned to face Ginesh. "Are you saying the goddamn rat doesn't like me?"

"I'm sorry, sir. No, I was just making an observation." Ginesh started moving toward Chaz's cage. "I'll move him."

"Good," McCabe said, "And keep him moved."

Once Christopher arrived, McCabe showed him what they had, then posed the problem to him.

"We might be able to play around with the frequency," Christopher said. "Find one that offers a clearer channel."

"Then do it," McCabe said. "See if you can get this to look like something besides an old porn movie."

Ginesh and Nancy hid smiles, but Christopher said, "Yes, sir."

For the next two weeks, Christopher worked alongside of Ginesh and Nancy making tweaks to the transmitters, and the frequency that they broadcasted on. Each adjustment was met with image improvement and enthusiastic support from Keith and Barney. In addition to working on this problem, Christopher was overseeing the development of the glasses at the nanotechnology center and coordinating it with Ginesh.

By Friday afternoon, on week two, the videos had improved to near HD quality.

"Looks like we're ready for prime time," Ginesh said.

"Not quite prime time," Christopher said, "but damn close."

Ginesh wanted to tell McCabe about the progress, but Christopher stalled him. "Let's try to finish the glasses first. I'd love to show him all of this at once."

I t took eight or ten tries to get the glasses to work at all, then another eight or ten before the image was crisp, but by the end of the next week, Christopher and Ginesh and Nancy had been able to receive good, clear images consistently.

"Okay, Ginesh," Christopher said. "Now, we're ready for prime time. Let's call McCabe."

Keith arranged a demonstration for McCabe, and everyone was in attendance.

McCabe watched while Nancy, Ginesh, and Christopher took turns demonstrating how easy it was to operate the glasses. You simply put them on, flipped a switch, and navigated to the dream spot. Navigation was as simple as eye movement; in fact, it was eye movement. If you looked up, the "screen" scrolled up. If you looked down, it scrolled down.

"How does it do that?" McCabe asked.

"There is a built-in laser that tracks the movement of the pupil, then it adjusts the screen accordingly."

"And this will work for different people?"

Christopher nodded. "When you first put the glasses on, the laser identifies the pupil, then records the position of the eye in relation to the screen. It should work for anyone."

"What about cost?"

"If we're talking high volume, it shouldn't be much," Christopher said. "No more than a few bucks."

"And how do the glasses become a screen?"

"When you flip the switch, the light reflection is changed and the glasses turn dark, then it's a simple matter of 'projection' from inside to make it appear as a movie."

McCabe looked at Christopher, Ginesh, and Nancy. "And anyone can wear these and make them work?"

"Yes, they adjust to the wearer's eyes. But why are you asking? I thought these would be for people to see their own dreams."

McCabe smiled. "That's how they'll be marketed, but I think the real market will be the people who want to spy on their loved ones. Husbands who want to watch wives, wives who want to see what husbands are dreaming, and parents who want to check on their children. That's where the real money will be."

Ginesh got a queasy feeling in his gut, but he didn't say anything.

"And how long will it take until the glasses start working?"

Ginesh stepped a shade closer. "The people will have to take the drug for about two weeks before the glasses work properly. Apparently, it takes that long for the drug to affect the neurotransmitters. Depending on the person, it could be earlier, but to be sure, I'd say two weeks."

McCabe furrowed his brows. "Two weeks? So we'll have a market for the drug *and* the glasses?"

Ginesh smiled. "Yes, people will have to take the drug almost continually if they want to use the glasses."

"This is better than I hoped for," McCabe said. "Two mega-selling products. We're all going to be rich. Think of it—from almost laid off, to filthy rich in an instant."

"I like the sound of that," Nancy said.

"Me too," added Christopher.

"You know I do," Ginesh said. "It couldn't have come at a better time."

"Like I always said, 'Good things come to those who cut corners.' " Then he laughed.

"What are we going to call them?" Ginesh asked.

"Dream Visors," McCabe said.

"To go along with that, I say we change the name of the drug to NeuroScan," Keith said. "It sounds right. Sounds techie."

"NeuroScan...I agree," McCabe said. "Let's do it."

"How are we going to get this pushed through?" Keith said. "They're going to want to see clinical trial data, FDA forms, all of that."

"Don't worry," McCabe said. "Theodore will take care of the FDA stuff, and our friend PJ will help with clinical trial forms. I'm sure he has paperwork that shows our requests for patients months ago. If he doesn't, he *will*."

"You sure about this?" Keith asked.

"Sure as rain," McCabe said.

Ginesh grabbed hold of McCabe's arm. "Senator, you mentioned that this will be used by young people."

"Yes. I should think so. At least I hope so."

"If that's the case, sir, we will need a few younger people to test the drug. Just showing it works on the elderly isn't enough. Younger people produce more hormones, have different metabolisms, and since we anticipate the devices being worn by teenagers, we better test it to ensure no surprises since they will have to take the drug to make the device work."

McCabe nodded. "I see. You're right of course. It wouldn't do to have issues like that after we release it. People might think we didn't conduct honest clinical trials." McCabe laughed then patted Ginesh on the shoulder. "Don't worry, son. I'll take care of it. Expect some patients soon."

"How soon?"

"I don't know yet. I have to get busy setting up a new company and I have to make sure my name isn't on it anywhere."

"Why a new company?" Keith asked.

"The government monitors clinicals associated with the military far too closely. Even more than private industry. We couldn't get away with what we need to if it were connected to DARPA."

"Okay, I'll leave it to you," Keith said.

JUSTIN

Washington, D. C., June 2028

Justin bounded down the steps, a smile on his face. "See ya, Dad. Be back around eleven."

"Whoa, young man. Where are you going, and who are you going with?"

"Just out. And I'm going with Megan and Vic. Don't worry. We're not going to be doing anything bad."

"Megan's fine. But you know I'm not crazy about Vic."

"I'd be worried if you were, Dad." Justin opened the front door, and said, "See ya."

Justin got in his car and drove off. Twenty minutes later, he was sitting in front of Vic's house. He beeped the horn to let him know he was waiting.

Vic ran out of the house, opened the car door, and got in the front seat. "S'up, dude?"

"Not a damn thing. Just going to get Megan, then we can hit the mall."

"Goddamn, you didn't tell me Megan was coming."

"What difference does it make?" Justin asked.

"All the difference, man. I would have spiced up a bit more. Megan's fine."

"Hey, dickhead. Watch your mouth. Megan is *my* girl."

"For now she is. But probably not for long. She's too fine to hang out with you for more than a few months."

"Screw you."

"Speaking of screwing, are you tapping into that fine meat yet?" Vic asked.

"None of your goddamn business. And stop talking about her like that, or I'll drop your ass off at the next corner."

"Whatever. But I'm not gonna stop thinking of her. That ass is way too fine."

Justin hit the brakes hard. He hadn't seen the stop sign at the corner. "Vic, we've been friends for four years, but it'll end at four years if you don't shut up."

"Done," Vic said, then made a gesture as if he were zippering his mouth shut.

Justin drove in silence for a few miles, then an oldie from Katy Perry came on the radio. "Turn that up," Vic said. "I love Katy Perry. She had a nice ass."

"Is everything dependent upon a girl's ass with you? Is that all you think about?"

"Well, yeah. What else should I think about?"

"How about intelligence, conversation, political views?"

"Now I *know* Megan's gonna be checking me out. If that's the kind of shit you're interested in."

"What are you talking about?"

"I'm talking about real life. A fine young thing like her doesn't give a shit about that stuff. She wants the same thing every girl wants—a nice hunk of meat. And if you don't give it to her, somebody else will."

Justin hit the brakes and pulled to the curb. "All right. Get the hell out. I mean it."

"All right, dude. Sorry. I won't say anything again."

"No. Get out!"

"What? Are you crazy? I can't get out here. This is a ghetto."

Justin clenched his teeth, raised his head, and turned it to the side. "All right, but I swear, one more word..."

"No worries. I'm through talking."

Justin picked up Megan, then set a course for the Pentagon City Mall. They were, of course, being tailed by Dennis.

"Does that dude follow you everywhere?" Vic asked.

"Pretty much," Megan said. "Sometimes it's a pain in the ass."

"I'll bet," Vic said. "Especially if you guys want time alone to...well, you know."

Megan giggled, but Justin said. "Vic! I told you to shut your mouth."

"Oh, hush up, Justin. Vic's just messing around."

"Yeah, Justin," Vic said, in a teasing manner.

Justin parked near Nordstrom, and luckily found a place to park not far from the mall entrance. They went inside, and took their time, slowly walking the first level all the way down to Macy's.

Justin picked up a pair of jeans and a few shirts, and Megan got a purse (like she needed another one) plus another pair of earrings.

As they walked past the swimwear section in Macy's, Megan let out a screech. "Oh, my God, look at that. Isn't it adorable?" She was looking at a bikini—tan, with a blue border.

"A little skimpy, isn't it?" Justin asked.

"I think you'd look like a fox," Vic said. "I mean, not that you don't already, just that a bathing suit like that would draw the attention of...like everyone."

Justin gritted his teeth and was about to say something when Megan said, "You think so? Really?"

"Absolutely," Vic said. "It would make me turn my head."

Megan took it off the rack and walked it to the cashier. "I'll take this," she said. "It'll be charge."

Megan handed the cashier the charge card and her license, then leaned on the counter, waiting.

"Megan Piersol? Is the—"

"Yes," Megan said. "He's my father."

As they left the store, Vic leaned close and whispered. "I'm guessing that happens all the time."

"*All* the time," Megan said. "I get sooo tired of it."

"Tired of what?" Justin asked, acting as if he hadn't heard.

"Nothing," Megan said. "Vic just asked me a question."

They cruised the second level, went down and hung out at the food court for a while, then decided to call it a night. The mall would soon be closing anyway.

On the way home, Justin decided to stop for coffee. As they were sitting at the table, drinking coffee, Vic pulled out a joint and lit it.

Justin snatched it from his mouth and dropped it in an almost-empty cup of hot chocolate. "What the hell is the matter with you?"

"What?" Vic said.

"For one thing, you can't smoke in here. For another, Megan's father has people following us. They'll see."

"Shit. They won't know what it is. They'll think it's a regular cigarette."

"Like hell. These people aren't dumb. And like I said, you can't smoke in here anyway."

"Chill out, dude. It's a joint, not smack."

"Wait till we get in the car," Megan said.

"Like hell," Justin said. "You can wait until you get home. Do it there if you want."

"For God's sake, Justin," Megan said. "Get off his case. Like Vic said, it's just a joint."

"*Just a joint* can get your ass in a lot of trouble, especially with your father."

"And such a pretty little ass it is," Vic said.

"That does it," Justin said. "I'm taking you home."

Megan laughed. "Come on, Justin. He just said my ass was pretty. It is, isn't it?"

"Of course it is, but it's not his place to say so."

Justin dropped Vic off in front of his house, took Megan home, then took the long way to his house. He had to let off some steam before facing his father, who had a way of always pissing him off.

It took fifteen minutes longer, and three missed calls from Megan, but he finally arrived. He parked in the garage and tried sneaking into the house, but his father called him before he got ten feet inside.

"Justin, is that you?"

"Yeah, Dad. What do you need?"

"I don't need anything, but you might want to hear about this. A friend of mine has a company that is conducting tests on people while they are in a dream state. It supposedly is no danger, and it pays well."

"Why would that interest me?"

"Because you're always complaining about money. I thought you'd want to know. Besides, most of the work is done at night, so it shouldn't interfere with anything; in fact, they need a few people for the trials, so if any of your friends are interested, you could take them, too."

Justin perked up. "No danger? What do they do?" He walked over an opened the refrigerator door, scanning the refrigerator shelves for a snack.

"Some kind of imagery that they hook up to your head. Sensors of some kind. Hell, I don't know. Ask them yourself. I told Ginesh, one of the scientists, that you'd be interested, so they're expecting you tomorrow night at nine."

"What the hell?" Justin said. "I have something to do tomorrow night."

"What? Screw around with Ellis's kid and that punk, Vic? You're probably not even getting any from her. Why are you wasting your time?"

"Dad, you can't talk about Megan like that. And her father is the president. Show some respect."

"Like hell. Ellis is a horse's ass, and he always will be. I'll show respect in public, but that's as far as it goes. Besides, I'm right aren't I? You're *not* getting any."

Justin slammed the door of the refrigerator shut and stormed out of the kitchen. "Sometimes I wish we still lived in Colorado."

"Yeah, yeah. Just tell your girlfriend that you won't be grabbing her ass tomorrow night—if you've gotten that far—because you've got something productive to do."

Justin reached the stairs and purposefully stomped as he went up each one. "You're an incorrigible son of a bitch. You know that?"

"Incorrigible? Your vocabulary is getting better. Your mother must have taught you that."

Justin got infuriated. "Don't talk about Mom. Ever."

"Why not? She's been dead for five years. And she wasn't a saint, you know."

"She was to me, so shut up. And leave me alone."

"I'll leave you alone. Just make sure you make that appointment tomorrow night. Directions and instructions will be on the kitchen table."

Justin stopped and leaned over the railing. "Why all the concern, anyway? What's in it for you?"

"Nothing."

"Bullshit. You never do anything unless something is in it for you."

"You're my son. Isn't that reason enough?"

"Did you just find that out?"

"Yeah, the DNA tests came back yesterday."

Justin's eyes moistened. "You're a real ass, Dad."

"I've been called worse," he said. "Just make sure you show up on time."

THE TRIAL

Washington, D. C., June 2028

Justin showed up a few minutes early, and he had Vic with him. He'd told a few of his friends about the test, but most of them didn't need the money and didn't have the ambition to do anything about it even if they did need money.

Vic leaned close to Justin and whispered. "You think this shit will get me high?"

Justin shook his head. "How the hell do I know? But I doubt it. I don't think they are doing tests to see if young kids can get high on this drug."

"I didn't mean that dumb shit, but some stuff has side effects that make you high. Maybe this is one of them."

"I don't think so," Justin said. "Now, shut up. Here comes somebody."

A tall, thin man appeared, and he looked as if he had Indian or Pakistani ancestry. He walked toward them wearing a wide smile, showing off gleaming white teeth.

"My name is Ginesh," he said while extending his hand. "I'm one of the scientists in charge of this trial."

"I'm Justin, and this is Vic."

"Then you must be Senator McCabe's son," Ginesh said. "He told us you'd be coming."

Justin smiled. "I'm a little nervous, Ginesh. I've never done anything like this before. Can you tell me what this is about?"

Ginesh shook his head as he walked down the hall. "I'm afraid not. You're trapped in here forever now." Then Ginesh laughed. "Certainly I can tell you. This is a test of a new product that will be similar to a pair of glasses, but they are designed, or at least we hope they are designed, to show a video of whatever you dream."

"So it's just wearing a pair of glasses?" Vic asked.

"Not quite," Ginesh said. "In order to activate the glasses you must take an experimental drug. We've tested this drug extensively with older people and they have had no adverse effects. With them it has taken about two weeks to work. I don't know if it will be the same with you."

"So you haven't tested this on younger people yet?"

Ginesh lost his smile. "Not yet. No. But there is no reason to be concerned. We don't anticipate any trouble."

"What would you do differently if you did anticipate trouble?"

Ginesh raised his brows. "Good question, and the answer is probably nothing. But we'll be monitoring everything and continually testing both of you."

"What about if I have to use the restroom?"

"Someone will be here all night. Just press this button and they'll come and unhook you then wait for you to return and hook you up again."

Justin took his coat off and set it on top of a desk that no one seemed to be using. "Okay, let's get started."

"Not so fast," Ginesh said. Then he pointed to several king-sized beds in the corner. "I'm going to hook you up to some equipment so that we can monitor your vitals, then we'll give you a pill to begin the process."

"What happens then?" Justin asked.

"Not much for at least the first week. After that, we will start testing the device to see if you are receiving images. If earlier research is an indication, you won't get full images for two weeks, but it doesn't hurt to try."

"It doesn't?"

"No. Not at all. Testing the glasses is simply a matter of putting them on and telling us what, if anything, you see."

"If that's the case, I'm ready," Justin said. "Vic, how about you? Got any questions?"

"I'm ready, dude. Fly me away."

Ginesh pointed to the call button, and said, "Just remember, if you need *anything*, use the button and someone will come right away."

Ginesh or Nancy came at seven every morning. Justin was usually awake, but Vic wasn't. The scientists checked their vitals, asked if they felt anything odd, then unhooked them from the equipment and sent them on their way.

At the end of day seven, things still looked fine.

"Don't forget to report if you feel anything different," Nancy said.

Justin waved as he left. "We won't," he said. "See you tonight."

The drive home was quiet. About halfway to Justin's house, Vic said, "Easy money."

"If you want to call putting your life at risk *easy*."

"Life at risk? I've put a lot worse than this in my body with no side effects. And no one was there to monitor it either."

A light-blue pick-up ran a stop sign at the next intersection, almost hitting them. Vic leaned out the window and screamed "Idiot!" and shot him the bird.

"Settle down, Vic. No harm done."

"Maybe no harm to us, but he's gonna hit somebody. Son of a bitch should be shot."

"A little severe, isn't it?"

"I'd do it. I'd shoot the bastard."

"You'd do it? You'd shoot somebody for running a stop sign?"

"Goddamn right I would. Without a moment's hesitation."

"You're a tough case, Vic."

"That's how you survive," Vic said, "By being a tough case."

fter three more days of clinicals, Vic turned to Justin on the way home and said, "Why don't you let me go to bed with her?"

"With whom?"

"There you go with your formal shit. Just say it like normal people do —with who?"

"All right, with who?"

Vic laughed. "Megan, of course."

"You're a sick son of a bitch," Justin said. "Forget we were ever friends. And we never will be again."

"Why not? You know Megan wants to do it."

"Screw you, Vic."

"You know, don't you? Ask her. She'll tell you."

"Tell me what?"

"Tell you that she wants to go to bed with a real man like me. She's got to be tired of trips to the mall with you."

"You can go to hell, Vic."

"You haven't had her yet, have you? Is she still a virgin? I like virgins. And man do they like me," Vic said, then he laughed.

"Get out of my life and stay out, you despicable son of a bitch. I don't ever want to see you again."

"That's fine," Vic said. "The next time you *do* see me, Megan will be in bed underneath of me, and she'll be loving it."

"Fuck you," Justin said, and brought the car to a screeching halt. "Get the fuck out. Get out, and you're never getting back in."

Vic looked over at him. "You mean that? You'd break up a good friendship over a girl?"

"You're goddamn right I would. Now get out of the car. And you can forget the clinical trials. You're out."

When he got home, Justin went immediately to his father. "I don't want Vic in these trials anymore. I told him he's out."

"Why?"

"Because he's an ass."

"That doesn't sound like a reason to me," McCabe said.

"He's an ass that said repulsive things about Megan."

"Ah. Now we get to the heart of the matter. What did he say about precious Megan?"

"Nothing."

"If he said nothing then there is no problem."

Justin sighed. "He said he wanted to screw her, okay?"

McCabe laughed. "Is that all? Hell, I can't blame him. The girl is a knockout. If I were younger, *I'd* want to screw her."

Justin kicked the sofa and said, "I can't believe you said that, but I should have known. You're a goddamn pervert. You'd screw a snake if you could."

"Maybe. But let's not talk about nasty things. Let's discuss more important things, like keeping Vic in these trials."

"No way. Not a chance."

"Justin, we need him for these trials. Even if you find someone to take his place, we will have lost weeks. Weeks that we can't afford."

"And what's so important about losing a few weeks?"

"It will delay the project and cost us money. Lots of money."

"Us? Who is *us*? It's you, isn't it? You're involved in this. I should have known you had your hand in it."

"Yes, I'm involved, and it could mean millions of dollars. So get your head out of your ass, and get Vic back in those trials. If you don't do it, I will."

"Then you'll have to do it, because there's no way I am."

HIDE THE STOCK

Washington, D. C., July 2028

By the end of week two, as predicted, both Vic and Justin were able to see their dreams come to life on video and in high quality.

Justin saw images of him and Megan skiing, hiking, mountain climbing, and camping in the forest. They were laughing and having fun, and he could not only see but "feel" the enjoyment.

Vic opened his eyes, looked at the monitor, and saw himself on a street corner in the city, smoking weed, and listening to old songs. He also saw himself making love to Megan. "Goddamn, she's better than I thought," he said, but to no one.

Justin must have heard Vic, and shot him a look to kill, then unhooked the last of the sensors on his forehead and stood to dress. He was supposed to wait for a technician to unhook him, but he did it himself.

As Justin was leaving, Vic hollered, "Hey, dude, can I catch a ride?"

Justin turned to him. "I'm sure you can with someone, but not with me."

Ginesh gave Vic money for the metro, which would take him to within a few blocks of his house. "Let me know if you need tokens," Ginesh said. "I'll pay for the metro but not a cab."

"You got it," Vic said. "That's great because it looks as if I'm going to need subway fare from now on."

His father was watching a football game when Justin walked in. "Hey, son, how'd it go?"

"The trial is over and it was a success, so you should be happy."

"A success? You were able to see the dreams?"

"Yes, and I'm fine, Dad. Thanks for asking."

"Don't be petty. This is about more than a few potential side effects; this is about us making a lot of money. I mean *a lot*."

"Not everything is about money," Justin said. "Maybe to you it is, but not everybody. Some people care about the well being of their kids, things like that."

"And I'm sure those people are living happily ever after in the ghetto somewhere. As for me, I'd rather have a house, a car, and things I can be proud of. Maybe some day you'll understand."

"I hope not," Justin said, and stormed off to the kitchen. As Justin grabbed a jar of pickles from the fridge, he could hear his father saying, "I can't believe he dropped that pass."

~

Ginesh was watching Chaz and two other rats run through the maze. He documented each wrong turn and how many wrong turns each rat made. It would be interesting to note the improvement, if any, and if it could be attributed to the drug.

His phone rang and vibrated on his desk. He walked over to answer it. "Hello?"

"Ginesh, it's Raji. I need you to come home. My water broke."

"What? Shit. Okay, I'll be right there."

Ginesh rushed over to where Nancy was conducting her own experiments. "Nancy, I'm sorry to do this to you, but I have to leave. Raji called, and her water broke."

"What! Then hurry up. Get your ass moving."

Ginesh grabbed his jacket and raced for the door.

"And drive safely," Nancy said. "And good luck. Call me when you know something."

"Will do," Ginesh hollered, then slammed the door.

Barney Franklin met with Keith early in the morning. "Looks like a go," he said with a smile. "It's not what McCabe wanted originally but it's something, and it's pretty damn good."

"And you're still working on the original idea?" Keith said. "The one using the audio to suggest things to dream of?"

"Working on it, but so far, nothing conclusive. We've had a couple of people dream what was suggested but it was generic stuff, so the dreams could have been coincidental. We're testing now with more specific and less common suggestions."

"Good. Keep me posted on results," Keith said. "I can't emphasize enough the importance of this."

"I know. But McCabe seemed exited by the commercial potential of this, also. Wouldn't it help if we had a commercial success?"

"If it works, yes. But who knows? It takes a lot more than technology to make a successful product."

"What do you mean by that?"

Keith looked at Barney. "I mean that just because you have a technology that works, it doesn't mean that there are people who want to buy the product."

Barney shook his head. "I hate to say it, Keith, but I'm siding with McCabe on this one. I think we have a winner. Not only is the technology good, but I think it will appeal to people's curiosity."

"I guess we'll see before long," Keith said. "In the meantime, don't quit looking for an answer to McCabe's real problem."

"Got it," Barney said. "See you later."

McCabe met with his team from the nanotechnology company, consisting of engineers, manufacturing personnel, project managers, and others.

"All right, here's the scoop. We've got a new product. Some of you have been working on it. We've run it through clinicals, tested it with animals and humans, and it appears to be working great. So great, in fact, that I'm considering launching it as a commercial product."

"What is it?" one of the project managers asked.

"A product that allows people to *see* their dreams. The dreams will be viewed on a pair of glasses, which will be our contribution, and the dreams are made visible by a drug that's manufactured by another company."

"Sounds cool," one of the engineers said.

"The question is, how much are you willing to bet on its success?"

"What do you mean?" the same engineer asked.

"We need to set up a new company, one that's not associated with the government in any way, and that company will need to be staffed. So whoever believes in the product might want to join. If it's a success, you'll be rich. If not, you'll be out of work. You need to make a decision by Friday."

"What about pay?" someone hollered.

"I'll keep everyone's pay the same. Benefits will be a little worse, especially vacation, but there will be generous stock options. That's where the *rich* comes in to play. If it sells, you can cash in. If not, you'll have kindling for the fireplace."

Before McCabe stepped down, he was bombarded with questions and he answered each one in detail. "One thing," he said, "Every one of you will have to sign a nondisclosure before coming to work and you will also need to sign a confidentiality agreement regardless. Part of that agreement will be that *no one* is permitted to mention that I am involved in any way. Is that understood?"

Every head in the room nodded, then McCabe continued to answer questions.

The next morning, McCabe met Keith at the coffee shop to discuss terms. "I think we should have the patents jointly owned," McCabe said. "If I have control of the glasses and you have the drug, we could each look for other partners. If we control them jointly, there will be no problem, forcing us to work out issues between us."

Keith thought about it for a minute then extended his hand to shake.

"Deal," he said. "If this is going to work, we need trust. And nothing ensures trust like an ironclad agreement."

McCabe laughed. "My thoughts exactly."

"One more thing," McCabe said. "I don't want to be identified with this project in any way, so my name will *not* be on the paperwork. I won't be an officer, and I will not sit on the board. It has to be that way if we expect any help or support from Congress. It can't look like I'm fighting for my own interests."

"That's fine, but what about the stock?"

"The stock will be issued in a name I'll provide. It's someone I trust but she's not connected to me in any public way."

Keith waited, pen in hand. "Well?" he said.

"Her name is Helen Kazinski." McCabe then proceeded to spell it for Keith.

"You sure you can trust her?" Keith asked. "This might become worth a hell of a lot of money."

McCabe smiled. "I can trust her. Don't worry. Just make sure my name isn't on the paperwork anywhere, as I said."

"And who is Helen Kazinski, if I might ask?"

"You may not ask, and who she is, is none of your business. You have the spelling of her name. Let me know what else you need—social, address, phone number, and anything else."

"I'll eventually need her signature," Keith said.

"When you do, let me know. Until then, you should have enough."

LAUNCH TIME

NeuroScan, the new company that Keith had created to handle the drug manufacturing, was a beehive of activity. A number of scientists from the old company had transferred to new jobs, but Keith also had to hire several new formulation scientists to work on scale-up issues. He was only able to do that because of the infusion of cash from McCabe.

The cash was keeping them afloat for now, but it came with a lingering sense of doom in the form of pressure to perform.

Ginesh walked into the lab, removed his coat, and sat down at the desk. He was only there a moment before he got up for coffee.

"Sleep in?" Nancy asked. "It's almost coffee-break time."

"Had to," Ginesh said, and he shook his head as he poured more coffee. "Ramesh kept us up all night. I guess he didn't feel good."

"What was the matter with him?"

"I don't know. It felt as if he had a slight fever."

"That had to be it," Nancy said. "Sweet little Ramesh would never keep you up on purpose." She smiled. "By the way, Ginesh, what does his name mean? I know you are big on giving out names that mean something."

Ginesh laughed. "Technically, it means *preserver* or *one who saves you from danger*, and Raji's parents were thrilled about it. But that was all just a lucky call. Raji and I are too Americanized, I guess. We just combined her name—Raji—with my name—Ginesh—and formed Ramesh. I didn't even know it meant anything until her mother told us."

Nancy joined him in laughing. "Just as well," she said. "Kids seldom like the names parents give them anyway."

Washington, D. C., March 2029

I t took six months to get production of the glasses up to speed and the same amount of time for the scale-up of the drug. Scaling up drugs was as much black arts as it was science—some said more. It was similar to baking—what worked in small quantities might not perform the same at higher levels.

Still, by mid-year, Keith and his team were ready, as was McCabe's team. As agreed, McCabe's involvement was nowhere to be found, at least not officially—on paper.

McCabe met Keith at their favorite coffee shop early in the morning. "We're ready," McCabe said.

"But for what?" Keith asked. "I know the product works, but like I said to Barney—it's one thing to create a new technology, it's another altogether to persuade people to fork over hard-earned money."

"It's not that much money," McCabe said.

"Huh? You could have fooled me. This isn't just a product for the idle rich, McCabe. If you plan on selling it in high volumes, it has to be bought by the masses, and that means you have to give them a reason to buy it."

"You can see your dreams. Isn't that enough?" McCabe asked.

"Not for me, it isn't. If I weren't involved in this venture, there is no way I'd fork out $300 bucks for a pair of glasses I didn't need, and another $130 *per month* for a drug that I didn't need either."

"You wouldn't?"

"Not a snowball's chance in hell," Keith said. "You'd have to give me a reason."

"Then we'll have to give them a reason," McCabe said. "A good one."

"While you think of a reason" Keith said, "tell me why you don't want your name associated with this."

"I told you before. Because there might come a time when people object to what we're doing, and I have to be able to defend this publicly without looking like it's self-interest. Besides, looking at a person's dreams is one thing, but looking at what they think is another."

Keith furrowed his brow. "We can't see what a person thinks."

McCabe smiled. "Not yet. But we'll work in it."

Three months later, the product was launched bearing the names McCabe and Keith had chosen—Dream Visors for the glasses and NeuroScan for the drug.

Sales did not skyrocket, but they *were* respectable. By the end of the first month, they were selling 10,000 glasses a month. That wasn't horrible, especially when combined with the companion drug sales, but it wasn't spectacular either. It was nowhere near the original expectations.

Three weeks later, McCabe met Keith for coffee again. It was becoming a morning ritual.

"Any ideas?" Keith asked. "Sales are not that remarkable."

"Not flying off the shelves, is it?" McCabe said.

"Far from it. And I don't know why other than what I said to begin with—the price is too high. People aren't willing to pay that much to look at their dreams."

"Have you had any reports of adverse reactions?" McCabe asked.

Keith shook his head emphatically. "None. Not a single one. So it's not that."

"And the product works as advertised?"

"Absolutely. At least according to the feedback."

"Then we need to *sell* it differently," McCabe said.

"Meaning what?"

"Meaning we have to give people another reason to buy it. A deep-seated primal reason."

"Like what?"

"Like jealousy or fear."

Keith took a drink from his coffee. "Explain. How does being able to see your dreams work in conjunction with jealousy or fear?"

"I'm not talking about seeing your own dreams. I'm talking about looking at the dreams of others."

"I'm still lost," Keith said.

"My God, but you're thick," McCabe said.

"Then enlighten me."

"We do what I suggested originally. Suppose you go to a party and some good-looking guy is flirting with your wife. The next morning, you get up and use her glasses to see if she dreamed about humping him."

Keith smiled. "Okay, I can see that. It's crude, but there are people who would do it."

"The best part about this is that the husband *and* wife would have to be taking the drug to be able to make the glasses work, so we'd be doubling the sales."

"But it's not doubling the glasses sales."

"No, it's not. That's something we need to work on. Perhaps make them fit one person only." McCabe shook his head. "Never mind. Forget I said that. If we did that, then they wouldn't be able to see what the other dreamed of."

Keith frowned, but a moment later it turned to a smile. "I don't think the one-person idea will work either, but we could limit the viewing experience. Let a person watch maybe ten times before the use expires."

McCabe thought about it, then he smiled. "I like it. In fact, I love it. People can use it ten times, then they'll have to buy new glasses."

Keith was shaking his head. "I don't think new glasses are the way to go. People will think we're greedy. But maybe we could make a renewable insert. Sell it for $29.99 or something like that."

McCabe didn't say anything for a minute, then laughed. "I like it, Keith. I like it." He dipped his biscotto in his coffee, took a bite, then said, "But we have to find a way to make people think of the things they could do with it—for those who don't think of it on their own. We want them using the hell out of these."

"We make some ads," Keith said.

McCabe shook his head. "No. We don't want to be associated with the ads, at least not the kind I'm thinking of. We need to come across clean." He took another nibble of the biscotto, then said, "Maybe we grant favorable treatment to one of the distributors if they run the ads for us, but run them as if they were their own."

"Depending upon what kind of favorable treatment, it might cut into our profits," Keith said.

McCabe laughed. "If this works, that will be a pisshole in the snow. Your idea for the inserts alone would cover that."

"Let me get this right," Keith said. "We tell people to spy on their loved ones—spouses and kids—we provide the means to do so, but we make it seem as if that idea belongs to someone else."

"That's the gist of it," McCabe said. "No one can blame you for making a well-intentioned product. If someone uses it improperly, well..."

Keith smiled. "Brilliant. I love it. And I think it'll work."

"I *know* it will work," McCabe said. "We just have to distance ourselves from the scandal that's sure to follow."

"What do you think the ads should be?"

"I'll leave that to the marketing experts," McCabe said. "I plan on calling a few after I leave. I expect we'll have a few ads to look at by the end of next week."

"In the meantime, we just keep chugging along," Keith said.

"Nothing's changed. If it does, let me know."

As McCabe got up to leave, he asked, "By the way, any progress on the original plan? The audio?"

Keith picked up his coffee cup to take with him. "Nothing yet, but we're still working on it. I'll get an update from Ginesh this week."

"Okay," McCabe said. "See you in two weeks. By then we should have those ads to review."

When they met two weeks later, Keith seemed a little more excited. "Got the ads?" he asked.

McCabe sat down, opened up a briefcase, and withdrew a couple of folders. He spread them out on the table.

"Picture this," McCabe said. "A deep baritone voice starts the announcement. You don't see anything, just hear it."

'People achieve what they dream. Let me restate that. A better way to say that is, people *do not* achieve what they *do not* dream.'

"Then the screen flashes to show a picture of a husband and wife sleeping. They will, of course, be young—in their twenties or thirties and good-looking. The ad will show a dream bubble over the man's head and pictures of him playing poker or bowling...or some other selfish activity."

"What will that do to help?" Keith asked.

"Patience, my friend," McCabe said. "Then the ad will close with a woman's sultry voice saying, 'Is he dreaming of making you rich or is he thinking of making himself comfortable?"

Keith didn't say anything for a moment, then he smiled. "That might work. Even though the majority of women work today, they still look to their spouse to at least contribute."

"Exactly," McCabe said. "And wait, there's more."

"We need something more provocative," Keith said.

"And that's what we have."

"The next one will show an image of her sleeping in bed, sexy as hell, probably with a flimsy nightgown on. Then you'll hear that same announcer's voice asking,

'What is she dreaming about at night? Or should I be asking...*who is she dreaming about?"*

Then flash to a scene at a party with her in an alluring dress. She is standing at the side of the room in a dark corner, holding a drink and talking to a handsome younger man. You are at the side, watching jealously. Then the voice comes back on, saying,

'Is she thinking of that guy at the party? Is she thinking of sleeping around?'

"Have a short break for listeners to form the image, then have the announcer come back on."

'You can find out, with the Dream Visors and NeuroScan.'

"Shit! I like that," Keith said. "That's the kind of ad we need. It might even tempt me to buy one."

"For the more loving couples, we could take a different approach. Try the positive side."

"Like what?"

"Something like,

'Find out what she's dreaming about for Christmas or her birthday, and surprise her.'

Or,

'Surprise her with the perfect gift—the one she's been dreaming of.'

"I love it," Keith said. "It's gold."

"Let's hope it turns into real gold," McCabe said, then he dumped his empty cup in the trash and headed out the door.

THE INVESTIGATION CONTINUES

Washington, D.C., March 2030

Langley got a call from Dennis first thing in the morning. Hell, it was before first thing. The caller ID showed Dennis' number, but only because Langley had entered it in manually. Previously, it had shown "unknown caller".

"This is Langley."

"It's Dennis. I'm returning your call."

Langley had to think for a minute, as it had been several days since he left Dennis a message. "Ah, yes. I called because I was looking over what you sent, and the files made mention of a witness who saw a young black man close by at the time of the attack. Possibly even following her."

"Turned out to be nothing," Dennis said.

"What was the kid's name, the young black man?"

"I don't remember."

"You think you could check? I know most of these kids. I've been working this area for a lot of years, and I know a lot of kids who make a habit of hanging out at that mall."

Langley heard the sigh through the phone. "Hang on," Dennis said. A moment later, he picked up again. "Mack. Mack Gattis. Mean anything?"

"I don't know Mack, at least not well, but I know his older brother and his mother and father. Can you meet me tomorrow about ten?"

"Yeah. Why?"

"If Mack is anything like the rest of that family, he wouldn't have told you shit without something in return. I say we give him something in return."

Dennis thought for a second, then said. "I don't make deals with criminals."

"Then you won't get shit done. I've been doing this a long time, Dennis. It's the way things work. Meet me in front of the Capitol Building at ten if you want to go."

"I haven't told you where he lives."

"I know where he lives. I told you, I know his family. You gonna meet me or not?"

"I'll be there. I hope it's worth our while."

"Bring a gun. It's not a nice part of town."

"I always have my gun. But what part of town is it?"

"Benning, across the Anacostia River."

"I'll bring two guns," Dennis said, then laughed.

At ten o'clock on the dot, Dennis pulled up to meet Langley. He got out of the car and walked to where Langley was parked. "We going in one car or two?"

Langley pressed the button to unlock the doors, then said, "Hop in."

They drove in silence for a few minutes, then Langley said, "I know you don't like me working this, and I can't say I blame you, but I might be able to help."

"How's that?"

"I know you guys can handle things on the technical side better than me, and I realize you have a hell of a lot more resources, but I've been on these streets a long time. I know the people and they know me. More importantly, they trust me. In the long run, that could help."

Dennis looked over to Langley, then said, "You might be right. Let's start out fresh."

"I'd like that," Langley said, and held out his hand to shake.

It didn't take long till they were crossing the Anacostia River. "Where to now?" Dennis said.

"Not far. Down by East Capitol and Texas. Some old projects near there."

"You might not be so welcome in that part of town, Langley."

Langley laughed. "You're not up to speed on that part of town then. *No one* is welcome. No matter what color they are."

Langley drove about three blocks south of East Capitol, then made a right and parked in front of a row of houses that had been built a long time ago. Back then, they were probably nice. Now, they were barely habitable.

Dennis opened the passenger door to get out, following Langley, but the detective stopped him. "You better wait in the car. You might be darker than the Gattisess, but they're a lot meaner. Besides, I'm sure I won't be long."

"Forget that. I'm going with you."

Langley shrugged. "Suit yourself."

Langley stepped slowly up the cracked concrete sidewalk until he reached the door. The screen was torn in several places and the frame was dented and scratched.

"Looks like they need a new door," Dennis said.

"Looks like they need a new house," Langley added, then he knocked on the door and shifted weight to his right foot while he waited for someone to answer. "By the way, I know these people, like I said, so it'll probably go easier if I do the talking."

"Take it away," Dennis said. "But if I see you faltering, I'm stepping in."

Within a moment, a middle-aged black woman answered, wearing a concerned look. She adjusted her glasses and stared, then seemed to recognize Langley. It must have been that recognition that forced a smile. "Grant! It's been a long time. Come on in."

Langley stepped inside and held the door open for Dennis. "Mama Gattis, you look as young as you did the last time I was here."

"And you're still full of shit," she said. "I feel ten years older and probably look twenty years older. But thank you, anyway." She sat in a chair
at the kitchen table facing the oven. "Have a seat and tell me why
you're here. It's not to say hello to me, so which of my boys is in
trouble?"

Langley laughed. "No one's in trouble. But I do need to talk to Mack
and ask him a few questions."

Mama Gattis shook her head. "When cops come down to this part of
town askin' questions, it's usually for no good reason. I'm bettin' it
ain't to ask him if he has the winning lottery ticket?"

"No, it's not that," Langley said. "But it's not for any trouble either."

"In that case, let me find him." She stood, then walked through the
living room and up the stairs.

A few moments later, she returned with Mack trailing behind her.
"Lazy sucker was still sleeping. That's why the young generation will
never accomplish anything. Too damn lazy. Not enough gumption."

Mack nodded to Langley, then pulled a chair out from the table and
sat. "S'up?"

Langley nodded. "Mack, I don't know if you remember me, but—"

"I know you," Mack said. "I remember seeing you with my brother."

"That's right, Mack," Langley said. "And I'm not here for trouble. I'm
here about a crime you might have witnessed. I need to know
anything you saw, or anything you might have seen, leading up to the
crime. And if you help us out, there'll be something in it for you."

"Like what?"

"Like a get-out-of-jail-free card for anything minor. You can't go killing
somebody and expect a pass, but little things I can work with."

"Sounds good," Mack said, then, "When? And where? I cover a lot of
territory."

"This would have been before Christmas, at the Pentagon City Mall. Probably not far from Nordstrom's entrance."

"I was at the mall before Christmas, that's for sure. But I don't remember seeing anything and I sure as hell wasn't shopping at Nordstrom."

Langley stared into Mack's eyes. "Come on, Mack. I'm not lookin' to bust some kid for carrying a dime bag or even breaking into a car. Most people don't know this, but the president's daughter was brutally beaten and raped at that mall two weeks before Christmas. It was a Thursday night and as far as we can tell it happened before ten. We saw her on video surveillance at about nine, so we assume it was sometime between nine and ten. And it wasn't far from the mall entrance on the south side, by Nordstrom on Hayes Street—unless the attack happened elsewhere and she was dragged there, which does not seem probable."

"Oh, my Lord," Mama Gattis said.

"Shit. I didn't know that," Mack said.

"Does that make a difference, knowing who the victim was?" Dennis asked.

Mack looked at him for what seemed like the first time. "I don't know you, dude. If I say anything it will be to Grant. And that's *if* I say anything."

Langley kicked Dennis' leg under the table and glared. "This is Dennis Markum. He works for the president. I'm helping him try to find out who did this."

Mack nodded, then looked at Dennis. "Yeah, it *does* make a difference. The president is an okay dude. He does good things. Not to mention that his daughter is a fox supreme."

Mama Gattis smacked him on the back of the head. "Mack, watch your mouth. Tell Detective Langley what he needs to know and don't hold nothin' back. He ain't here to arrest you for some petty drug-dealing shit. A girl got hurt. So tell him."

"What do you mean, watch my mouth? I didn't say nothing but the truth. She's stone cold. Anybody who's seen her knows that."

"You don't say that about the president's daughter," his mother said. "Now get to talking."

"That's bull," Mack said, then he turned to Langley. "Yeah I might have seen something."

Langley pulled out his notebook and a pen. "Go ahead, Mack. Tell us."

"I don't know if it means anything, but about 9:15, me and a couple of other dudes were hanging out in the parking lot—"

"Doing what?" Dennis asked.

Mack leaned forward, closer to Dennis. "None of your goddamn business. What we were doing has nothing to do with this case."

"Excuse Mr. Markum," Dennis said. "He was just being his rude self. He obviously didn't understand that you were trying to help."

"Got that shit right," Mack said. Then he took out a smoke and lit it. He took a few drags before continuing. "Like I said we were hanging out when we saw her. And a guy was following her. It wasn't obvious to most, but I could tell. I've followed enough people."

"How did you know it was her?" Dennis asked.

"Come on, man. She's a fox. And she's the president's daughter. I might be poor and ignorant, but I ain't blind."

"Why didn't you report this?"

"Ain't stupid either. Dude like me, from this part of town saying he was at the same place and at the same time that the president's daughter was attacked...You do the math."

"Why didn't you do something?" Langley asked.

"Like I said he was following her. For all I knew he was checking out her ass. Can't blame a guy for doin' that. Anyway, she went into Nordstrom a few seconds later."

"What did he look like?" Langley asked.

"Average. Maybe a little less than six feet. Waist-length leather jacket, black. Dark hair. I don't know much more than that."

"White or black?" Langley asked.

"White."

"And that's all? You didn't see her again?"

Mack shook his head. "My business was outside the mall. I never went in." He tapped Langley on the arm. "By the way, how'd you keep this quiet?"

"She was taken to the hospital as a Jane Doe. No ID. It was only when one of the nurses recognized her that they called the White House. The president asked them to keep it quiet after that."

"I looked at surveillance. I don't remember seeing anyone enter the mall within a few minutes after Megan went in," Dennis said.

"The dude that was following her waited five or ten minutes before he entered. He'd have probably just looked like a straggler on surveillance."

"We'll have to recheck that," Langley said.

"Wait a minute. Now that I'm going over it in my head again, I think he entered with a crowd of people. Maybe five or six of them."

"Were they with him?" Langley asked.

Mack shook his head. "I don't think so, and I don't think he was with them. I think he just waited for a group and tagged along."

Dennis took a drink from his water. "If it was a group, we'd have paid it no mind."

"Then it looks like we need to look at that surveillance again," Langley said to Dennis. He stood, shook Mack's hand and thanked him. "Mack, you've been helpful. And now, I owe you one. Call it in anytime."

Then Langley kissed Mama Gattis on the cheek. "Mama Gattis, it's been great seeing you again."

Mrs. Gattis kissed his cheek and said, "Don't make yourself a stranger. This place needs the kind of policing you do."

"I'll check on who patrols this area," Langley said. "I'll tell them to keep a close eye out for you."

THE AUDIO PROGRESS

Washington, D. C., March 2029

Ginesh sat in the chair drinking coffee while Nancy crunched numbers. "It would be good if more than one person worked on this. Maybe we'd get something done."

"I'm trying to figure some things out," Ginesh said.

"It looks like the only thing you're trying to figure out is how to get comfortable in that chair. It *is* possible to drink coffee and work at the same time. I know because I've done it; in fact, I do it every day."

"And yet, we're nowhere," Ginesh said. "But don't worry, I have plans."

"What kind of plans?"

"Plans to isolate whether this thing works or not. From the results we have so far, it's difficult to tell. What is showing as positive could be coincidence."

"And how do you plan on eliminating coincidence, boy genius?"

Ginesh smiled and pulled up a chart he'd made. "It won't eliminate coincidence, but it should limit it. We interview each subject and find out what they *never* dream about, then use that as the choice for audio on an individual basis."

Nancy thought for a moment. "All right. That will work better than what we're doing now. Let's give it a try. Today we'll come up with the questions, and tomorrow we'll do the interviews. Then we'll schedule testing based on subject."

Ginesh smiled. "I agree. Let's get started."

Nancy took patients whose names started with the letters *A* through *M* and Ginesh took *N* through *Z*. They focused the questions not on what the people usually dreamed of, but what they *never* dreamed of.

Some were dreams regarding sports. Mr. Campbell said that in forty years, he had never dreamed of playing professional sports. Another was music—that person had never dreamed of being a musician. Some people had to give the question a lot of thought, while others answered right away. And so the interviews went, until they were all completed.

Once finished, Ginesh and Nancy scheduled individual rooms for patients so that there was no chance of one hearing the audio that was being broadcast to another. In the morning, each person's visor was scanned to see what they dreamed of the night before. This went on for two weeks, and in two weeks, nothing matched. Not a single person had dreamed of what audio had been broadcast.

"As we feared," Ginesh said. "Our process is working, but it's proving the trial is a failure."

"Maybe we need to try something different," Nancy said. "Maybe we should increase the drug again."

Ginesh shook his head. "They're already getting two times the maximum recommended dose. We don't dare go any higher. Besides, I thought you were the cautious one."

"Then try it on the rats. See if it bothers them."

Ginesh thought for a moment, then looked over to the cages. He focused his gaze there for a long while, then said, "Okay, Nancy. We'll try it."

He walked over, opened the cage, reached in to get Chaz, and carried him back to the testing area. "Give him his new dosage," Ginesh said, then he raised Chaz up to his lips and kissed him.

"You're disgusting," Nancy said. "It's a goddamn rat."

"I know what he is," Ginesh said. "But he has a life. Who are we to mess with it?"

Nancy shook her head, spread the pill contents in with the rat's food, then handed the dish to Ginesh. "Here you go— rat dinner for one."

Ginesh set the plate on the desk, then allowed Chaz to feast. It didn't take him long, and when done, they began the test. It was a little different with Chaz. Instead of using audio projections, they broadcast images of things like cheese, rat traps, snakes, and so on. If the images struck a chord, the rat would respond with similar transmissions. After a week of testing, nothing had happened.

"It looks like another failure," Ginesh said. "We should stop before the NeuroScan does something to him."

"I don't really care about the rat," Nancy said. "We need to keep going to see if we can get anything. So far we have nothing, and we're fresh out of ideas."

"What are the sales like on the visors?" Ginesh asked. "Have you heard anything?"

"I've heard they're not good enough," Nancy said. "Which is all the more reason why we need a positive outcome."

"All right," Ginesh said. He picked up Chaz, kissed him on the head, and put him back in the cage. "We'll try this again tomorrow, Chaz."

~

Megan walked down the hall, smiling, saying hi to everyone she saw. The other kids knew who she was, but they liked her for her personality; she was nice to everyone.

Just as she was turning the corner, she felt a tap on her butt and spun around. "What the hell...?"

She dropped her indignant expression when she saw who it was. "Vic, what do you think you're doing? And where have you been? I haven't seen you in forever."

"I don't know if it's been forever," Vic said, "but I haven't been around because of Justin. Didn't he tell you?"

"Tell me what?"

"Tell you that he threw me out of his car, and said he never wanted to see me again."

"What? No, he didn't tell me. Why did he do that?"

Vic lowered his head and turned to the side. "No reason."

"What do you mean, *no reason*. There must have been a reason. Tell me."

"I can't," Vic said. "It's kind of embarrassing."

"It can't be too bad, Vic. Just tell me. I won't say anything."

Vic shrugged, then said, "I told him that I thought you were the finest woman I'd ever seen and that I'd give anything to make love to you."

Megan blushed. "What?"

"I'm sorry," Vic said. "I didn't mean to embarrass you."

"I'm fine, Vic. But I had no idea you felt that way."

"Shit. I feel that way and more. I'd...well, I'd do about anything to be with you."

Megan blushed more. "Really? You really feel that way?"

Vic grabbed her by the shoulders and pulled her toward him, then he kissed her passionately. He shoved his tongue into her mouth, and Megan couldn't resist. She almost returned the kiss.

A few seconds after Vic grabbed her, a group of kids walked by. If nothing else, it provided a reason for Megan to break off the kiss. "Vic, I can't," she screamed, and then smacked his face. "I can't do this to Justin. You better leave."

"You made my day. All I wanted was a kiss." Vic said.

~

Jon Clarkson saw Justin about to enter the restroom. "Justin, wait up."

When he caught up to him, he said, "Dude, I was just coming from Mr. Hasker's class and I saw Megan and Vic making out in the hall."

"Bullshit! No way Megan would do that."

"Whether she would or not is no longer in question. She *did*. And they were going at it hard, dude. I mean, like it looked as if they would get down and do it right then."

"Screw you," Justin said. "There's no way Megan would do that."

"No way or not, she did," Jon said, then left.

After Jon left, Justin punched the wall, drawing blood from his knuckles. "That son of a bitch."

RATS HAVE DREAMS

Washington, D. C., April 2029

Ginesh got to work early, but he was still surprised when Nancy's car wasn't there; she was *always* in early, and she knew they had a meeting with Mr. Ratcliffe. He had texted them both last night.

It wasn't often that Keith Ratcliffe held a meeting with anyone at Ginesh's level, so it must be important. He and Nancy had been working on this clinical trial for months, and even though they didn't have anything to show for it, he felt they were making progress.

Maybe the progress isn't fast enough. Maybe he's going to fire us? It would be just my luck, Ginesh thought *After two years of trying to have a child, Raji had finally gotten pregnant and given birth. I now have more than Raji and myself to look after. If I lose my job now, I'll be in deep shit, as they say here in America.*

As Ginesh pressed the button to lock his door, he noticed Nancy's car as she turned into the parking lot. He waited as she pulled beside him then got out of her car. "What the hell, Nancy. Mr. Ratcliff will probably be waiting. Where have you been?"

Nancy slammed her door, then gestured to the front bumper. "You see that? Some asshole slammed on his brakes for no reason, and I rear-ended him. That's why I'm late. I'd have been here half an hour ago if not for that."

Ginesh walked to the front of the car and leaned toward it. The left side of the bumper was smashed in, with dark-green paint from the other car stuck to it. "This is not good, Nancy. But are you all right? Any pains?"

"I'm fine," she said. "But the damn car isn't. Neither is his. And my insurance rate will probably go up because of it." She slammed her fist on the hood. "I can't afford this shit."

Ginesh patted her shoulder. "I know," he said. "But we need to get going. Mr. Ratcliff is probably waiting."

"Waiting with more bad news is my guess," Nancy said. "He's probably going to lay us off."

When they walked into Ratcliff's office, Barney Franklin was already there, sitting in a stiff-backed chair to the left.

"Ginesh, Nancy. How are you?" Barney asked.

A sick feeling rumbled in Ginesh's gut. "Fine," he said. Then he turned to shake hands with Mr. Ratcliff. "Good morning, sir. You wanted to see us?"

"I did," he said. "I know that you and Nancy have been working on the Dream Visor trials, and now you're on the audio trials. We *need* something positive. Sales of the visors have not been as good as expected. They started out good, but now they've slumped, so we need to show something on another front to keep money coming in."

"Yes, sir," Ginesh said. "We're working on it. We started a new treatment program with the rats, and even though we haven't seen any positive results, I'm confident we will."

"Confident enough to bet your job on it? Because that's what you're doing. I think we need to escalate to human trials. I'll get the patients."

Ginesh said, "You can't just *get* patients. You have to apply for a trial, get funding lined up, lay out a plan. There's a lot to do. You know that."

"Don't worry about it, Ginesh. I'll send patients over. You just be ready for them."

"Yes, sir," Ginesh said. After a few more questions regarding the trial and some idle chatter, he and Nancy shook hands with Keith and Barney and left.

At the lab, Ginesh began preparation for the new trials, but decided to continue testing the rats while waiting. Keith said new patients would arrive in a week or so, but Ginesh thought he might as well take the time to continue working with Chaz.

On the fourth day, while working on her computer, Nancy's attention was diverted to the monitor next to hers—the one used to watch the rats. On the monitor were images of inside the maze, images that shouldn't have been there, and the blinking light indicated that the monitor had received images. She'd had the sound turned off because she hadn't expected anything.

She got up from her chair and bent over to stare at the monitor. After a few moments, she called Ginesh. "You've got to come here. Something weird is going on."

"What?" he asked.

"I don't know. Just come here. And hurry."

Ginesh got up and hurried over to stand beside her. "What?"

"Look at the screen," she said. "That's inside the maze, but not where we have cameras."

Ginesh leaned closer, then said, "What the hell is going on? What is that? What are we looking at?"

"I don't know," Nancy said. "I honestly don't know."

"I think we're seeing Chaz's dreams," Ginesh said. "He dreamed about the maze and we're seeing it transmitted on the screen."

"Impossible," Nancy said. "Rats don't dream."

"Maybe they do," Ginesh said. "Maybe they do."

Nancy studied the image more. "Ginesh, look closer. Chaz wasn't in this part of the maze yesterday, and as far as I know, he's been awake all day today."

Ginesh spread his hands, palms up. "So?"

"So, how is he dreaming of an exact place that he's never been to?"

"I don't know," Ginesh said. "But if they're not dreams, what are they?"

"Memories," Nancy said. "I think we're seeing images of memories of where he's just been."

"That's impossible," Ginesh said. "You can't see memories."

"Until a short while ago you couldn't see dreams either. Now look what we're doing."

Ginesh thought for a moment. "We need to test this on humans.

"Not yet," Nancy said. "Let's do this with Chaz a few more times and see what results we get. And see if there are any problems."

"I don't want to risk Chaz," Ginesh said.

Nancy smiled. "I don't either, but it's better to risk Chaz than to risk the human patients."

"I guess. Let's get started then."

Nancy rearranged the maze and put colored and numbered stickers on various walls for easy identification. Afterward, they placed Chaz at the beginning of the maze and stepped back.

Chaz walked all the way through, squeaking and squealing the whole way. Once he got to the other end, he stopped, as if to rest.

"Anything?" Ginesh asked.

"Nothing yet," Nancy said.

They waited, watching Chaz for several minutes. Nancy had her arms crossed in front of her, and Ginesh held his hands in his pockets. Both appeared nervous.

After several more moments, an alert sounded on the monitor, which Nancy had now adjusted so she could hear the sound. Nancy rushed to it. "Oh, my God. It worked. Ginesh. It's a memory."

In a flash, Ginesh was standing beside her looking at the monitor.

"Look," Nancy said. "The maze wall has the green sticker with a *four* on it. It's the one we just put on. It wasn't there before."

"Son of a bitch," Ginesh said. "Are we really seeing Chaz's memories?"

"I say we are. Notice the slight delay. I think that's caused by memory compression."

"What do you mean?"

Nancy paused, trying to think how to explain it best. "Have you read any of the recent papers dealing with long-term memory consolidation?"

"Yes. A few. It's an interesting theory."

"It's more than a theory," Nancy said. "And this proves it. Memory is compressed at different frequencies, not much different than computer files. Some files are for instant retrieval and some are compressed for long-term storage, to be recalled later."

"So why are we just now seeing these memories? Why didn't we see them before?"

"Because of the different frequencies. If Neurscan enhances the neural receptors and transmitters, then maybe it took a stronger dose to affect this frequency?"

"I'll be a monkey's ass," Ginesh said. "This is amazing. We need to tell Barney."

"No time like the present," Nancy said. "Maybe it will be enough to keep us afloat."

EXPLAINING MEMORY RECALL

Washington, D. C., April 2029

"Come in," Barney said. "Have a seat. You want coffee or tea?"

"We're good," Ginesh said. "We have some news we feel will brighten your day."

"I need that, so spit it out."

"Spit it out?" Ginesh said.

Nancy laughed. "He probably doesn't understand *spit it out*. He's not very good with idiomatic expressions," she said. "I have found that I need to speak clearly for Ginesh to understand completely."

Barney laughed. "*Spit it out* means 'Tell me. Be on with it. Hurry up.' "

"Ah," Ginesh said. "Now I understand."

He shifted in his chair and said, "Anyway, while working the trial, we made an exciting discovery. I think Nancy can explain it better, so I'll let her."

"I'll try to make say this in an easy-to-understand way. Perhaps the best way is to cite a <u>Newsweek article</u> on the subject."

"I'm all ears," Barney said, further confounding Ginesh's understanding of English.

Nancy produced a paper she had printed out before arriving at Barney's office and read from it. "There has been research that suggests an approach to dreaming that focuses on the relationship between sleep and memory. In the papers I read, the scientists suggested that dreams reflect a biological process of long-term memory consolidation that serves to strengthen the neural traces of recent events, to integrate these new traces with older memories and previously stored knowledge, and to maintain the stability of existing memory representations in the face of subsequent experience."

"Now I feel like Ginesh," Barney said. "I don't know if I understood one word of what you said."

"Let me try another way," Nancy said.

Ginesh interrupted. "Perhaps it will be easier if we just accept that we can see Chaz's *memories*. We don't need to know how it works, just like you don't need to understand how a TV works to enjoy watching a show. Signals are broadcast and signals are received. This uses the same principal."

"I'll buy that," Barney said. "Now finish telling me in a language I understand what you found. And remember, even though I'm head of R&D, I finished school a looooong time ago."

"Good enough," Nancy said. "Let's leave it at this. The brain compresses memory on various frequencies. We're able to lock onto this frequency, we assume, because of the increased dosage of Neuro-Scan. It must be allowing the neural transmitters we're working with to send images to the nanochip receptors, which then transmit the images to the monitors, allowing us to see a person's memories. In effect, it's like tuning your radio to different channels. We stumbled onto the one that works for memories."

"But this is on the monitor. Will it work on the visors?"

"We haven't tested it on the visors, but I don't see why not. We're using the same technology. I think it would simply be a matter of adjusting the visors to the proper frequency. Ask Christopher. He should know."

"How far will the memories go back? Will we see only new memories or old ones too? How long will it last? Can they be recalled?"

"Hold on, Barney," Nancy said. "We just discovered this. We don't have all of the answers, at least not yet. Give us some time."

"Is this something like that old movie, *Total Recall*, I think the name was?"

Nancy shook her head. "Nothing at all. I remember that movie. That movie involved people buying premade memories for enjoyment, like a vacation or something, and while the one guy was getting a vacation, they implanted a fake memory into his brain, overriding all else."

"How is this different?"

"In every way possible. First off, it's not buying premade memories, it's not having fake memories implanted in your brain; and you don't have to go anywhere to have the *procedure* done. This is simply putting on a pair of glasses—assuming Christopher can get them to work—and watching someone else's memory. Oh, and this is real. The other stuff wasn't. And this doesn't erase your own memories or override them in any way; this simply gives you something else to watch, like flipping the channel on your TV."

"And you're sure of this?"

"No, I'm not sure of this, because we've just started with it. Some of this consists of educated guesses. But I'm fairly confident it will prove to be true."

"Fairly confident? We have to be more than fairly confident."

"No shit," Nancy said. "Hence, the request for clinical trial patients. We can't be certain until we test it on humans and can ask follow-up questions."

Barney took a second or two to digest the information, then said, "Okay, we don't have a lot of time, so get back to the lab and find the answers. I want to know about everything: which memories are stored, how they're stored, why they're stored, all of it."

"You may have to wait longer than you want, but if we're to have any hope of getting those answers, we need patients," Ginesh said.

"I'll get the patients. Don't worry. Just get to work. Prepare tests to verify. Prepare questions. Do whatever the hell you have to do."

Nancy and Ginesh stood to leave. "You've got it," Nancy said. "It shouldn't take too long."

"And once we see if it works on humans, we'll be sitting on a gold mine," Barney said.

Ginesh looked sideways at Nancy, then nodded. "I like the sound of a gold mine," he said.

Back at the lab, Ginesh and Nancy framed the questions they had devised to ask the patients, then they organized the questions they had about memory storage, highest priority first.

The storage questions were the easiest, as they had no control over them, and they didn't know the answers to most of them.

"Which memories are stored?" Nancy asked. "How are we going to know?"

"By determining which ones are *not* stored," Ginesh said. "It will be easier to figure out what *isn't* stored than to know what is stored. At least I'm assuming it will."

Nancy thought for a moment, then nodded. "You're right. So we ask each people what they thought of during the day and compare it to what is stored on the monitor."

"Better yet, we video each person during the day then compare the video to what's stored on the monitor. We then see what is omitted. This way, we're not relying on the faulty memory of the patients. It will require watching a lot of boring videos, but what the hell."

Nancy smiled. "Perfect. Good idea, Ginesh."

"Now we need to know *why* certain memories are stored."

"I don't think we're going to get an answer to that one," Ginesh said. "I say we leave it alone for now."

"Okay, then we focus on *when,*" Nancy said. "How long does it take to store a memory and then for it to be transmitted?"

"I think that will be easy enough to determine," Ginesh said.

"Does it work on the visors? Again, easy enough to determine," Nancy said. "If we see it on the monitors but not the visors, then we'll know they need adjusting."

"Can we see old memories? Or just new ones? That won't take long to tell," Ginesh said.

"The rest of the questions we probably can't answer until we use the visors," Nancy said. "Things like, how the memories are stored, in what order, how they are retrieved, are the visuals as good as the dreams, and so on."

"I think that wraps it up for now," Ginesh said. "We're ready."

"Except for using real people," Nancy said. "Remember, we have to increase the dosage of NeuroScan yet again. Should we increase the frequency of the present dose or up the amount? Do we know how they'll react? Will there be problems?"

"Chaz did okay with the increase," Ginesh said.

"Chaz is a rat," Nancy said. "And he's only one rat. It's not like we tested this on 1,000 or even 100. We tested it on *one* rat." She stared at Ginesh for a long time. "Do you feel comfortable with basing conclusions on that? I don't."

Ginesh shrugged. "Regardless, it has to be done, so let's be on with it. I've got a one-year-old son who gets hungry several times a day. I want to be able to feed him."

The next day, they informed Barney that they were ready, and he arranged for the patients to show up. Subjects started arriving two weeks later at about 4:00, and Ginesh and Nancy began preparations. All of the patients had already been taking NeuroScan, so their bodies were prepped.

Nancy began administering the increased dose, giving it to them in their evening meal, then she and Ginesh set the video to record mode and got the patients situated for the night. Afterward, Ginesh and Nancy went home, leaving the night crew to babysit.

They checked the monitors in the morning but nothing showed. And for four more days nothing showed, but on day five, a few alerts appeared. Patient six showed images of playing gin rummy with patient five; however, five did not show anything. Patient nine showed winning a game of chess with patient two, including the celebratory dance.

By ten o'clock Nancy and Ginesh had watched most of the memory recordings and had formulated their questions so that they were ready for the patient interviews. They started with number six.

Nancy began the questioning. "I want you to put on your visors and watch the video. Tell me what you can of the experience."

"I can tell you about it without those visors," he said. "I kicked Joe's ass. Beat him 120 to 56. Kicked his ass."

Ginesh leaned forward and pushed the "on" button on the visors. "Just tell us what you see, and if it coincides with what you remember."

Patient six watched the video. Ten minutes later, he removed the visors. "I'll be damned," he said. "That was more than a video. It was like reliving the experience."

"What do you mean?" Nancy asked.

"It was like I was right there, playing cards again. I could see i—and even more, I could *feel* it. On that last hand, when I hollered *gin*, I felt the excitement all over again. It was like it happened twice."

The report from patient nine was similar. He saw his chess match with patient two, and he said the experience was relived as if it were happening again.

Ginesh looked at Nancy and smiled. "We've done it," he said. "It works."

Nancy high-fived him. "I don't know if *we've* done anything, but it does work. That's all that matters."

THE PRACTICAL USE

Washington, D. C., April 2029

"Tell me about it again," Barney said. "Keith and I want to be sure to get this straight when we report to McCabe."

Ginesh rehashed his explanation, then Nancy went over it again. "The most interesting thing," Nancy said, "is that every one of the patients who produced memories said they could not only *see* the memory in the visors, but they could *feel* the experience as well."

Barney looked to Nancy and then Ginesh. "Why would that be? What would make them feel the memory?"

"I can't answer that," Nancy said. "Can you, Ginesh?"

He shook his head. "I have no idea. Perhaps the cells that store memories of sensations are close to the neural transmitter and their data is sent along with it. I don't know. But why question it? Just go with it and see where it takes you. Remember your American saying, 'Don't look a gift horse in the mouth.?'"

Barney said, "Yes, I'm familiar with that saying, but I prefer the one that warns you to 'Beware of Greeks bearing gifts.'"

"I'm glad I'm not so cynical," Nancy said.

Barney snorted. "I hear you, and I know how young people are, but some day you'll wish you were as cynical as I am."

Ginesh turned to Keith. "Any questions, Mr. Ratcliff?"

"None that Barney hasn't asked. We may have some once we speak to McCabe, but for now, I think we're covered."

"Okay," Ginesh said. "Then I guess we're back to work."

"Back to work is right. We're not through yet," Barney said. "We still haven't found an answer to McCabe's audio problem."

"We may never find an answer," Nancy said, and before Keith could interrupt, she added, "but we'll keep trying."

Ginesh and Nancy returned to the lab, and Keith left to meet McCabe for an impromptu meeting at the coffee shop.

McCabe arrived ten minutes late. He plopped down in a cushioned chair next to Keith. "Was our table taken?"

Keith gestured to both sides. "Take a look around, McCabe. It's packed in here. I have no idea why these seats were open. Maybe someone just left when I got here. In any case, be happy; these seats are far better than the normal."

"I guess so," McCabe said, then he sipped from the drink Keith had ordered him.

"What have you got to discuss that's so important?"

Keith waited for a young couple to pass by and get out of earshot, then he continued. "Ginesh and Nancy have made a breakthrough. We are not only seeing dreams, we're seeing *memories*."

"What?"

"You heard it right the first time, McCabe. Memories. As in, whatever you experience is saved to memory. I don't know much about it yet, but it's significant, and it's quick."

"If what you're telling me is correct, this could be big."

"You haven't heard the best part. The patients said they not only *see* the memories, but they *feel* them too."

"What do you mean?"

"I mean just that. The patients said that while they were viewing the experience, they felt it all over again, as if it were the first time."

"Does that work with other people?" McCabe asked.

"Now it's my turn to ask *What do you mean?*"

"I mean suppose you dreamed of taking a cold swim on a hot afternoon. From what you're saying, you would feel that refreshing sensation all over again. My question is, if you gave your visors to someone else and let them watch it, would they feel the experience or would they only see it?"

Keith didn't take long to think. "I don't know, but it's an excellent question. We'll have to find out."

McCabe drank more of his coffee while he thought. "You know, Keith, if this turns out to be as you say, it could be bigger than the dreams."

Keith furrowed his brows. "How so?"

"Think about it. Suppose you went to dinner at a fantastic restaurant. Instead of just telling someone about it, you could actually share the experience. Or better yet. Imagine you just returned from a vacation to Italy or Greece, or wherever. Rather than show boring pictures of where you went, let your friends go along for the ride. They can climb the same mountain you did, swim in the same sea, and marvel at the same ancient sites."

McCabe gulped the rest of his drink and beamed. "Oh, my God, this could be huge! Forget everything else we're doing and focus on this."

"But we're working on the audio," Keith said.

"Forget the audio. This could be real money. I mean *real* money."

Keith made notes on his phone while McCabe ordered another drink. When he sat back down, McCabe said. "Is there any way to limit the viewing?"

Keith looked at him with a puzzled expression. "What do you mean?"

"Imagine the scenario I mentioned earlier about the vacation. Why should we let all of this person's friends experience a trip to Italy for nothing? We should charge them for it."

"How?"

"By doing what I said before. If we limit the viewing to where only one person could view it or it could be viewed only one time, then whoever else wanted to *experience* the trip would have to pay."

Keith started to get excited too. "Okay, I see what you're saying. People could sell their memories."

"Exactly," McCabe said. "Exactly."

"So if you ski, you could go on a skiing trip down a dangerous trail, then sell the experience to people who maybe have always wanted to ski, but never could."

"Even to people who *used* to ski. Maybe now they're seventy-years-old and can no longer do it. With this, they could. Older people could relive their youth."

"How much would we charge for this?" Keith said. "Wait a minute, how would *we* charge? We don't own the visors. Whoever owns the visors would control the experience."

"I guess you weren't listening earlier. Limit the viewing. Figure out how to limit the number of times a person can view a memory. After that, the person has to pay for new visors or new storage or something. I don't know the details, but I'm sure you can figure it out."

"If we limit the visors to one use or even two, then we'd be limiting the user the same way. That might be a deterrent to sales. No one would want to pay for their own memories."

"In what way?"

"Come on, McCabe. If someone goes on vacation then decides to *sell* that vacation, as you said earlier, they could only do it one or two times. They couldn't earn enough to pay for even a small part of it."

McCabe thought for a moment then shook his head. "I don't know how, but find some way to make the owner of the visor pay us for use but, at the same time, allow them to sell the experience for a profit."

Keith raised his brows. "Tough challenge."

McCabe laughed. "That's what challenges are. I'm sure you're up to it." He stood to leave, then said, "And don't forget the ads for the Dream Visors start running tomorrow. We need those ads to work if we hope to spur sales."

"All right," Keith said. "See you later."

THE AD CAMPAIGN

Washington, D. C., April 2029

The ad campaign for Dream Visors kicked off with a bang, shocking people and instilling ideas at the same time. Pretty soon, sales of the Dream Visors soared. Existing inventory soon depleted and backorders piled up. In two weeks, seventeen million units had been sold and orders for thirty-one million more were pending. All in all sales totaled more than one billion dollars in one month —records.

It had been two weeks since McCabe and Keith met, so at 8:00, McCabe parked the car and walked to the coffee shop. Keith was at his usual spot at a table in the rear.

"We've made it," McCabe said. "It's been a long journey but we've made it."

"And not a moment too soon," Keith said. "We were running out of money."

"We won't run out of money now," McCabe said. "We'll never run out again."

"I guess I should be thankful," Keith said.

"Thank American greed, jealousy, suspicion, and more. They are the things driving sales."

"If sales continue at this rate, we'll be sitting on a pile of cash, a huge pile of cash."

"Keith, we'e already sitting on a huge pile of cash. If sales continue, we'll be sitting on a mountain of cash. And if the second product is as much a success we'll be rich beyond dreams—so rich that we won't have to worry about anything again. You can buy that mansion you always dreamed about on the Eastern Shore, and I can move to the beach in California."

"Good," Keith said. "Let's make sure it happens."

Almost two months passed, and though sales continued to climb, so did divorce rates and teenage runaways. Both of these statistics were attributed to the distrust and suspicion that grew out of use of the Dream Visors; in fact, distrust and suspicion grew in direct proportion to the sales increase of the product.

Keith met McCabe at the usual place and the usual time. "We've got to do something about these ads," Keith said. "People are starting to place blame on the visors for the divorce rate. That's not good."

"I can't help it if people are distrustful of their spouses and children. They should practice more of what they preach."

"Spouses we could live with," Keith said. "But teenage kids are something else. If parents end up blaming the visors for the problems they have with their kids, we're in trouble."

McCabe nodded. "Then we tone it down. We continue the ads from the vendors, but we put out our own ads denouncing the others, saying how it's wrong to spy on our children or distrust them."

"That won't be enough. We have to do something that is viewed as proactive. People must think we're on the good side, that we're trying to prevent bad things from happening."

"How do we do that?"

"Put out ads that talk about how wrong it is to do these things. At the same time we'll reinforce the right thing to do. That will give ideas to people for the wrong thing to do, and that will, in turn, sell more visors."

The skin on Keith's forehead wrinkled. "Explain."

"Put out an ad showing a husband dreaming of buying his wife jewelry for Christmas or planning a surprise birthday party. Then show the wife sneaking a peek with the Dream Visors and ruining it. Simultaneously, a voice would come on saying

'Don't spoil what he has planned. Show some trust.'

"This might embarrass honest people to listen to the ad, but it might also give the idea of *sneak peeking* to people who hadn't thought of it."

Keith thought for a moment, then said. "I like it. It will make us seem like the good guys."

"Exactly. And in the meantime, our third-party ads could be cooking up something else. Show a picture of a husband or wife sleeping in a hotel room. Then a voice comes on saying

'What is your spouse dreaming about while they're away? Is it you? Or someone else?'

And just when the voice says

'Someone else'

"...an image of another woman or man lying next to them appears. Maybe they're both in underwear and partly under the covers."

"Fantastic," Keith said. "And with the teenagers, we prey on other common fears, fears every parent has."

"Like what?"

"What do you mean *like what*? You're a parent."

"True, but I don't worry about my kid; he's good. I don't think he's ever done anything wrong. So I repeat my question, 'like what'?"

"Drugs or sex. That's 'like what'," Keith said. "We show a teenager dreaming of getting high or of having sex, then the voice in the ad says

'What are they thinking of doing when you're not around?' Let Dream Visors show you.'

"What else could we do?" McCabe asked.

"Suggest using the visors for assisting video production. Imagine you work for a corporation and want to advertise it as a benevolent, caring company. Dream of a representative from the company giving away food, or helping the homeless. Instead of having to pay for the production, dream about it, and voilà, you have it on video."

"I like that," Keith said.

"Or you dream about a trip to the zoo and then show the video to your kids and let them enjoy that experience instead of playing video games or watching mindless TV."

"I like that, too," Keith said.

"Perfect. Let's get these ideas to the ad agency so that they can refine them."

THE SOLUTION

Washington, D. C., June 2029

Keith met McCabe at the same place they always met. He was smiling when McCabe sat. "I think I've got the solution," Keith said.

"I'm listening, but you'll have to tell me what I'm listening to. It's been a while since we met. You've got the solution to what?"

"What we spoke about the last time we met. Even if it's been a while, you should remember. It's about how to limit the viewing of the memories."

"Let's hear."

"We make the files unable to be downloaded, but the files could be transferred to another pair of visors using a common miniature USB connection; however, make it so the user can only transfer one file, and the size of the file will determine the cost of the insert. So a full-blown vacation memory might take up several hundred gigabytes and cost $69 while a ski trip or a fishing expedition might only cost $29. A trip to the Super Bowl might be $69 and a common weekend game only $19."

McCabe was nodding the whole time Keith talked. "So a savvy marketer could pay for his trip to the Super Bowl by selling enough memories of it."

"Exactly," Keith said. "Even if the trip cost him two thousand dollars. If you figure he could sell them for sixty-nine dollars apiece, he would only need to sell thirty of them to do better than break even. Anything after that is profit."

McCabe thought for a moment, then said, "But what about if a person isn't a good marketer, or if they don't have many friends?"

Keith smiled. "This is the best part. If they desire, a person can 'sell' us their memories for marketing and they still get half the sales price. So that same Super Bowl trip that cost him two thousand would require about sixty sales, but *we'd* be the ones selling it. And if we have our database set up properly, can you imagine how many people will want to buy a Super Bowl package? And don't forget we'd get half the sales."

"So if we sold a thousand packages, we'd get thirty-five thousand?" McCabe asked.

"And if we sold 10,000 packages, we'd get $350,000," Keith said. "And considering it *is* the Super Bowl, I think even ten thousand is underestimating."

McCabe's grin stretched ear-to-ear. "And if we were smart, we could send our own rep, pay for the game, then earn a hell of a lot more than 50 percent."

"And if we're lucky, the rep will 'experience' other things worth selling."

"Son of a bitch. Goddamn. We've got us a winner, Keith."

"Think about it," Keith said. "There could even be third-party vendors and brokers spring up to offer deals. Madrid vacations, vacations on the Riviera, Venice tours, all for ninety-nine dollars."

"Exactly," McCabe said. "I can almost hear the spiels now—'Choose from two hundred vacations and forty-seven locations for the same price. Or, take two vacations. Why limit yourself to one choice for seventy-nine dollars when you can choose from among nearly fifty choices for just twenty dollars more?'"

McCabe paused to ponder and drink his coffee. "Keith, I think this is going to be bigger than the Dream Visors."

"I agree," Keith said. "Think of how much a ski vacation would cost, then calculate how much you could sell it for. The same thing goes for anything. Sell a trip to New York to someone in Iowa, a hunting expedition to a big-city person, a fishing trip, anything. This will give a person the ability to do almost anything free of charge; in fact, if they have any marketing skills, they can earn a profit. Hell, we could make a new occupation—memory seller. All the person has to do is experience things worth selling."

"We need to get in on the third-party end too," McCabe said. "I see it being lucrative. After all, how are people from New York going to sell to buyers in Iowa or Kansas?"

"The Internet."

"Yes, there's the Internet, but these people have to be able to be found. A vendor who's selling millions of them could afford to advertise and let people know where they can be found. But an individual or a small company couldn't."

"But where do we steer them? There are millions of sites for booking vacations or hunting or fishing expeditions, almost anything you want."

"I'll have to give that thought," McCabe said. "In the meantime, get your people working on the memory transfer issue. We need that perfected."

"That falls in your lap," Keith said. "That's a visor problem. Christoper and his team should handle it."

"You're right. I hadn't thought about it. I'll get hold of Christopher today."

In two weeks, Christopher had the answer. He hadn't proven it in real-life experiments, but theoretically it should work.

He joined McCabe and Keith for coffee so that he could explain the details. After ordering his drink, he sat down alongside of McCabe.

"Okay, tell us how this works," McCabe said.

Christopher looked to his left, then right, then leaned over the table and whispered. "I used the basic concept that Keith suggested but changed it up a bit. We transfer the files from the user's visors using CDTR (close data transmission and reception) instead of a USB connection, and we transfer the files to a backup storage device, similar to an old hard drive. It would be quick using CDTR, so a person could activate the transfer before sitting down for coffee and be done with it before the cup is empty."

"Sounds all right," McCabe said. "But why not use the USB? It sounded easy."

"It was easy," Christopher said. "But that was part of the problem. Almost anyone could do it, and we'd lose control. This way, we control every aspect of the transfer. Let me finish explaining and you'll see."

McCabe looked at Keith, then nodded. "Go ahead. We're listening."

"As soon as the transfer is completed, it kicks off an automatic second transmission—this one uses WIFI4 though, so wherever the transmission is being done has to be accessible to WIFI4."

"That shouldn't be a problem. It's damn near ubiquitous," Keith said.

"That's true in New York and in most major cities," Christopher said, "But it's not true everywhere, although it's happening fast."

"All right, continue explaining," McCabe said.

Christopher took a bite from his cinnamon twist, before continuing. "As I said, the second transmission uses WIFI4, and it's hooked up to an online storage system that we will have set up. It then transfers the data to that location, which categorizes it—like, vacations to England, or hunting trips, sports, etc. It then scans the file and adds searchable keywords, then it codes everything and prices it according to category. Now, for anyone who wants access, it's simply a matter of paying for it. Once a file is paid for, it's available to download." Christopher smiled. "Simple as that."

"And you could have a lot of different enticements," McCabe said. "Have a fifty-dollar-off coupon on the visors for first-time visitors."

"Or a free 'mini vacation' for first-timers who already have visors," Keith said.

"Or let someone just choose what they want in a select price range," Christopher said. "That might be better, as not everyone will want the same thing."

"I kind of like it," McCabe said, "But I still like the USB option. Not everyone has WIFI4."

"I didn't mention the other factor," Christopher said. "With this method, there would be no need to be in proximity. A person from Philadelphia could sell their memory to someone in San Diego or, just as easily, sell it in Singapore, and they would have the transaction completed in minutes. All that would be required is access to the Internet."

"But we'd still be excluding all of those people who don't have access to WIFI4."

"True, Keith. But if these visors are as big a success as we think, we can provide the access. Build free WIFI4 access in local coffee shops, or wherever, and allow people to use it; in fact, we may even be able to charge the coffee shops to install it, as it will be beneficial to their customers, probably even drawing new customers."

Christopher looked at Keith and McCabe. "Besides, doing it the way you originally suggested, not only is it dangerous because the buyer and seller have to be in contact physically, but it creates a logistics nightmare. How is a guy from the East Coast going to sell to a prospective buyer in Montana if he has to hook up a USB plug? Doing it the way I propose, it's no more difficult than hitting a key on the keyboard. And doing it your way, even assuming the owner can transfer to a hard drive himself, he still has to upload it somewhere and then have it accessible for transfer to the purchaser. Doing it my way, we take care of all of that. For a price, of course."

"Okay. I like it," Keith said. "It answers all of the questions and solves all of our problems. It even solves problems we hadn't thought of."

"I like it too," McCabe said. "I say we go for it." He looked at Christopher. "How fast can you set this up?"

"It's going to take a while. I haven't tested it yet, so we'll need a few volunteers in various locations, then we need a few trial runs to work out the bugs, of which there will be some."

"I thought you had software to work that out beforehand," McCabe said.

"We do," Christopher said, "and it's damn good, but no matter what you use, there *will* be problems, things that none of us or the software anticipated."

"So how long is a while?" McCabe asked.

"Probably a couple of months. And before you say that's too long, remember that you have to build the online storage system and the accompanying database. My guess is that my team will have our part done before you have completed yours."

"Shit. I forgot about that," McCabe said. "We also have to set up the site. I don't even know what to call it."

"How about *memoryvisors.com*?" Christopher asked. "I thought of that while I was working on this. It's simple, and after all, it's what it is, right? You're selling memories that have been stored in visors."

McCabe thought for a moment, then smiled. "I like that too, Christopher. I like it a lot."

"I do too," Keith said. "Let's plan on it. I'll get the website today. Assuming it's not taken, and—"

"It isn't," Christopher said. "I checked."

"Fantastic," McCabe said. "Keith, get it done. I'll get started on the storage and database issues. Get Ginesh and Nancy to line up a few patients for testing. Let's get moving, people. We don't want delays."

"We won't have any," Christopher said. "Not from my end."

THE LEGAL QUESTION

The Dream Visors were still fresh on the market—as far as new products go—and already they were drawing heat from the righteous members of Congress. They seemed to be catching the blame for almost everything wrong with society.

Washington, D. C., September 2029

Congresswoman Rankle started out the session with a proposal. "We need to look at these Dream Visors more seriously. I don't know about the rest of you, but in my district, divorce rates have gone through the roof, teen runaways are sky high, and violent crime is escalating at unprecedented levels. And I place the blame squarely with the makers of the Dream Visors."

"How can you blame them?" the senator from Mississippi asked. "We're talking dreams here. If someone gets that worked up over dreams, then there's a lot more wrong than they care to admit."

Rankle stood again and shouted. "Bull! Most marriages are on rocky ground as it is. Give either one of partners a reason, and they run to the attorneys. Well, these damn visors *are* the reason. Without them, the marriage might continue on rocky ground, but it would still continue. The relationship with the teenage kids might be tenuous, but at least that relationship would continue also."

"I agree," the congressman from Connecticut said. "I say we get rid of these accursed visors."

McCabe presided over the meeting, and he was getting a sick feeling in his gut as things continued. Still, he had to maintain his composure. He pointed to his left, "You, Senator Fiore. Do you have something to add?"

Fiore stood and turned, looking at the entire Congress. "I do. I want to echo what Congresswoman Rankle said. In Illinois, we have had divorces increase by 27 percent, and I too, place the blame on the visors. It's even affected my household, and I don't even use the damn things. And that's the problem. My wife wants to know *why* I won't use them, asking me if I'm afraid of what she'll see. So I'm damned if I do, and damned if I don't."

A huge round of laughter erupted from the audience, then Fiore said, "That's the whole thing, though. I shouldn't have to defend myself from dreams I don't even have. And I shouldn't have to prove my innocence by being subjected to taking drugs that I don't want to take."

"I agree," shouted the congressman from Oklahoma.

"Bullshit," yelled the representative from Dallas.

"I'm not taking any drugs," said the senator from Vermont. "If my wife wants to see my dreams, she'll have to develop mind-reading powers."

Within minutes, shouts from representatives around the country were clamoring to be heard. It was getting out of hand.

McCabe banged his gavel on the podium. "All right. It's obvious that something needs to be done. I say, let me speak with the owners of this company and see if we can talk sense into them. Who knows? They may be reasonable."

"What are you going to ask them?" came a question from a representative on the side of the room.

"I'll ask them to step up like responsible human beings and put a stop to this," McCabe said. "If things continue at this rate, we'll be a country full of divorcees. Then they'll have no one to sell their product to. After all, who wants to see their own dreams? I know I don't want to. Mine scare me enough the first time around."

Everyone chuckled at that, then a few of them shouted support for McCabe's proposed plan.

"I'm with McCabe. Let him talk to them."

"I agree," both senators from Texas said. "It can't hurt."

"Can't stop it anyway," a congresswoman from Nevada said. "It hasn't hurt anyone. Even if it is causing a commotion. I've known video games to stir up as much trouble. Hell, in my house the Sunday and Monday-night and Thursday-night football games cause more trouble than those damn visors."

"Yeah, another woman yelled. "And the endless array of basketball games. I can't watch a damn show of my own without being interrupted."

"All of what's been said is true," McCabe said. "And it all needs to be addressed. I plan on discussing it with the CEO as soon as I can set up a meeting."

"He better have answers," Rankle said. "If not, we're going to shut him down."

"I'll make sure to mention that," McCabe said.

On his way home, McCabe called Keith. "I don't know if you were watching, but be prepared for an onslaught of reporters bearing questions before long. My guess is tomorrow morning."

"What kind of questions?"

"The bad kind," McCabe said. "Just be ready to deflect them. Do what we talked about."

Keith's voice rose. His frustration was growing. "What did we talk about? I don't remember."

McCabe sighed. He felt as if he wanted to punch something, or someone. "We talked about toning it down. We said we'd continue the ads from the vendors, but we would put out our own ads denouncing the others, saying how it's wrong to spy on our children or distrust them. And don't forget, the reporters can't know about our involvement with the other ads, so we make sure to mention that we have nothing to do with those, and that our ads will send a positive, family-reinforcing message."

"And that's it?" Keith asked.

"Shit! No, that's *not* it," McCabe said. "I was counting on you to contribute *something*." This time, he did punch the steering wheel. "Never mind. I'll get something to you tonight. Keep your phone with you. And don't say anything to anyone until you get my messages."

When Keith walked out the door to go to work, the clock showed the time to be 7:00, and already three news vans were parked in front of his house. Fortunately, McCabe had gotten back to him the night before, so he felt he was prepared—at least as prepared as he was going to be.

A young, female reporter shoved a mic at him when he was barely ten feet from the door.

"Mr. Ratcliff, would you like to comment on the things happening since the launch of Dream Visors?"

"Did you see the hearings yesterday?" came another question fired from an older reporter who stood to his left side.

"Do *you* think the visors are causing divorce?" another woman said. "What does your wife think? Do you use them?"

Keith figured he'd better stop and answer a few of these questions or he'd never get anything done. He stopped walking and held up his hands. "Okay. Okay. One at a time. First, as far as commenting on what may or may not be happening as a result of the Dream Visors, 'no', I won't. I won't comment because I have no idea if those things are the result of Dream Visors or not."

He took a few steps toward his car, then turned to the older gentleman who had asked him whether he had seen the hearings. "As to your question, sir, yes, I did see the hearings, and while I thought some genuinely good questions were raised, I thought some were rather silly."

He then turned right to the last woman. "And as to your question regarding 'Do I think it's causing divorce?' I don't know. I hope not. But if couples are so unstable and untrusting as to use this product as a tool for their own jealousy...then I cannot help them. I don't think anyone can. The ads I see that suggest 'spying' on your spouse or children are irresponsible, and they shouldn't be on the air. That's not what the visors are meant for."

Keith laughed. "As to what my wife thinks—you'd have to ask her, but I think she likes them. And yes, that should answer your final question, and I'm afraid that will have to be your final question because I have to get to work."

"What about future products?" one guy asked.

Keith stopped again to answer. "Future products, like everything we work on, are confidential. But I'm sure there will be future products, as my wife saw them in one of my dreams."

Everyone laughed, then Keith got into his car and started the engine. He had been nervous as hell but he had survived, and he had handled the reporters well. At least he thought he had.

LET'S GET IT APPROVED

Washington, D. C., September 2029

McCabe looked over his notes on the way in. He also watched the news reports showing the reporters drilling Keith on the Dream Visors. McCabe smiled. Keith had done a good job. No damage done.

He got out of the car, briefcase in hand, and started walking to the waiting members of Congress. People tried stopping him a dozen times to discuss the matter, but he didn't have the time. "I'll talk about it when it's done," McCabe said.

The room was full of chatter when he walked in, so he decided to get right to it. He opened his briefcase, took out a few talking points he'd prepared, then set up on the podium to talk.

The noise in the room diminished until it was quiet enough for McCabe to speak. "As I said I would, I had a talk with Dream Visor's CEO last night, as did the reporters this morning from what I saw on my way in.

"He was not only receptive to my suggestions, he seemed genuinely concerned and mentioned he knows a few people who ended up divorcing as a result of using the visors. But as he also mentioned, those people had rocky, unstable marriages to begin with.

"As my mother always used to say, 'you can't make good soup using bad broth.' And I think that applies doubly when we speak of marriage. If a marriage cannot hold up to a little bit of jealousy, then maybe it shouldn't exist to begin with."

McCabe stopped to drink water and wipe his brow. "Despite his insistence that the visors were not directly at fault, Keith Ratcliff agreed that there was a causal effect, meaning that without the visors this escalated divorce rate would not be happening. With that in mind, he agreed to create ads to promote proper use of the visors and condemn the improper use of them. This will, hopefully, put an end to the jealousy and envy, which comes as a result of the spying."

McCabe took another swallow of water, then continued, but in a louder voice. "I say we give NeuroScan and the Dream Visor team another shot. Keith Ratcliff seemed genuine, and he appeared to be concerned with the public. He is going to create ads to promote the good the visors can do—like help psychiatrists diagnose people who have mental issues—and he is working on future products that will be even better."

"I hadn't thought about the diagnosis aspect," said a senator from North Carolina. "My ex always had her shrink ask her about dreams, but she could never remember enough to tell him. Or she'd recall bits and pieces. This way, the shrink would have it all."

"Exactly," McCabe said. "And Keith assured me that using the new CDTR—for those of you not technologically savvy, that's close distance transmission and reception—the glasses only need to be within range, which I believe is about ten feet or so. Don't quote me on that, though."

A few chuckles were heard, then the congressman from Florida spoke. "You mean you won't have to wear them?"

"Not at all," McCabe said. "According to Mr. Ratcliff, simply setting them on the nightstand would suffice. Of course you'd have to leave them turned on."

"That brings up another question," one of the senators from New Mexico said, "How long does the charge last or the batteries?"

"Not that it has anything to do with this session, but Mr. Ratcliff told me that a charge will last eight hours and batteries about twelve. So a fully charged unit has the potential for twenty hours of continuuos use. But don't take my word for it; call technical service."

McCabe quieted the laughter, then held up his hands. "All right, people. Settle down. We went off on a tangent but it was for a good reason. There had been initial reports of people getting hurt due to the frames of the visors pressing into the bridge of their nose, or even breaking during the night and the broken frames or lenses cutting them. This innovation will put a stop to that. If the visors are on the nightstand, there will be no problem."

More questions started pouring in from the audience. McCabe held up his hands signaling the people to stop. "All right. Listen up. We're here to discuss the problems associated with the use of the visors related to divorce and runaways. We're not here to talk about how long batteries last. Let's leave that analysis to CNET."

An echo of agreement rose from the crowd.

"Now, let's talk about something else," McCabe said. "When doing research in preparation to speak to Mr. Ratcliff, I uncovered rumors that there was another product coming out soon and that it would put the Dream Visors to shame."

"What is it?" somebody asked.

"I don't know what it is exactly," McCabe said. "As I said, these are nothing but rumors. But it this alleged new product is supposed to be more advanced than the Dream Visors, then I'd buy some stock without delay."

"Are you buying any?" someone asked.

"I already have some that I bought shortly after the first product came out," McCabe said. "But I intend to get more. I didn't get enough stock the first time, but I'm not going to miss the boat this time."

"What's the new product about?"

McCabe thought before he answered. He didn't know whether he should answer, and then realized he shouldn't as it might be viewed as insider trading. "Ratcliff didn't tell me anything—damn him—but I've heard that they're working on a device that will allow you to *see* your memories."

"What? See your memories? What do you mean?"

"I don't know much about it," McCabe said. "But from what I understand, it's almost like wearing a video camera, only better. You will have access to a video image of whatever it is you experienced, and you can relive it."

"Can other people see it?" someone asked.

McCabe thought before answering. "I don't know. I haven't seen the product, only heard about it, and not from Ratcliff."

"That will be against the law," Rankle said. "A product like that can't be allowed to be sold."

"Why not?" McCabe asked.

"It's an invasion of privacy," Rankle said. "Think about it. You can't record a person's phone call without permission, so how could we let people record something else?"

"Like what?" someone asked.

"Like anything. If we're talking about recording memory, a person would be recording what you thought was a private conversation and you would have no control over it."

"That's true," the Indiana senator said.

"You'd have no expectation of privacy," the senator from Minnesota said. "I don't see a problem. Besides, it would eliminate misunderstandings. No one could say, 'I didn't say that', because it would be recorded."

"I'm all for that," Congressman Nirrota said. "It would go a long way in settling marital disputes. Maybe it would even help fix the divorce rate."

"No expectation of privacy?" Rankle said. "Suppose you were in the restroom? Wouldn't you expect privacy there?"

"I hadn't thought of that," the representative from Wyoming said. "I wouldn't want *that* recorded."

"I don't know," McCabe said. "As far as I'm concerned, if you need privacy, you're probably doing something wrong. And if you're doing something wrong, why should you have privacy? People can record me any time they want. If they are interested in what I have to say, let them hear. I have nothing to hide."

"I'm all for that," Minnesota shot back. "If I hear one of my kids whispering on the phone, I know they're up to something."

"Another thing," McCabe said. "I just thought of this, but I think it's important. We all know about the crime rate, and how it's been rising. Something like this could go a long way to bolster eyewitness testimony."

"How's that?"

"Right now, eyewitness testimony is almost useless. Any defense attorney worth a dime can discredit it. But it would be tough as hell to discredit a video. The images would be staring the jurors in the face. A defendant couldn't say, 'That wasn't me', when the jurors are looking at a video of him doing the act. Or he or she couldn't say 'That wasn't my car', when we're staring at a license plate that shows it was."

The representative from Idaho jumped to his feet and applauded. "It's damn near as good as DNA," he said. "Count on my vote. And put me on the list to buy a few, too."

"Let's not get carried away," McCabe said. "We don't even know if this product will work. All we have is a rumor. I'd have rather had the CEO's word, but he declined to give that. If it does work, however, I say we go for it. I'd love to put some criminals in prison using something like this. It's about time technology worked in our favor."

"I agree," the representative from Illinois said. "As far as I'm concerned, we could use a few more deterrents. If criminals knew that half the city of Chicago would have virtual video cameras focused on them, maybe they'd think twice before doing something."

"Why would they care?" a woman asked. "They don't care now."

"Because as McCabe said, it's easy to discredit an eyewitness, but it would be tough as hell to deny it's you on camera."

The more the room debated, the more people swung to McCabe's position. Pretty soon, everyone but Rankle and a few others supported the memory device, a device that wasn't even released yet. McCabe smiled. *Victory.*

"Okay," McCabe said in a raised voice. "I say it's time we end this. If there are no real objections, I say we let NeuroScan continue as is with Dream Visors and future devices as long as there are no additional problems."

A resounding approval met McCabe's proposal. He smiled again. *Another victory.*

On the way to his car, McCabe ran into Theodore Kelly, head of the FDA.

"Senator McCabe, good morning. I hope your day is going well."

"It's going better than yours is going to. If you had stayed alert during evaluation of the Dream Visors, you'd have noticed their tendency to break during sleep or to dig gashes into people's noses."

Theodore looked puzzled, then said, "I didn't know that was my job. I rightfully presumed that was taken care of during clinical trials."

"It's your job to protect the people. That means from all issues related to medical products. You don't take the word of the people who conducted the trials."

"I understand that," Theodore said. "The issue must have slipped by us. It won't happen again."

"I'll make sure of that," McCabe said. "I intend to have people monitoring your every activity. I'll make sure of your competence, though I have many doubts."

"Have no fears then, Senator. I'll ensure all future products are thoroughly scrutinized."

"Make sure it is so, Mr. Kelly. I'll be watching." After having his say, McCabe got into his car and had the driver take him home.

As he walked inside, Justin greeted him.

"Saw you on TV, Dad. You looked good in that segment with the FDA guy."

"You mean good old Theodore? He's not so bad."

"I'll bet he watches out for things now," Megan said. "You made him look foolish."

"Let's hope he remembers," McCabe said. "For all of our sakes."

A VISIT FROM THE FDA

Washington, D. C., September 2029

Two hours later, there was a knock on Senator McCabe's door.

McCabe opened the door and said, "Come in, Theodore."

Theodore removed his scarf and coat, handing them to McCabe. Then he said, "What the hell was that all about today?"

"I had to make it look good for the press," McCabe said, "and I didn't have time to brief you. I presumed you would catch on."

"And if I hadn't?"

"But you did, so the matter is over."

"And what do we do now? About the visors, I mean."

"I'm sure you can expect a few questions—or more than a few—questions regarding the visors, but more importantly there will likely be a lot of questions about a new product that we'll be launching soon."

"I didn't hear about any new product."

"You would have been told. But that's not important. What *is* important is that we will need rapid approval for this new product. If we don't get it, all of the money we've made so far will be jeopardized. Even worse, we may be caught regarding the manipulation of the files. So the paper trail for the trials better be good."

McCabe handed him a glass of wine, then sat. "You can take care of this?"

Theodore took a drink, then shook his head. "I don't know if I like this. We could all get in trouble."

"We could always get in trouble, but how would it look if people found out you had 800,000 shares of stock in Dream Visors? What would that look like?"

"I have no stock. All I have is the one time payment you gave me, and that was in cash."

McCabe smiled. "Remember when I had you sign all of those papers? Some of them acknowledged your receipt of the stock grants, gifts from the corporation for 'services rendered.' It will be amusing to see what the public thinks of that."

Theodore gritted his teeth. "You son of a bitch. How could you?"

"Very easily. It's relatively simple to dupe people into signing anything, especially when the contracts are long and complicated. You didn't even know what you were signing."

Theodore seemed to be in thought for a moment, then he smiled. "I guess there's worse in life than being rich."

"I'm sure there is," McCabe said. "But I don't want to know about it."

Theodore looked at his near-empty glass, sipped it, then said, "How about the current product? Is there anything I need to do?"

"There's no need for you to do anything. Keith has already made adjustments so that people are not required to wear the glasses to bed; they can set them on their nightstands or anywhere close by."

"And the other problems?"

"As far as I know, there are no other problems. If you are aware of any, let me know now."

Theodore thought for a moment, then shook his head. "No, I don't know of any. Aside from the social implications that claim they are the cause of the rise in divorces and such."

"I'm not worried about that angle," McCabe said, then offered him another glass of wine. "Red or white?"

"I'll have red, please."

McCabe poured red into a waiting crystal glass, handed it to Theodore, poured himself one, and sat at the table next to Theodore."

"You know we have to be careful not to be seen conversing with each other in private," McCabe said. "For example, you should not have come here tonight. You shouldn't call, either. You can get a message to me some other way, and we will arrange to meet."

Theodore gulped his wine, set the glass on the table, then said, "I don't understand why you're such a stickler for secrecy. It's no big deal."

"No big deal? Your cut of this is looking like it's going to be about forty million by the time we're done. You call that no big deal?"

"Forty million? That *is* a big deal, and I want anything to jeopardize it."

"Good. Then listen to what I say, and if we see each other in public, pretend to be adversaries. Otherwise, we don't meet unless I say so."

"Okay. I'm good with that."

"Then we might as well put the policy to practice starting now. And that means goodnight, my friend."

Theodore slugged the last of his wine, the one McCabe had refilled, then said goodbye.

"Don't be seen," McCabe said. "It would be better if you went out the back door."

Theodore grabbed his coat and scarf, put them on, then moved toward the back entrance. "I guess I'll see you when I do."

"I guess so," McCabe said.

Megan was coming down the back stairs just when Theodore was leaving. "Hello," she said.

"He nodded, but then quickly exited the door without saying a word.

She poured a glass of juice for herself and a diet drink for Justin, then took them back upstairs.

As she entered Justin's room, she asked, "Who was that downstairs?"

"I didn't see anybody."

"He was with your father in the living room. I swear it looked like the guy we saw on TV, the one your dad was fighting with about those visor things."

"No way. He wouldn't be here."

"I'm telling you, he was. And even weirder, he left by the back door."

"The back door? No way. Nobody but the servants use that door."

"Then you better get up to speed because this guy left through the back door, and I can tell you he was no servant, unless servants wear cashmere coats with white silk scarfs."

"Impossible. I need to get to the bottom of this," Justin said. He set his drink on the nightstand and went downstairs.

He walked into the living room and called, "Dad. Dad, are you here?"

"What is it?" McCabe responded from the other side of the sofa, where he had lain down to rest.

"Megan swears someone was just here and used the back door to leave; in fact, she says he looked like that guy on TV today, the one from the FDA."

McCabe sat up and laughed. "What? No way. I can promise you, if it had been him, I'd still be throwing punches."

Justin laughed in return. "Okay. Just checking. You know how women are."

"That's for sure," McCabe said. *They're loud-mouthed bitches.*

McCabe waited for Justin to get up the stairs, then he went and got his burner phone from the coat pocket. He dialed Theodore.

"Hello?"

"I told you we'd have problems. You were recognized."

"Recognized? By whom?"

"By Justin's girlfriend, that's who. And she's the goddamn daughter of the president."

"Oh, shit."

"Shit is right. What am I going to do now?"

"I don't know. What the hell can you do?"

"You've screwed this up but big, Theodore. I mean big."

"So what are you going to do?"

"I don't know. I'll think of something."

WHO FOLLOWED MEGAN?

Washington, D.C., March 2030

Langley and Dennis drove back at a slow pace. "That was pretty good, Detective," Dennis said. "My men had checked this out before and ended up getting nothing. Now we have a potential lead."

"Don't get too excited," Langley said. "All we have is a guy who was possibly checking out her ass, and there's no law against that. If there were, we'd have more than half the city locked up."

"Including me," Dennis said. "I've stared at a butt or two myself."

"Haven't we all?"

"Where do you want to do this?" Dennis asked.

"I'm guessing you have the surveillance at your place, not to mention the equipment to manipulate it if we need to. We might as well go there."

"Ever been to the White House?" Dennis asked.

"The White House? No. Is that where we're going?"

"You'll need to surrender your gun at the gate, but that will make things go smoother. If not, it would be jumping through hoops to get you in."

"I've got no problem with that. Rhonda is going to shit when I tell her where I was."

"You can tell her you were here," Dennis said. "but, remember, we still want to keep this quiet."

"Got it," Langley said. "By the way, you weren't very nice to the Gattis boy back there. You don't have to be so rough on them you know—the ghetto kids, I mean. I'm guessing it hasn't been that long since you got out of there."

Dennis turned to look at him. "What makes you say that?"

Langley laughed. "Come on, Dennis. You barely needed directions to get there, and you knew where you were going once we arrived. And I'm gonna' make a wild guess and say the president doesn't get down there much, so I figured you didn't get the experience on the job."

Dennis laughed. "Okay. Got me. I guess I have a thing for the bad kids that live here."

"Nothing wrong with that, as long as you remember that living here doesn't necessarily make anyone a bad kid."

"Agreed," Dennis said.

hen they arrived, Langley handed his gun to the guards at the gate. One of the guards poked his head in the window and said to Dennis, "Everything okay, Dennis?"

"It's Mr. Markum to you," Dennis said.

The guard waved them on, smiling. "Pretty shitty attitude," Langley said.

"It's code," Dennis said. "If I had just responded with 'fine' or 'okay' then he would know something was wrong. If I respond sarcastically with 'It's Mr. Markum to you,' then he knows things are fine."

Langley smiled. "Pretty good. No one would suspect."

"I hope I never have to find out," Dennis said.

Dennis led them to a room set up with several monitors and computers of all types. A technician was working at one of the desks.

"Steve, I need the surveillance video from the night Megan was attacked. It was Pentagon City Mall."

"I got it," Steve said. "Let me load it. I'll have it ready in five minutes."

Dennis and Langley chatted for a few minutes while Steve prepared the video. When he was ready, he called them in. "All set up, Dennis."

Dennis and Langley took seats on either side of Steve, and Langley told him the time to go to. Within a few minutes, they saw someone join up with a small crowd of people and walk in, then a moment later, he broke off and went his own way.

"Follow that guy," Langley said. "Jump to each camera but don't lose him. I want to see where he goes."

It took the guy about ten minutes to catch up to Megan, then he tailed her at a distance for another fifteen minutes. When she reached the intersection, on her way out, she took a turn toward Nordstrom. He turned the opposite way, toward Macy's.

"Doesn't look good," Dennis said. "This is almost the time she was attacked."

"Keep following him," Langley said to the technician. "Let's see where he goes."

A moment later, he pulled out his cell and dialed: he spoke for a few seconds and then went into Macy's. A few minutes later, he exited the mall using the Macy's exit and climbed into the passenger side of a car.

"Looks blue to me," Dennis said.

"Almost black," Langley said. "I can't make out the plate, though."

"Zoom in," Dennis said to Steve. "See if you can get it."

Steve played with the image, but when he zoomed in, it became too fuzzy. "Can't get it," he said.

"Focus on those three girls," Langley said.

"What about them?" Dennis asked. "There's no way to track them."

"Look closely. They're wearing visors, and two of them are carrying bags." Then he spoke to the technician working the surveillance video. "Rewind that to where that group was still inside the mall."

"How far back do you want to go?" Steve asked.

"Until one of them bought something. They had to have bought something, because two of them are carrying bags."

Langley's idea must have finally hit Dennis. "Goddamn!" he said. "Good job. I'd have never thought of that."

The tech stopped at the perfume counter in Macy's. "Here it is," he said.

"And look, she used a credit card," Dennis said, unable to contain his excitement.

"What time is it on the video?" Langley asked the tech.

"Looks like nine thirty-six."

"Now we just pull the receipts from Macy's at that time and see who the credit card belonged to."

In no time, they got an address and went to see the girl. After explaining what they wanted, the girl said her visors had already been downloaded but she gave them the name of her friends who were wearing visors. One of them had downloaded also, but the other hadn't.

After extracting the data, they were able to ID the license plates of the car that picked up the suspect. The car belonged to a Darius Finch.

They brought Darius in for questioning. He was resistant, but Dennis and Langley kept up the pressure.

"Why did you pick him up?" Dennis asked.

"I didn't pick up anybody."

"Bullshit. If you keep up the lies, you're going down for first degree rape. If you cooperate—"

"Whoa. Whoa. I didn't do anything," Darius said.

"Then tells us what went down. We have surveillance of you picking somebody up outside of Macy's, so don't try to lie."

"Okay. I picked him up. Big deal. He needed a ride home."

Langley leaned across the table and smacked him in the face. "You just picked him up? What? You don't think we know you dropped him off again by Nordstrom? The question is, did you get out and help him rape the girl, or did you wait for him to finish?"

"Whoa. I told you. I didn't do shit. I just drove him."

"Did you see him rape her? Did you do anything to stop him?"

"No. I didn't see anything. It wasn't until a few weeks later, when I heard about it, that I put two and two together. I still don't know if he did anything for sure, but it seemed awful coincidental."

"So you had nothing to do with it?" Langley asked.

"I told you. I didn't do anything but pick him up at Macy's then drop him off at Nordstrom.

Langley looked at Dennis. "What do you think?"

"I think he's going to have to give us the name of who he picked up, and pass a lie detector about the rape. If he does that, and if he testifies..."

"I can't testify," Darius said. "Vic would kill me."

Langley smiled. "Now we're heading in the right direction. We've got a first name. Give us the rest of it and we'll be happier."

"I can't. He'll kill me."

"Think of what he'll do when both of you are doing twenty years for the rape. Give it thought, because that's what's going to happen. This is the president's daughter we're talking about. If you think we can't make it happen, you're dreaming. You're already convicted; you just don't know it yet."

Darius looked from Langley to Dennis, then back. "Okay. Okay. I'll do it. I'll tell you."

Langley stood and gestured to Dennis. "Take his statement. I'm through with this piece of shit."

Ten minutes later, Dennis joined Langley in the hall. "Nice piece of work back there."

"Thanks. I felt like hitting the son of a bitch."

"Me too," Dennis said. "But then we couldn't use his statement. So it's a good thing we didn't."

"I assume you got the kid's name then?"

Dennis smiled. "Name and address. Vic Todd's the name. And here's the address," he said, handing a slip of paper to Langley.

Langley looked at the address then tucked the paper into his shirt pocket. "Now let's get the prick that did that to Megan."

PREPARATION FOR SECOND LAUNCH

Washington, D. C., October 2029

Time seemed to fly by, and before Keith knew it, the time to launch the second product was at hand. It was two days before the announcement, and they still didn't have a name for the product. Keith figured he would discuss that with McCabe at their coffee-shop meeting.

He waited impatiently for McCabe to arrive, then nervously broached the subject. "McCabe, before we get into anything else, we need to discuss a name for this product."

McCabe thought for a moment, then said. "Let's keep it simple and in line with the first. I propose we call them Memory Visors."

"Sounds too much like the others," Keith said.

"Exactly," McCabe said. "That's what we want. Product recognition. *visors* tells you the product, and *Memory* or *Dream* tells you which product line you're speaking of. It couldn't be simpler."

Keith took a moment to digest the information, then nodded. "I guess I could live with that. In a way, it even makes sense."

"In a way? Of course it does. Don't be an ass. It's perfect." McCabe spread some strawberry cream cheese on his bagel, then sipped his coffee. "I'm assuming everything is a go for launch day?"

Keith nodded again. "All set. And we've got plenty of inventory, too, so even if sales are higher than expected we'll have it covered."

"And we're set with ads?"

"Ready to go. Scheduled to run on every major network during prime time and in every major newspaper on page three."

"And the stock?" McCabe asked.

"Stock is up 21 percent as of this morning. Most of that in anticipation of the new launch, but a decent portion due to continued record-breaking sales of the Dream Visors."

"Are the buys coming from institutional investors or the common folk?"

"Both," Keith said. "A few large blocks went to retirement funds and credit unions, but millions of shares went out as sales of five or ten units."

"Good. Good. That will help keep the price stable. Individuals tend to hold on to stock longer than the big investors do. So if anything goes wrong, we've got more time to react."

"I don't anticipate anything going wrong. Have you tried it out yet?"

"Not yet, no."

"You should. It's amazing. And it's addictive. Once you get a taste of reliving a memory, there's nothing like it."

"Tell me about it."

Keith blushed. "Well, for example, the other night Marcy and I made love, then the next morning I replayed the memory and it was like screwing all over again. I actually *felt* it. In fact, it was so real that I had an orgasm again."

McCabe leaned over the table, eyes widened. "Are you shitting me?"

Keith laughed. "No. I'm not. If I didn't have things to do, I'd replay it all day long."

"Jesus Christ! Mother of God! This is huge. Think of it. People can basically make their own porn movies."

"They can do that now using any phone with a camera."

"Yeah, but they won't do it. They're too prudish. But this...this will remove those inhibitions. Free them to act out their desires and fantasies."

"How is that going to help us?" Keith asked.

"Because we're controlling how many times they can view it, remember? You've already said you wanted to replay your own experience all day. Would you be willing to pay a few bucks to do that? It might even make it more desirable."

"I don't think I'd pay for it, but...who knows? Maybe I would."

"The question is how to take advantage of this." McCabe thought, then thought more. "Maybe we let people have one view free, then offer the option to buy a package of replays. So if they wanted to watch something ten times, it would cost X amount."

"We'd have to give them a discount. It'd be their own damn memories."

"Of course, and it would need to be a steep discount. But could we tie it into the person's DNA? Make sure they are the only ones viewing it?"

"I'm sure we can," Keith said, then, "How about the database work? Have you tested it?"

"I haven't, but I know that Ginesh and Nancy have. They said it works fine. Simple to use. Easy to understand. And thought-provoking. It gave them ideas that they didn't have when they navigated there."

"Great. That's exactly what we want. What else do we need to do?" Keith said.

"Did you get some bloggers lined up to write about it?"

"I thought your people were doing that," Keith said.

"No. Son of a bitch! We need to get some people. I want their posts to coincide with the launch. We want exposure."

"With the FDA scrutiny, even if it's fake, we'll need good press."

"Don't worry," McCabe said. "I've got bloggers who owe me favors. I'll line up some interviews, then have them follow up with product reviews. Then I'll have future posts cover the social impact angle."

"Okay, but don't let this slip. It's important; in fact, it's all important. If we get off to a big start, momentum will help sales continue."

"I agree that momentum is the key," McCabe said.

"I'm not worried about getting off to a big start either, but how do we keep the momentum going?"

"Sex," McCabe said.

"What?"

"Sex. You said it yourself this morning. Sex sells. It has always sold. They use sex to sell cars, clothes, lipstick—hell, even milk."

Keith thought back to his favorite ads and realized McCabe was right; most of them involved some sort of sexual innuendo.

"Keith, the ad business is built around only a few basic tactics. *Fear*, like the fear pharmaceutical ads use to convince you that you need to use their product; *embarrassment*, like the ads used for bad breath or dandruff; **comedy,** like the ages-old Wendy's commercial about

'Where's the beef'? And the biggest of all—*sex, used for almost all the rest.*"

"Damn, McCabe, you're right. I can think of a few others, but most fall into those categories."

"You bet they do. At least the ones that have the most impact. So there's no sense in venturing far from what works."

"We could have ads that imply spouses could make love one time and enjoy it forever."

"Or as long as their wallets hold out."

Keith beamed. "Now, I'm getting exited. This could be really big." He looked over and McCabe was leaning against the back of the chair, staring out the window at nothing. "What's up, McCabe?"

McCabe shook his head as if to clear it. "Nothing. Or should I say everything. I just thought of something while we were talking. Suppose someone had sex with a hot chick—a really hot chick. Then he put it up for sale. People could buy the experience and relive it, just like you said you did. It would be safe, they could do it in the comfort of their home or hotel, and it would be with a hot woman, not a prostitute in an alley in Brooklyn."

Keith thought for a moment, then said, "Holy shit. I think you're onto something. You might have just created an entire country full of pimps."

"Let's hope not. We don't want pimps. We want Johns."

"But can we do this? Is it against the law?"

McCabe thought. "I don't know. It would be pushing the law to be sure. And I'm sure the privacy nuts will have a field day with it, so it would be better off to make this another third-party operation. All we care about are the sales of the memories."

"We'd have to figure out a way to hide this, like a black-market operation."

"Shouldn't be too difficult. There will be plenty of money involved, and where there is plenty of money, there is talent to make things work."

"Okay, then we need to get working on it."

"I'll see to it right away," McCabe said. "Leave it to me."

"Speaking of things you're seeing to, did you ever take care of that problem with the president's daughter? Theodore asked me about it."

"Not yet, but I'm working on it."

THE DARK WEB

Washington, D. C., November 2029

Christopher walked into McCabe's office carrying two briefcases. One contained his laptop and several folders stuffed with printed material. The other held only one thing—a pair of Memory Visors that he used for testing purposes.

"Launch day is getting close," McCabe said. "I've got to know that we're ready. Tell me everything. Security, safety, transmission...all of it."

Christopher opened the first briefcase and removed two folders, which he set on McCabe's desk. Then he opened the second briefcase and took out the visors.

"Security is simple," Christopher said. "The visors, when originally bought are imprinted with the owner's DNA.

"Hold on. How is it going to get a person's DNA?"

Christopher sighed, then flipped open one of the folders and pointed to a diagram. "Do you see this hollow spot on the top rim of the glasses?"

McCabe leaned forward and looked closely. "Yes."

"Well, as you know, for years everyone has had their DNA recorded at birth. For those of us who are too old, we get it done with driver's license renewal. Between those two segments, it takes care of 90 percent of the population. The rest won't be able to buy visors unless they register their DNA."

"What does this have to do with security?" McCabe asked.

"Be patient," Christopher said. "DNA verification could be carried out through a 'well' on the top of the visors where either a drop of blood or a sample of saliva would go." He pointed to the hollow spot on the diagram. "See this here?"

McCabe nodded.

"DNA is then matched to the person's retina via a scan. This allows only the proper person, albeit, the owner of the visors—to operate it. No one else can do it. That ensures that whoever wants to use visors will have had to have purchased it."

"And what about buying the memories?" McCabe asked.

"You must be a registered owner/purchaser of a pair of visors to buy a memory, because you must view a memory with your own visors. Whenever you 'buy' a memory, the verification procedure built into the visors first verifies your identity, then it ensures it is you with the retina scan. Once the retina scan activates, if the glasses are removed from the proximity of the person wearing them, the transaction is terminated."

"All right, I like that," McCabe said.

"Assuming it is not terminated," Christopher said, "you go to a site where there is an encrypted link that you click. That link takes you to a 'hidden' website that allows you access to a database of pleasure."

"And I presume there is additional security there?" McCabe asked.

"The site only accepts the credit card you registered when you originally purchased the visors. And the database is set up similar to the main one, only the categories are different."

"Different how?" McCabe asked.

"Similar, but 'darker.' We have categories for people who are seeking thrills that might be on the other side of the law, such as theft or robbery."

"How are those two different?"

"*Theft* might be pickpocketing or stealing something where there is little or no danger of being caught. Whereas *robbery* might be breaking into a person's home while they are in the residence—say robbing a bedroom while the family is eating. Something like that."

"All right. I like it. Go on."

"There are also other categories in thrills, such as *speed*."

"And what is speed?"

"Like driving fast, way faster than the speed limit. Having a race with another car, like kids do. Speedboats. Anything involving speed that is against the law."

"Oh my God, this is good. What else?"

"Drugs. Enough said about the legality, but the subcategories are almost endless. You can have categories for marijuana, speed, benzos, other pills, glue, cocaine, acid, meth, and heroin. You can have sub-categories within sub-categories too, like PCP or angel dust, hash and oxycontin. The possibilities are endless or almost endless."

"Goddamn, Christopher. You're getting me excited."

"There's more. Think of violence and sex. If there is anything that will be bigger than drugs, it's one of those two."

"How so?"

"Sex I don't think I need to explain. Have a high school jock make it with the head cheerleader—or anyone for that matter, as long as she's hot. He then 'sells' the sex experience. What red-blooded American male isn't going to want to access that?"

"I'm getting horny just thinking of it."

"Or how about visiting a prostitute and getting 'unusual' things done —things your wife won't do?"

"Or how about 'not so consensual' sex, or the ultimate taboo, rape?"

McCabe wrinkled his brow. "What do you mean?"

"I mean just what I said. Maybe someone almost forces a woman to have sex or, on the other hand, maybe someone rapes a woman and sells the experience. Do you know how many people would pay to see and feel that if there was no chance of getting caught?"

"How about the police? Won't they be eager to bust this operation?"

"I'm sure they'll be eager to bust it, but with the safeguards we've built in, I don't see how they will. First of all, everything is verified by DNA, so a person can't buy anything without us being able to check their records."

"Yeah, but couldn't the police create a false record, using fake DNA, and pretend to be that person?"

"Great idea, but we already have birth and license DNA for all of the states. Every request is compared against that in a matter of seconds. If an anomaly shows up, the transaction is canceled until we can figure it out. So, in other words, no, you can't create a new record and have that person be you. It won't work."

McCabe sat back in his chair as he thought. "How about if the cops have someone that is cooperating? They go to his house and, using his glasses, they access the database. When he downloads the memory, we're done."

Christopher shook his head. "Already thought of that. First, whoever accesses the database *must* be wearing his or her own glasses. This is verified with DNA as I already mentioned, and compared to a retina scan. If the glasses are removed, or even moved far enough away for someone else to view them, the session is terminated and the connection broken."

McCabe kept thinking of ways that the police might foil them. "What if the police put a miniature camera next to your eye to view it, and worse, to record it?"

"The camera, no matter how small, would interrupt the signal of the retina eye scan and, that would terminate the viewing."

McCabe thought for a moment. "How about if the camera were far enough back, out of the range of interference?"

"There would still be some kind of glare. These visors are extremely sensitive. Remember, they have to do retinal scans. Retinal scans map the patterns of a person's retina. The blood vessels within the retina absorb light more quickly than the surrounding tissue and need appropriate lighting to work properly."

Christoper stopped to sip his drink. "If I'm boring you, stop me."

"Not at all," McCabe said. "Continue."

"A retinal scan is performed by casting an unperceived beam of low-energy infrared light into a person's eye as the person looks through the scanner's eyepiece. Any glare or reflection will trigger a 'cease connection' signal that will terminate the session. Also, remember that while we might not be able to see the waves, any camera that is recording is sending waves—even very low-frequency waves—and that will be detected by the retinal scan."

"So there's no way for the police to view the website?"

"None that we can think of. I believe all safeguards are in place."

McCabe smiled. "Then it looks as if we're ready to launch." He thought some more, then said, "What about registered users who get a new credit card or the card they have expires? Won't the system flag that?"

Christopher shook his head. "Good thinking, but if they get a new card, they simply log in as usual. The system will allow them to add a new card although it puts them through the verification process again. And if it's an expired card, the system can easily tell by checking the expiration date of the previous card."

McCabe reached over and patted Christopher on the back. "Damn good job. I'm impressed with the thoroughness."

"Thanks. I'd say we are done," Christopher said. "I know I'm ready. Or at least ready for the sales to roll in."

"Christopher, I don't want you to quit on this development. This is new. There will be enhancements that could be made for a long time. I am charging you with continual monitoring of the database and analysis of the categories. Furthermore, you are now in charge of future development for all database-related products."

"Not to sound ungrateful, Mr. McCabe, but I'll need help if you want me to do all of that."

"What kind of help?"

"I need a database expert for that part of the project. I need another one for category analysis, as it's a full-time job, and I'll need an engineer to help for future addenda to the security of the glasses so that we can keep complete control over their viewing. The last thing we want is the police or FBI getting into this database."

"And you're sure they can't?"

"I've only given you the surface reasons why it's secure. We've hired hackers, good hackers, to try to bust it. I've put up a sizable reward if they succeed, but so far nothing; in fact, nothing even close."

"Christopher, that's the kind of progress I like to hear. And that's what you should like to hear also; it will mean a lot of money for you."

Christopher smiled. "Nothing motivates like money—the mother of innovation."

"And the father," McCabe said, then he and Christopher laughed.

LAUNCH DAY IS HERE

Washington, D. C., November 2029

Keith drove into work with a queasy stomach. He was a little more nervous than most days—make that a lot more nervous. Today was launch day; do-or-die day for the Memory Visors. Everyone, himself included, expected it to be a runaway success—anything less would be viewed as a failure.

He drove through the gates to his office, past the six vans belonging to news companies, past the reporters and cameramen who were waiting to pounce on him, and past the just-now-arriving employees who were trying their best to dodge questions from the reporters.

He pulled into the space marked "Reserved for CEO", got out, and headed toward the building. He didn't get ten feet before being besieged by reporters, cameras shoved in his face, and a barrage of questions shouted from all of them.

"Not now," Keith said. "I'll be out in half an hour. I've got to get my coffee."

He used his free hand to brush away the cameras, and he increased his pace in an attempt to get away.

He pushed through the front door, then let the officer on duty block the entry.

"They look like a pack of vultures," Ginesh said.

Keith laughed as he brushed a few sprinkles of snow from his coat. "They *are* a bunch of vultures, but right now they are the kind of vultures we need. They are going to be responsible for kicking this off with a bang."

"And suppose they don't deem it worthy of being kicked off with a bang?"

"They will. There's no way they can't."

Keith went to the cafeteria and had his coffee, then, as promised, he was out in front of the reporters within half an hour. "I told you I'd be back," he said.

"What have you got, Mr. Ratcliff?"

"Tell us about the product."

Keith lowered his head and blushed. "There have been plenty of leaks about the product and more than a few hints, but today you get to see the entire show."

He reached into his briefcase and pulled out a pair of visors that looked almost identical to the Dream Visors. Then he held them up in front of his face and put them on. "These," he said, "are Memory Visors."

"Memory Visors?" one guy asked. "What the hell are they?"

"Memory Visors are just what they sound like," Keith said. "They record whatever you experience as long as you are wearing them or have them available nearby."

Questions started pouring in. He held up his hands to forestall them. "This is not only a visual experience but a sensory one as well. Meaning you see *and* feel the replay of the memory."

"What do you mean? Explain it better."

"Let's try it this way," Keith said. "Suppose you went to the amusement park and rode the roller coaster. You could go home, let your wife or son or daughter replay the experience. They would not only see the twists and turns but they would feel them, as well as the ups and downs. Of course, whoever wants to experience the memory must be taking NeuroScan to do so, the same drug that allows access to the Dream Visors. And they must purchase the 'experience'. As we all know, nothing is free in life."

"Does the same amount of NeuroScan work for both?"

"This is a slightly higher dose of NeuroScan but only slightly. And it takes about the same amount of time to become 'prepped' for the experience—about two weeks. And no, we have had no adverse effects."

"You said the visors could be nearby. How close do they have to be? Can they be in a pocket or in a lady's purse?"

"Absolutely. My wife made sure of that. She said there was no way she would be caught dead wearing those ugly things, so I guess we're going to have to hire a fashion consultant for future versions."

All of the reporters laughed. The one from Channel Five said, "Will distance affect image quality?"

"Yes. The first few feet should deliver the same high-definition picture as the Dream Visors, but get ten to fifteen feet away and quality will suffer. Still workable, but not high definition by any means."

"So what good are these Memory Visors? What will people use them for?"

Keith smiled. "For everything. But instead of me trying to convince you, take a look at the first ad."

He pulled up a video player on his tablet, turned it so it faced the reporters, then hit play. The ad began.

With Dream Visors you could only see dreams—*now you can see* everything. *Everything you remember, that is, and while wearing a pair of Memory Visors, you will be able to remember* everything.

Keith held up his hand. "The ad says while wearing a pair of Memory Visors, you will be able to remember everything. Remember, though, you *don't* need to be wearing them. We have to correct that in the ad. You only have to have them nearby."

"So this is like walking around with a twenty-four-hour video camera strapped to your forehead?"

"Yes and no," Keith said. "Yes, it will record whatever you see, but it will also record what you experience or feel. So if you fall and hurt yourself, a camera might record the fall, but this will allow you to feel it all over again, assuming you want to. That's the other good thing about this—the visors will store things as events and they can recognize the difference between...say a spat with your partner or a love-making session with your spouse."

"You mean you could record...*that*?" an elderly reporter asked.

Keith smiled. He was hoping someone would ask that. "Absolutely," Keith said, then smiled. "And you could *feel* it all over again. So for those of you who don't think you're getting enough, you can replay your session as often as you want."

"What about the quality of the video?"

"I'm glad you asked," Keith said. "This is critical. With a video camera you would have to focus the lens, make sure the audio was right, the lighting, etc. With Memory Visors, you don't need to worry about any of that. The lenses are your eyes; the audio is replaced by your ears;

and the lighting is whatever you can see with your eyes also. So if it's dark outside and are having difficulty seeing, the video will reflect that. If there is a plane flying overhead making a lot of noise, the sound on the video will reflect that. And if the sun is glaring in your eyes, it will appear that way on the video. So for better *and* worse, the video will be exactly what you see and hear and feel. That can be both bad and good. If conditions are ideal, like the bedroom..."

"It looks like this is another play toy for the idle rich."

"Not at all," Keith said. "We see many practical applications. For example, it will be irreplaceable for training purposes. Suppose you're trying to learn complex schematics for an electrical circuit, you could use this to replay the session at a later time for clarification. Or suppose you are witness to a crime, this would allow the criminal to be identified clearly, not relying on the vagaries of eyewitness identification."

"I hadn't thought of that," a young woman said.

"And for college students it would be invaluable. They would have the option to replay a lab session or a seminar whenever they want."

"Damn," one of the men said. "My kid could use this for sure."

"How about—"

"Sorry. That's going to have to suffice for now. There will be plenty of time for questions later. I've got Thursday almost completely open. We can talk then." Keith took his briefcase and laptop and went inside while the reporters hurriedly packed things back in their vans.

His phone rang before he got in the door. "Hello?"

"Keith, excellent job," McCabe said. "I watched it live. It was fantastic. It was so damn good, you almost convinced me to go buy one."

Keith laughed. "Thanks, Rich. I was nervous at first, but once we started talking it flowed naturally."

"And it showed. You looked calm and confident. This is going to send sales through the roof."

"You think so?"

"Trust me."

"I hope so, because sales of Dream Visors are down."

"Really?" McCabe said. "Is that this morning's report?"

"Yeah. I was going to call you tonight."

"How much are we down?"

"Not much—2 percent. But that's still down. Not a good precedent to set," Keith said.

"No. It's not. Any indication of why?"

"Can't be certain, but sales were off the worst in Rankle's district. I'm betting if we look closely, the other districts where senators or representatives opposed us would follow suit. I think it's a good thing we came out with the Memory Visors when we did."

"You'll get no argument from me on that," McCabe said. "Still, we should try to counter their effect. Give it some thought."

"I will, but I'm guessing we'll run into more obstacles and more objections with this one."

"I've got it covered," McCabe said. "Don't worry."

Keith's wife had dinner waiting for him when he walked in the door.

"I saw the interviews," she said. "You were great."

"Thanks. I was anxious at first, but then lightened up."

"You think this product will be a hit like the last one?"

Keith sat in his spot at the end of the table, picked up his fork and knife, then said, "I think it will be a hit, I just don't know if it *should* be a hit."

"What do you mean by that, dear?"

"I mean that almost everything offers the chance to be used for good or bad purposes. I worry about people using this the wrong way. Look what happened with the Dream Visors. People started using them to spy on their spouses and children. They did things they shouldn't have."

"Dear, I wouldn't worry about it. Like you said, almost everything can be used for good or bad. A blanket is meant to keep you warm, but you could also smother someone with it. That fork you're holding is meant to eat with, but you could also stab someone. Just eat your supper and stop worrying. You're a good man. Be happy about that."

Keith cut a piece from his meat and used the fork to put it in his mouth. "I know what you're saying, but this offers more chances than most." *Especially for the bad.*

NEED A RIDE?

Washington, D. C., November 2029

The visors had only been out two days when Vic saw the opportunities. When he was growing up he had been forced to look for ways to make money and that situation hadn't changed. He saw an opportunity with the visors, and since he was prepped as a result of the clinical trials, he didn't have to wait for the drug to take effect. It would give him the head start he needed.

Vic went down to the basement of his home and lit up a joint. He sat in the corner, listening to some old rock music and took deep drags, inhaling all the good smoke, letting it set his mind at ease.

When he was finished and sufficiently high, he crushed out the joint, then went upstairs and took the necessary steps to initiate the sale.

It didn't take long for a green light to indicate that the transaction had been completed. Now all Vic had to do was wait. Wait and hope it worked.

Three days later, he had his answer when a text arrived on his phone saying he had money waiting in his PayPal account. He quickly checked it and found out three hundred dollars had been deposited. Nothing great, but not bad for getting high. Vic was excited.

He knew this wouldn't last long, as either the police would break it up, or the rest of the country would find out about it and give him competition. Right now, he had to be one of the only ones who was prepped with the drug. Even the previous users of the Dream Visors didn't have enough NeuroScan in them; Memory Visors required a higher dosage.

Working from that knowledge, Vic tried benzos the next night, then LSD, then cocaine, and finally, heroin. First, he did heroin in pill form, then he shot it up. He put them all the memories up for sale immediately after. Each one drew more money and fetched bigger individual prices than the previous one. LSD got more than benzos, cocaine more than LSD, and heroin the most. Vic thought about it and guessed it was the risk factor. A lot of people wanted to try heroin but were afraid. Experiencing it this way removed fear from the equation.

The magic was that people got the feeling of the high without the danger or risk. No risk of addiction and no legal risk. It was perfect. And Vic earned enough to not only pay for his drugs but a lot more besides.

He earned a profit of almost five grand from the cocaine and nearly double that from heroin. He put up another heroin high, but it did no better than the first. Next, he thought of other experiences to sell. *What would people be willing to spend good money on? What are they afraid to do themselves?*

While Vic gave this thought, he pondered other highs to sell. He put up a drinking high for sale, then a glue-sniffing experience. The alcohol didn't sell well, but the glue did above expectations.

Still, Vic had to come up with something new. Right now, he had the black market for memories to himself, but that wouldn't last long.

He put a lot of thought into his dilemma, even going so far as to ask other people what they were afraid to do but would love doing. He got all kinds of answers, some of which were unexpected.

Speed topped the list, including car racing and boat racing. It was followed by sky diving and bunji jumping, then rock climbing and white-water rafting. Vic made plans to experience all of these things as soon as possible, then sell the memories.

Vic made it through the day, ignoring all of the chatter from students about illicit sales of memories available on the Internet. By the end of the day, he had talked to dozens more people about their desires, but had no new ideas. He left school as soon as the bell rang and made his way to the metro.

~

McCabe sat across from Keith in a chair reserved for interviewees. "Any activity yet?

"We've had a flurry of drug sales all week, all from the same person. It's beginning to worry me. It won't be long before the police find out and come knocking on our door. And it won't be long after that before the reporters show up. They're all going to want the person's identity."

"I'll get Christopher and his team working on better masking. He assured me it was difficult to find, but I want to ensure that it's impossible. As to the reporters, let's keep the knowledge away from them as long as possible, then we'll do the same thing we did with the Dream Visors, pretend we're protecting the people. It shouldn't be too difficult."

Keith nodded, but then he said, "But why not really protect the people? We could. We could prevent things like drug use and sex from being sold. After all, we're facilitating it."

"But that's where the money is. It would cut hugely into our profits."

"Yes, it would cut into profits, but we'd still be making a fortune. It's not like people wouldn't want it for legitimate use. Come on, Rich. How much money do we need?"

McCabe reached over and patted Keith on the shoulder. "I understand your concerns. But it would be like the difference between medicinal marijuana sales and street sales. Massive. I don't know about you, but I don't want to throw millions down the drain."

"Flushing millions down the drain isn't so bad if you have plenty of millions to play with."

"When I get enough so that I don't worry about losing some, I'll let you know. In the meantime, keep working like it's our first dollar."

Keith sighed. "All right."

"Who is the person selling the drugs? It must be somebody we know if they're already prepped with NeuroScan."

"I thought we were protecting people's identity?" Keith said.

"We are. This is me. Now, give me the goddamn name."

Keith hit a few keys on the keyboard, pulled up a database, and said, "Some young kid named Vic Todd. I think he was one of the clinical trial patients."

"I know him," McCabe said. "Thanks."

Vic got off the subway and started the long walk home. It wasn't really a long walk, but it was cold and nasty out so it sure as hell seemed like it.

He had only gone two blocks when a large blue sedan pulled to the curb. The passenger side window rolled down. "Vic, you need a ride?"

Vic looked over, saw who it was, and waved him off. "That's all right, I'll walk. It's not far."

"Nonsense," Senator McCabe said. "It's cold. Get in."

McCabe drove him to his house, but there were no cars in the driveway. "Nobody home?"

"I suspect not," Vic said.

"Then come on over to our house for dinner. We have plenty."

"I don't think that Justin will be happy about that," Vic said.

"Happy about what?"

"About me coming to the house. He and I haven't been on the best of terms."

Vic lowered his head and mumbled. "Because of something I said."

"You mean what you said about Megan?"

"He told you about that?"

"Yeah, he told me, and I told him to grow up. For God's sake, a girl as pretty as her..."

I t wasn't long before they pulled up to McCabe's house. They got out and went inside to the kitchen. "You want a drink before dinner?" McCabe asked.

Vic was surprised, but he shook his head and said, "No thanks."

Morgan came in to check the oven, and McCabe asked him how long it would be before dinner.

"It's going to be another hour, sir. I got started late."

"That's all right, Morgan. Just get me another drink." Then he looked over to Vic again. "You sure you don't want one?"

Vic almost declined again, but instead he said, "Sure, I'll have one if you don't mind."

"Of course I don't mind. I offered it to you."

Three or four drinks later, McCabe and Vic were talking like old school chums. "I keep telling Justin that he's missing out on a gold mine," McCabe said.

"What do you mean?" Vic asked, now interested. "What gold mine?"

"Megan. I told Justin that all he has to do is wear his visors when screwing her—assuming he is screwing her—then sell the goddamn experience on that website. He could auction it for a fortune. Who wouldn't pay to have sex with a fox like her? And especially her being the president's daughter?"

Vic's interest grew, but he said, "Justin would never do that. Number one, Megan would find out and then she'd kill him."

"You said 'number one'. That implies there is a number two. What is it?"

Vic waved him off.

"No. Go on. Say it."

"Number two is, we're assuming he really is screwing her, like you said. And I don't think he is."

McCabe laughed, but then he nodded. "I told him how to fix that. We'll grant him the benefit of the doubt and presume he is getting some. If he is, he tells her the next day that someone stole his visors. Then, when the video is known about and circulating the Internet, she won't know who did it. She'll think it must have been the work of whoever stole his visors."

"Pretty slick," Vic said. "But the visors don't work like that. Another person can't see what's on them." Vic laughed. "Damn shame, though. I bet he could get a thousand dollars for that."

McCabe slammed his glass on the table and laughed. "What? A thousand dollars? Try more like twenty or thirty thousand. Hell, it might even bring twice that."

"No way," Vic said.

"Guaranteed," McCabe said. "I'd never tell him to do it for five or ten thousand, but twenty or thirty or forty...that's another story."

"That *is* a lot of money," Vic said. "But like I said, the story wouldn't work. The visors need the original person to work them."

McCabe brushed his hand in the air. "I doubt if Megan knows that. And so what if she does. It's sex, for God's sake."

"But it's sex with the president's daughter." Vic said.

"Yeah, but it's not like he'd be doing anything really bad. I mean its a goddamn sex video. At the turn of the century, sex videos were like rites of passage. Paris Hilton, Kim Kardashian, Pamela Anderson, and about a million others. It didn't hurt them. Why should Megan Piersol be any different?"

Vic laughed. "You got that right. Besides, as good-looking as Megan is, she's just begging for it. It'd be a shame for someone to not take advantage of it."

"Wouldn't it?" McCabe said, and smiled.

Two hours later, after a few more drinks, McCabe bid goodnight to Vic and had Morgan drive him home. "Vic, I enjoyed the company. But don't tell anyone what we talked about. People will think I'm crazy."

"You got it, Mr. McCabe. You can count on me."

I hope I can count on you, Vic, because that's what I'm counting on.

A KISS FOR CHAZ

Washington, D. C., November 2029

Ginesh came in at the usual time and, as usual, Nancy wasn't there. He finished the coffee he had bought at Starbucks, dumped the empty cup in the trash, then went to Chaz's cage to say good morning.

He reached in, picked up Chaz, causing him to squeal and leaned forward to kiss him. Instead of his ritual kiss, though, Chaz bit Ginesh's lip and took a piece of it with him.

Ginesh screamed and dropped Chaz on the floor. Blood streamed from his upper lip and pain shot across his face. "Son of a bitch! Goddamn! What the hell did you do that for?" Ginesh kicked the cage on the bottom level, then went to the bathroom for a bandage.

He rinsed the wound, applied antibiotic ointment, taped his lip with a small bandage, then returned to the lab.

Nancy was now at her desk. She seemed startled to see Ginesh with the bandage on his face. "What happened?"

"Goddamn Chaz bit me," Ginesh said. "Tore a piece of my lip right off."

"Why did he do that? What did you do?"

"I didn't do anything," Ginesh said. "That's the thing. I went to give him a kiss, like I always do, and he bit me—ripped a piece of my lip clean off."

"And you're sure you did nothing else? Nothing to piss him off?"

"Not a goddamn thing," Ginesh said. "And he's still loose. I dropped him when he bit me."

"Oh, shit," Nancy said, and started searching the lab. "Close the door so he can't get out."

She and Ginesh started a methodical search of the lab and within five minutes found Chaz hiding under a desk. Hesitantly, Ginesh reached down to pick him up.

"Be careful," Nancy said.

"No need to warn me of that," said Ginesh. "My lip reminds me every moment."

He extended his hand, then placed it on the floor about a foot away from Chaz. "Come on, Chaz. Come on, boy. Let's go back to the cage."

Much to Ginesh's surprise, and delight, Chaz scurried over and climbed onto the palm of his hand, then he sat up straight. Ginesh smiled. "Look at that, Nancy. He's acting normal now."

Ginesh slowly raised his hand and even more hesitantly than before, leaned forward to kiss Chaz. Chaz gave him a kiss and a squeak, then lay down as if to sleep.

Ginesh placed him back in the cage and sat next to Nancy. "He must have had a scare or something. He seems back to normal now, though."

Nancy shot a skeptical glare at Ginesh. "He may seem normal, but I'd keep a close eye on him. Something made him bite. I'd like to know what."

"It could have been anything," Ginesh said.

"My point exactly. It could have been anything, so let's keep an eye on him and see if we can determine what *anything* might be."

The rest of the day was filled with anxiety, for Ginesh, Nancy, and probably for Chaz. Ginesh had Chaz run the mazes several times more than normal and both he and Nancy picked him up twice as much as usual to judge his reaction. At the end of the day, there had been no more incidents.

"I told you," Ginesh said. "I must have frightened him or startled him."

"That doesn't excuse what he did to you," Nancy said. "I still think you need to see a doctor."

"Nonsense. They'll push for rabies shots and other bullshit. Then they'll want to put Chaz down. And I can tell you, I'm *not* putting him down. It was an accident. It won't happen again."

"Okay. It's no skin off my back," Nancy said. "Or my lip."

"Smart ass," Ginesh said. "You're just jealous because they don't like you."

"Yeah, that's it. I'm jealous because a pack of rats don't bite me. Damn. Why didn't I see that before. I'll have to consult my shrink about that."

"Screw you," Ginesh said. "I'm going home."

"Don't forget to kiss Chaz goodnight."

~

Ginesh walked in the door earlier than usual. "I'm home," he shouted.

Raji came to greet him, surprised when she saw the bandage. "What happened? Are you all right?"

Ginesh reached to embrace her. "I'm fine. A tiny bite, that's all." Then he looked all around. "Where's my baby boy?"

"He's in bed already. He got tired from playing in the park. But tell me about your lip. You said a bite? From one of those rats?"

"Don't start acting like you were born here, Raji. We know what rats are like; we grew up with them. I must have scared Chaz. That's all."

Raji frowned as she lifted the bandage. "Scared or not, that's no excuse. You know what would have happened to a rat who did this to you back home."

"But we're not *back* home. We *are* home. And I'm *not* going to treat an animal that way. If I thought Chaz bit me on purpose that would be one thing, but I believe it was an instinctive reaction. Nothing else."

"I understand, Ginesh. I just don't want you getting some disease. We're finally making it. We've got a child, and with our stock we'll be able to afford to buy a house."

Ginesh hugged her. "Raji, I'm not going to get the plague from Chaz. Don't worry. Things will be fine."

"When will this all be done? When will it be over so we can get our money? I'm tired of waiting, Ginesh. I just want to sell the stock and get it over with."

Ginesh kissed Raji's neck and rubbed her back. "It will be soon, Raji. It will be soon."

THE RATS REVOLT

Washington, D. C., November 2029

Two days went by with nothing to show for the time spent. On the third day, Ginesh got in early and walked over to Chaz's cage. He was about to say "good morning" to Chaz when he noticed something dripping from the cage.

He increased his pace, then examined the liquid leaking from the floor of the pen. *It was blood.*

"What the hell?" Ginesh said. Then he looked closer and saw that the rat who shared the cage with Chaz was dead—and not just dead, but its body had been ripped apart, pieces of skin strewn about the cage.

Instinctively, he wanted to reach in and pull the dead rat out, but then a sensation from his lip reminded him of what happened when Chaz had bitten him. So instead of opening the cage, he put on a pair of heavy gloves before he opened the door.

Chaz acted as if nothing was wrong, huddling in a corner and chittering. Ginesh took hold of the carcass and quickly yanked it out, doing his best not to disturb Chaz. *What the hell is going on?*

Moments later, Nancy arrived, perky as ever and wearing a smile as wide as the Potomac River. "Good morning, Ginesh. I trust you had a good night."

"I had a good night," he said. "But this morning has not been good. Look what happened," he said, and held out his hand.

Nancy rushed over, eyes going agape when she saw what Ginesh held. "What happened, for God's sake? Who did this?"

"Chaz," Ginesh said. "But I don't know why. I found it like this when I came in this morning."

"What is going on with Chaz? First your lip, now this."

Ginesh shook his head, bewildered. "I don't know. This can't be explained by someone or something startling Chaz. No one was here."

"So why did he attack his cage partner? Nothing has changed to make him behave that way."

"That's what we need to find out. *Something* has changed, or he wouldn't be acting this way. It's up to us to discover what the catalyst was. What was the last thing we changed? Think."

Nancy looked at her computer screen. "No sense in stressing my brain. I'll check the chart and see what we changed and when we did it."

"Good," Ginesh said. "I'm curious."

A few moments later, Nancy turned to look at Ginesh. "Nothing since the dosage increase when we were beginning work on the Memory Visors."

"But all the rats have had an increase in dosage. The people too. Have any of them reported problems?"

"Not that I know of," Nancy said. "Maybe we better check."

Ginesh thought about the turmoil it might cause, and said, "Let's do some more work on the rats, first. We'll take them through the mazes tomorrow, give them some time out of the cage. Maybe that's all they need."

"I have a feeling it's a lot more than that," Nancy said. "But I'm willing to give it a try. What do you want to do?"

"We'll create a few typical rat runs for the maze, then let them loose two at a time. If nothing happens, we'll let a few more go in."

"And you think that's smart, considering what we've seen the past few days?"

"I think it's smarter than crying wolf to Barney or Mr. Ratcliff."

"I don't consider reporting an adverse event 'crying wolf.' It's procedure; in fact, it's required. We are required to report serious AEs as soon as they happen. And I consider this a serious AE."

"You want them to shut this down?" Ginesh asked. "We have twenty thousand shares of stock in this. If the trial shuts down due to an AE, we're screwed. I don't know about you, but I'm counting on that money."

"It's your conscience," Nancy said.

"Chaz can take care of himself."

"Obviously he can," Nancy said. "His former cage partner will attest to that. But I was speaking of the *humans* who have been doing the trial. Those people from Silver Spring and those two kids from Bethesda."

"We haven't heard of anything wrong," Ginesh said.

"We haven't asked either. And maybe they don't know if something is wrong. Maybe they are not associating any problems that they might be having with the trial."

"Okay," Ginesh said. "You win. We'll check the patients. But after the maze run."

"Fine by me," Nancy said. "And for your information, Ginesh, this is not for *me*. It's not *my* win. It's for the patients. It's the right thing to do."

Ginesh worked for several hours setting up a complicated and sure-to-be frustrating maze run, complete with a plate of crumbled cheese and peanut butter at the end as a reward for those who found their way through. He had many false turns built into the layout, and it was the longest one they had used to date. This was one that was bound to frustrate the hell out of them. If there was going to be a fight, this should bring it on.

By the time he was finished, it was late afternoon. "You want to do this now?" he asked Nancy. "Or wait until morning?"

Nancy turned to look at the clock, then shook her head. "I've got a date for the movies tonight. It will have to be tomorrow."

"Okay," Ginesh said. "Fine by me, because if we did it now it would probably mean we'd be staying late, and I promised Raji I'd bring home Chinese food for dinner."

"Where are you going for the food?"

"Da Hong Pao. Raji loves the dim sum from there."

"Then you better get going. It gets crowded at dinner time."

"You don't have to suggest it twice," Ginesh said. He grabbed his briefcase and said, "See you tomorrow."

Ginesh got sweet-and-sour chicken for himself, and he stopped to get more tea for Raji. She loved tea.

During dinner, Ginesh told her what had happened with the rats, and he told her about the conversation he had with Nancy.

Raji sipped her tea, swallowed a bite of her food, then said, "I'm siding with you, Ginesh. There's no sense in raising an alarm unless we have reason to believe something is definitely wrong. Too much is at stake."

"Good," Ginesh said. "Then we'll see what happens in the morning." He reached over and put a few bites of food from his plate onto Ramesh's, who immediately started gobbling it up. Ginesh laughed. "He's eating like a big person, now."

"And pretty soon, he'll *be* a big person. All the more reason to make this trial go smoothly."

In the morning, Ginesh and Nancy picked up two pair of rats and placed them at the beginning of the maze.

"They haven't eaten since dinner last night, so they should be motivated," Nancy said.

"They should be more than motivated," Ginesh said. "They should be starving."

After ten minutes into the run, there had been no trouble. All four rats had made a few wrong turns, but they were all back on track and heading toward the reward at the end—food.

Then Carmel (a big brown-and-white rat) cut off Misty, and a huge fight ensued. Before Ginesh could break it up, the other two rats joined in, and all four were attacking the others.

"Get the gloves," Ginesh yelled to Nancy.

She rushed over with two pair of gloves. They put them on, then quickly grabbed hold of the rats and placed them in separate cages.

"That didn't go so well," Nancy said. "What happened?"

"Nothing," Ginesh said. "Everything was going fine, then they began fighting. I think you're right. We need to visit Silver Spring."

"I'll call Mr. Connor at Spring Meadows. I'm sure we'll need an appointment."

SILVER SPRING

Washington, D. C., November 2029

In the morning, Ginesh met Nancy north of the city at a coffee shop off Route 29. They had coffee, discussed what they wanted to accomplish, then headed toward Silver Spring.

"Don't forget," Nancy said. "Don't ask the patients if they are feeling aggressive of late—ask them if *anyone else* has shown signs of aggressive behavior. We're much more likely to get a response that way."

"Got it," Ginesh said. "People don't want to talk about what's wrong with themselves, but they're more than willing to discuss someone else's shortcomings."

"Exactly," Nancy said.

Thirty minutes after leaving the shop they arrived at Spring Meadows. "We're here to see Mr. Connor," Ginesh said. "We have an appointment."

"Your name, please?" the receptionist asked.

"No need," said a voice from down the hall. "I know these people."

P.J. Connor walked briskly toward them then shook hands. "Ginesh, Nancy. Good to see you again."

"I'm surprised you remembered our names," Nancy said.

"I try to pay attention to things like that," Connor said. "Follow me. You want coffee or tea?"

"We're good," Ginesh said. "We stopped on the way up."

Connor took a seat at the head of the conference table in what was marked "Eagle Room", then he said, "Okay, you didn't stop by for coffee, so what *do* you want? I didn't hear from McCabe."

"We have run into potential problems with the rats," Ginesh said. Adverse events that are, as yet, unexplained. We need to see if any of your patients are experiencing the same thing."

"What kind of problems?" Connor asked.

"Unusually aggressive behavior," Nancy said.

"Mildly aggressive," Ginesh said.

Nancy shot him a glare. "I beg to differ, sir. It's been overly aggressive. In a person, I'd label it as psychotic. They have been attacking cage partners and others for no apparent reason. There has even been a death."

Connor nodded. "We can't have that. What would you like to do?"

"I think we should interview the patients and determine if any of them are experiencing the same issues. And we need to do it before we have a situation."

"I agree," Connor said. He picked up the phone and dialed someone on the intercom. "Rosie, I'm sending two people your way in one moment. Allow them access to the patients."

Connor turned to face them again. "When you exit the door, turn right then go to the end of the hall. You'll see Rosie at her desk, and she'll show you the way to the patient ward."

Ginesh and Nancy walked down the hall, eager to see Rosie. Even more eager to interview the patients. When they finally reached her desk, Rosie was there, waiting.

"Follow me," she said. "I'll take you to them."

onnor watched as Ginesh and Nancy walked toward Rosie's desk. When they were far enough away, he returned to the conference room and dialed the phone.

"Senator McCabe," a voice said.

"McCabe, this is Connor. We've got a problem."

"What kind of problem?"

"Your scientists think that they should be reporting adverse events. I don't have to tell you that it's far too late for that. That product will be in the hands of millions of people by late next week. We can't have reporters questioning why negative reactions to the drug were not looked into earlier."

"No. I've got you. Son of a bitch. Okay. I'll take care of it. Leave it to me."

~

Rosie led Ginesh and Nancy to the patient ward, then left them alone after instructing the guards to allow the scientists access.

Ginesh walked up to the first man. His name was George Bidden—patient number six, if he remembered correctly. "Good morning, sir. I don't know if you remember me, but my name is Ginesh—"

"Of course I remember you. You're the son of a bitch that stuck me with needles all the time," he said, then laughed. "No, seriously, what can I do for you?"

Ginesh sat in a chair next to George. "We are just following up on the tests. I wanted to see if you remembered anything else, or if there was anything that didn't seem right."

"I remember darn near everything. I even remembered a gin rummy game that Fred and I played last week. But as far as trouble—no, nothing. I feel great and have been feeling great."

"That's fantastic," Ginesh said. "That's just what we wanted to hear."

"How about the rest of the people?" Nancy asked. "Have you noticed any of them acting strange or more combative than normal?"

George looked as if he were giving it consideration, then he said, "I don't know if I'd call it combative, but Kevin has been arguing more than normal. Of course, he always did like to argue."

"But has it been more than usual?" Nancy asked.

George cocked his head sideways again and looked up at the ceiling. "I don't know. I said it was, but it's hard to tell. Kevin loves to argue with people. It makes it hard to tell if it's more than usual. Hell, if his sports team loses, he'd argue with God."

"Okay," Ginesh said. "Thanks."

Next up on the list was Martha. She was busy playing chess with her friend Lucy.

"Martha, I'm Nancy. Remember me? From the lab?"

Martha nodded slightly. "I remember you. I shouldn't but I do. What do you want?"

"I just wanted to ask if any of the other people who took part in the trial were acting strange. If they had shorter tempers? Anything like that?"

"If you're asking if they are a bunch of cranky old bastards, the answer is yes. If you're asking if they are crankier than they were before, I'd have to say no. A couple of them are even happier."

"Happier in what way?" Ginesh asked.

"Just happier. Like they are more full of life. Ask around if you don't believe me. Other people have noticed. I know because they've mentioned it to me."

"But no one has been acting more aggressive or violent?" Nancy asked.

"I didn't say that, but you didn't ask."

"I asked if anyone had a shorter temper?"

"Having a shorter temper is different. Stuart has been more aggressive than before. He even got into a fistfight with Bob. And it was over nothing as far as I could tell."

"What do you mean? What started it?"

"Bob asked Stuart if he could have his cottage cheese, like he has for years, and Stuart leaned across the table and smacked him."

"Just smacked him?"

"Like you'd smack a dog," Martha said. "Then Bob grabbed him by the collar and punched him. Punched him hard."

"And that's been the only thing?"

"Only one I've seen," Martha said.

"Okay, thanks," Nancy said, then stood to leave. Before going, she handed Martha one of her cards. "Call me if anything changes."

As they were exiting the facility, Nancy tapped Ginesh on the arm. "What do you think? Should we report it?"

Ginesh thought about the money he'd be losing if things went wrong, and he thought of the disappointment Raji would have. "I don't see enough of a reason to yet. But we should continue to monitor it."

"And how are we going to continue to monitor it?" Nancy asked. "We don't have the patients showing up here anymore, and they've stopped taking the drugs."

"I don't know," Ginesh said. "Let's look at someone who hasn't stopped. Maybe those kids who were taking the trial. Maybe they're still taking the meds."

Nancy shrugged. "Worth a shot."

LET'S GET HIGH

Washington, D. C., November 2029

As more and more people got up to speed with NeuroScan, Vic's marketshare of the drug high declined—slowly at first, then rapidly. By the end of the second month, his earnings had dipped to a level so low that he could have earned more working a paper route.

He thought of how to improve his situation, but he didn't know what to do. In a desperate attempt to salvage what he once had, he purchased the leading "marijuana high" on the market in order to see what it had that was so appealing. In other words, why was it selling versus his. They both dealt with getting high, so why should one be different than another?

Vic went online via his visors then navigated to the drugs category, then purchased the number-one-selling memory. It cost twenty-nine ninety-five, which was ten dollars more than his, and yet it was selling at twenty times the rate. Vic had to find out why.

He downloaded the memory to his visors, then closed his bedroom door; he needed privacy to watch. Once the download was completed, Vic turned off the light and started the memory viewing.

An image of a young man leaning against the brick wall of an alley appeared. The alley was dark, and it was strewn with garbage. It gave Vic a creepy feeling—a scary feeling.

The man looked both ways, then reached into his pocket and pulled out a cigarette. Upon closer inspection, it was shown to be a joint. He put it in his mouth, holding it between his lips, then took out a pack of matches, struck a match and lit the joint.

He took two long drags on the joint, making the cherry glow brightly. He inhaled a long, slow drag, held it in for a moment, then did an extended exhale. Vic felt the rush in his head, his senses growing numb and more alert. He felt as if he were floating. It was a magnificent feeling, one he'd had before, but stronger. *This must be some good shit.*

Footsteps echoed down the near-empty street, causing the man to yank the joint from his mouth and cup it in his hand. He held the joint to the right of his leg, making sure the cherry wasn't visible from the street.

The footsteps grew louder, meaning whoever it was, was coming closer, and the man kept the joint hidden from sight. A moment later, a cop appeared at the mouth of the alley. He turned, peering down the alley and moving in that direction.

The man looked as if he would run, then the cop said, "Hey, you. What are you doing?"

"Nothing," the guy said, and turned to walk away.

"Don't even think of going anywhere. Stay right where you are."

"I'm just getting my car," the man said. "I need to be somewhere."

"Where you need to be is right here," the cop said. "Don't take another step."

The words had barely escaped the cop's mouth when the man took off. He ran toward the back of the alley at what appeared to be full speed.

The cop hollered. "Stop! Halt," but to no avail.

Vic could almost feel the muscles in his legs tense. He actually *did* feel them, but when he checked they were not tensed—it just felt as if they were.

"Where the hell are we going to go?" Vic asked himself before realizing it wasn't actually him in the alley.

A few seconds later the man approached a chainlink fence about ten feet high.

What the hell is he going to do now?

His dilemma was soon solved as the man leapt to the fence and climbed it as if he were a monkey. He scrambled over the top and dropped to the concrete on the other side, falling to his knees as he did so.

The cop screamed one more warning to stop, then fired a shot just as the man turned the corner.

Vic breathed a sigh of relief. He just then realized he felt as if he were out of breath, and he felt as if he'd been punched in the chest. *That was exhilarating.*

The young man continued down the alley at a slow jog. Near the end, he stopped, lit up another joint, then continued on his way.

He walked about four blocks, checking his surroundings all the time, then finally reached a metro stop. He got on, paid his fare, and rode the red line to Woodley Park.

Vic smiled. He had reason to smile. He still wasn't selling nearly as many memories but now he knew why. Why would someone want to see a kid getting high in the comfort of his basement when they could experience a life-and-death situation in a darkened alley in the depths of the city?

I know I wouldn't.

Right then and there, Vic decided to put an end to his plain-vanilla highs. Things were going to be different. He intended to push the limits of getting high, and he intended to make them sell.

A LONG DAY ON THE METRO

Washington, D. C., November 2029

As Vic thought about what to do regarding his memories, he recalled how great it felt when there was danger involved. When the cop was chasing the guy over the fence, when he had to jump from ten feet up, and especially when the cop shot at him. Vic thought he could feel the ache in his legs for two days afterward. Only logic and common sense made him realize that he couldn't really feel the pain. He might recognize what the pain felt like at the time of viewing, but afterward the pain would be gone; he'd feel nothing.

Now, all he had to do was come up with something to make people feel the same way, or better.

But what?

He took time to analyze the memory more and finally realized that it was the combination of danger and high that was so compelling. It was almost as if he *had* to continue, go on, maybe even buy another memory. If he hadn't been doing this for research only, he probably would have bought another memory. It was that good. Now, he had to make his that way. And he had to make more than one, so that the other memories would be available for purchase after someone viewed one of them.

After much thought, Vic decided to start out with a simple but exciting scenario. He rolled a few joints, put them in his pocket, and walked to the metro.

He boarded the train and looked for any big, muscular construction worker. He soon spotted one—a guy about 6' 2" and maybe 240 pounds.

Fortunately, a seat next to the guy was vacant. Vic sat down, nodded, then took out a joint and lit it.

"You can't smoke here," the guy said.

"Fuck that," Vic said. "I'll smoke where I want."

The guy clenched his jaw, then said it again. "I said, you can't smoke in here."

"And I said 'Fuck that. I'll smoke where I want.' And you're not doing anything about it."

The words had barely escaped Vic's mouth when the guy next to him snatched the joint from his mouth and crushed it out on the floor. "I think I did do something about it," he said.

Vic sneered, pulled out another joint and lit it. He inhaled deeply to kickstart it. Within seconds, he felt the sensations—felt as if a ball were spinning inside his head, rolling around like a pellet in a roulette wheel. Vic turned to the guy next to him and smiled. He dragged long on the joint, then he exhaled into the guy's face, a vaporous cloud forming around the man's head.

The guy coughed, then he cocked his right arm back and punched Vic in the face. It broke his nose; blood spurted out all over his clothes and the seat.

"Oh, shit!" Vic said, then stood, holding a handkerchief he had pulled from his back pocket under his nose. "You broke my goddamn nose!" he said.

"You should have listened," the guy said, and with no remorse.

Vic walked toward the front of the car, found an empty seat and sat. He then used a metro map to find his way to an emergency room, where he had them reset his nose. *Might as well get two memories out of this.*

Having the bone reset in your nose is not fun, so this might make a good memory. Not great, but good.

After getting his nose fixed, he took the metro to his stop, walked home, and uploaded the memories. Afterward, he went to bed. It had been a productive day.

In the morning, Vic brushed his teeth, then checked the visors. His "high" memory was number two. Not bad for an overnight climb up the charts.

He quickly moved to "medical procedures" so that he could check his nose reset. It was nothing great, but it sat at number fourteen. Still not bad. It would be good residual income.

Besides, with his high already at number two on the charts, there was a chance it would overtake the top spot. The top spot was already earning about five thousand per month on a regular basis. He'd do a lot more than get a broken nose for that kind of money.

While other ideas festered in his fertile mind, Vic decided to do little things to add to his supplemental income. Things like smoking a joint in the school lavatory, going to the ghetto late at night and hollering "nigger," jumping from the top of two-story houses, or leading cops on high-speed chases.

Before two weeks were out, Vic had earned the top spot in drugs, had maintained his place in medical procedures, and had two in the top ten for thrills.

Smoking a joint in the lavatory had flopped as did the jump from the roof, so he didn't try anything like that again. On the other hand, the trip to the ghetto and the high-speed chase had been surprisingly wild successes. So much so that he was already formulating plans for more dangerous thrills of a similar nature.

The broken-nose sensation had also been a big success, as evidenced by the rise to the number-one spot. Why someone wanted to feel as if they'd been punched in the nose was a mystery to Vic, but for that kind of money, he didn't ask questions.

ONE HUNDRED MILES PER HOUR

Washington, D. C., December 2029

All morning during classes, Vic had been trying to think of new memories to make that he could sell, preferably for a decent price. He was wracking his brain, and though he thought he had a few good ideas, he wasn't sure.

The bell rang, indicating lunch, and Vic exited class and headed toward the cafeteria.

The usual crowd was gathered at the end of the table and seemed to be actively engaged in heavy conversation. Vic walked up and slapped Jibs on the back. "What's up? What are we talking about?"

"I don't know what you're talking about, but we're discussing an old movie, *Fast and Furious*."

"*Fast and Furious*? What for?"

"Because it was the epitome of nineties race-car movies guys with big muscles, fast cars, and girls with big tits."

'What more could you want, right?" Vic said. "But aside from the bull-shit you just fed me, why were you really talking about it?"

"Aaron just saw a rerun and we were talking about the part where they were going about 150 mph."

"And probably not wearing seat belts," Jibs said.

"Is that exciting?" Vic said.

"Exciting? Hell yeah, it's exciting. Can you imagine going that fast?" Jibs hit Aaron on the side of the arm. "Listen to me asking Vic that question. He's probably *been* that fast."

Aaron laughed and another guy, Frank, joined in.

"Is that something you would all want to do?" Vic asked. "If you couldn't get hurt, I mean."

"What do you mean, like the Memory Visors thing? Hell yeah."

"How much would you pay for something like that?"

"I can't speak for the rest of them," Jibs said, "but I'd spend thirty bucks easily, and I'd do it more than once."

"Me, too," Aaron said. "I'd pay fifty bucks if the memory was long enough."

"Fifty for me, too," said Frank. "What the hell is fifty bucks? It costs that much or more to take a chick to the movies."

Jibs looked at Vic and smiled. "I think you've got your answer, Vic. Go for it. You've got a built-in customer base. It's memories on demand."

At the end of lunch, Vic walked back to class, but he had a notepad full of ideas. Now, he knew what to do.

He went home after school, rolled a few joints, then drove off in his father's rebuilt 88' Mustang, something he had been forbidden to touch.

Vic headed out toward a long section of barely traveled road past Tyson's Corner. If he timed it right, the road would basically be his.

There wasn't anyone there when he arrived, so he parked the car, lit a joint, took a dozen hits, then stomped on the gas pedal and took off. In less than a minute, he was racing down the potentially slippery surface at more than 120 mph. He rolled down the window and let the icy, chilled air chafe his face to add another dimension to the thrill.

This wasn't going to be just a thrill; this would be a thrill while high, and with the added sensation of being flogged by icy winds while performing the act.

Vic held both hands on the steering wheel so that he would have better control of the car. All he needed was to lose it. At this speed it would almost surely mean death.

He got the car up to a speed of 142, then he hit an icy patch on the road and started skidding. "Son of a bitch!" Vic hollered, certain that he was going to die. But he fought for control, turning into the skid and slowly pumping the brakes. It took about thirty seconds to come to a stop, but he was able to pull it off with no damage to the car or himself. Vic leaned his head back against the seat, took a moment, and breathed deeply. He was alive.

And best of all, his pulse was racing and his adrenalin was sky high. This thrill was bound to sell. After all, he had an initial group of customers waiting, and once they viewed the memory they were sure to spread the word. Like almost any entertainment product—movies, books, games and more, word-of-mouth worked better than anything.

Vic drove home slower than usual. Perhaps his near-death experience had put the fear of God in him. Despite what he had to go through to create this memory, Vic was ecstatic. He had what was sure to be a financial success, and he also had a great new idea. His buddies at lunch had given it to him. He would pre-sell his memories. In other words, he would get people to subscribe to a site where they would anonymously list what kind of thrills, drugs, sex, and other stuff they were interested in, and how much they'd pay for it. If he got enough subscribers for any particular memory, he'd make it.

When he got home, Vic parked the car in the garage so that his old man wouldn't miss it. Hell, he was probably so drunk he wouldn't have missed it for a week.

After parking the car, he sneaked in the back door and went down to the basement. Once there, he donned his visors and began the process of uploading the memories and putting them on sale.

In addition to the night's thrill, he had a few cocaine highs that he hadn't used yet, and he felt they might make good supplemental income.

The next day at school, he told his friends about the availability of the particular memories. All of them seemed excited, asking lots of pertinent questions. Vic thought that they got more excited because they knew the person involved, and that was fine with him.

Before going to bed that night, he checked sales. He had already sold more than four thousand dollars of this one memory alone. *In one day.*

By the end of the week, he'd sold fifteen thousand dollars worth of memories, and though sales had dropped off, they were still strong.

Vic smiled, and he went to bed smiling. He was quickly becoming wealthy, and for doing what he liked doing.

Whoever said life's not fair?

Vic had to make a few pick-ups of weed paraphernalia that night, and he had to pick up some additional needles for heroin injection. Despite the danger of heroin, Vic feared the danger of infection from the needles more. He refused to re-use them or use a dirty one.

As he turned off the freeway to head for home, he gave thought to what he felt would be the best memories. Thrills would sell well, as he'd already seen. He was also counting on drugs, as that was an easy memory to create.

But sex will sell the best. That means I'll have to convince Joan to become a movie star—or a memory star—because, like it or not, she has a body that is on fire. *A body that people will pay for.*

"And they will pay *dearly* for it," Vic said.

ANY SYMPTOMS?

Washington, D. C., December 2029

Shortly after dinner, Vic heard a knock on the door. He opened it up, and said, "What are you doing here? I thought I'd seen the last of you."

"So you remember me," Ginesh said. "I didn't know if you would."

"Sure I remember you. Ginesh, right?"

Ginesh smiled at the recognition. "You have a good memory. I'm lucky if I remember my wife's name."

"What's up? Anything wrong?"

"No. Nothing like that," Ginesh said.

"So what are you doing here? I know you didn't drop by to visit."

Ginesh laughed, an uncomfortable chuckle. "You're right. The makers of NeuroScan wanted me to follow up with everyone to ensure things were going well. Make sure there were no adverse effects."

Vic swung the door open wider. "Come on in. Have a seat."

After Ginesh was inside, Vic led him to the living room and sat on the sofa. "I've never heard of anyone following up like this. Is this normal? I thought once you were done with the trial, it was over."

"It usually is," Ginesh said. "But NeurScan is very conscientious. They want me to talk to everyone who participated in the trial and ensure that there are no problems."

"So a cover-your-ass strategy, right?"

"What do you mean?"

"I mean NeuroScan anticipates selling the hell out of these visors, which I'm sure they're already doing, but they want to make sure that, in case there are any problems, they can head them off at the pass."

"You should have been a scientist," Ginesh said.

"You don't need to be a scientist to figure that out," Vic said. "But to answer your question, no, I've had no problems. Nothing unusual physical or mental. And just between you and me, I've been doing plenty of drugs."

"I'm glad you told me," Ginesh said, "But I don't need to know about the drugs. That's your business."

"I thought you always worried about drug interactions?"

"We do," Ginesh said, "But we only concern ourselves with prescription drugs. The illegal drugs are a person's own business."

"Let me get this straight. About one third of the damn people in the country smoke weed, but you don't care if it interacts with your drug. But you *do* care about some rare anti-psychotic that is only taken by about ½ of 1 percent of the people?"

Ginesh's skin was dark, so he knew the flush didn't show; nonetheless, he felt it. "Yes, I guess so."

"Figures."

"For what it's worth," Ginesh said. "It's not up to me. I'm simply performing my job."

Vic nodded. "I know. I was just making an anti-establishment observation. That's all."

"To get this straight, you have had no problems since terminating the trial?"

"None."

"And your medication has stayed the same?"

"I'm not on any medication," Vic said. "The chart should show that."

Ginesh glanced at his notes. "Of course. I'm sorry."

"And you've started no new medication since the end of the trial?"

"I just told you, I'm not on any medication. And I also told you I have taken drugs. Lots of weed, some acid, cocaine, glue, heroin, and meth once or twice. It's a healthy combination."

"Good God," Ginesh said. "It's a wonder you're still alive."

"Maybe that's what's keeping me alive," Vic said. "Who's to say? It's obvious you're not keeping track."

"And you're still using NeuroScan?"

"Every day," Vic said. "Just check your dark web charts."

"I don't know what you're talking about. Dark web?"

Vic looked at him quizzically, then laughed. "You don't know? I believe you don't, Ginesh. I really believe you don't know." Then he laughed more.

Ginesh put his notebook away, then looked at Vic. "Please tell me what you're talking about. I don't know anything about it."

"Okay," Vic said. "But sit back and listen. This is going to take a while. You want a beer?"

Ginesh accepted Vic's offer for a beer, then relaxed while Vic explained what the dark web was and how people sold memories there."

"You mean people are selling illegal acts?" Ginesh said.

"Of course," Vic said. "That's why I'm doing all of the drugs. There's big money in this. Next week I'm starting on sex."

"This is wrong," Ginesh said. "This is not what the visors were meant for."

"Maybe not what *you* meant them for, but the people who made them knew. They're the ones who made the dark web database and they control the uploads and downloads, not to mention they take a healthy chunk of the sales."

Ginesh gulped the rest of his beer, then stood to go. He reached to shake hands with Vic. "I am sorry for this. I had no idea what they were doing. The visors were meant to be used for good things."

Vic laughed. "Hey, don't apologize to me. I'm making a fortune getting high. I love it."

"Okay, thank you," Ginesh said and walked out the door.

On the way home, he called Nancy. Stock or not, this was not right.

"Hello?" Nancy said.

"Nancy, this is Ginesh. We need to talk. Can you meet me? Maybe at the café by DuPont Circle. I'll be there in twenty-five minutes."

"I can make that, yeah. Why? What's up?"

"Nothing I want to discuss over a cell line. Just meet me."

About thirty-five minutes later, Ginesh arrived. He rushed in and sat at the table Nancy had secured.

"What's so important?" Nancy asked.

Ginesh proceeded to tell her what Vic had said about the visors and the dark side of the web. He then told her how it was being controlled by NeuroScan or Memory Visors or both, and that, according to Vic, it was a thriving business.

"I can't believe it," Nancy said. "Who would be doing it? You don't think it's Barney, do you?"

"Maybe it's Keith," Ginesh said. "He's CEO."

"Or McCabe," Nancy said. "I've never trusted him."

"I hate to say this, but whoever it is must be stopped. It's not right. I don't mind breaking a few rules, but I'm not going this far."

"You know what that means?" Nancy asked.

"More than likely it means that Raji and I won't be buying a new house anytime soon. But that's okay. I can live with that. I cannot live with this on my conscience."

"And we can't just blow the whistle on the dark web aspect," Nancy said. "I'm sure they have their asses covered, so if we let it leak about the dark web, it will only spur sales."

"So what do we do?" Ginesh asked.

"I don't know," Nancy said. "Let's think about it and talk tomorrow."

"Okay. Sounds good." Ginesh stood to leave. "See you tomorrow at eight."

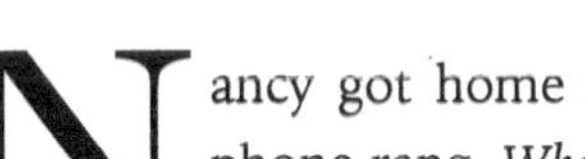

Nancy got home around 7:30 PM. At about ten o'clock her phone rang. *Who the hell could that be?*

"Hello?"

"Nancy, this is Martha from Spring Meadows."

At first, Nancy didn't recognize her, then she remembered. "Martha, how nice of you to call."

"It's not nice of me to call, and I'm sure you won't think so either when I'm done."

"Why? What's wrong?"

"Everything is wrong. I lied to you when you were here. I said nobody has shown any effects, when a lot of people have. I know six people who have darn near become bullies since we started that trial. Fred is nasty as hell and fights with everyone, and Ginger will slap you if you say good morning to her the wrong way."

"Why didn't you tell me this when I was there?"

"Because they were watching. They told us not to tell *anybody* about the problems or we'd be sent away to another facility, and not a nice one. And the morning you came up, Mr. Connor had someone remind us not to say anything."

"So there have been problems?"

"They've been fighting like trained pit bulls, not the nice ones."

"And Connor hasn't reported it or intervened?"

"The ones that have been fighting he's taken off the meds. That seemed to help but it took a week or so."

"Okay, thanks, Martha. And don't worry, I won't say anything about our talk."

"Please don't," Martha said. "I don't want to look for somewhere else to stay. I'm too old for that."

"Okay," Nancy said. "Thank you."

A TRIP TO THE MALL

Washington, D.C., December 2029

"I'm leaving, Dad," Megan hollered as she reached for the doorknob.

"Wait a minute, young lady. Where do you think you're going?"

"To the mall, shopping. Summer's not too far away."

"Summer? It's not Christmas yet."

"But after that it won't be long before summer," Megan said. "Besides, you don't wait for June to shop for summer clothes; you do it in the winter."

The president shook his head, opened up the paper, and sat. "Wait for Dennis. I'll tell him to send someone with you."

"Come on, Dad. Not tonight. I can't go anywhere without them, and I'm getting sick of it."

"That's life, dear. And crime is rampant nowadays. I think it's those damn visor things. We can't be too safe."

"It doesn't have to be the way life is. Just let me go by myself. I'm not going to be long and besides, I'll be shopping for girl things. It's embarrassing to do that if they're looking over my shoulder."

The president didn't say anything for a long time, then said, "Okay, I'll make a deal. They'll go with you, but I'll have them wait outside in the parking lot. They won't follow you inside. I don't imagine much can happen inside the mall."

Megan smiled. "It's about time you got with it. That sounds like a plan I can live with. Thanks."

The parking lot was full when Megan arrived, forcing her to drive around looking for empty spaces. Dustyn followed right behind her.

At the far end of the lot where Megan always parked, she finally spotted two spaces that were empty. She pulled into one and Dustyn parked in the other. Megan started for the mall, then Dustyn got out of the car and began walking alongside her.

"Where do you think you're going?" Megan asked.

"I'm walking you to the mall," Dustyn said. "Once we get there, you can proceed on your own, but I'll escort you to the entrance."

Megan smiled. "Okay. I'll go along with that, but only to the entrance."

Dustyn smiled also. "You drive a hard bargain. But don't worry, I'll be waiting for you when you get out."

"I figured you'd say that, but there is no need to wait. I'll call you when I'm ready. Besides, I might be a long time. You know how women are with shopping."

"You promise you'll call?"

"I will."

"Okay," Dustyn said. "Remember, I'm only a few seconds away. Call if you need *anything*."

Megan laughed as they approached the Nordstrom's entrance to the mall. "Don't worry, Dustyn. I'm fine. Now, go."

Dustyn walked back to the car while Megan entered the mall. She shopped for almost an hour in Nordstrom, then browsed the stores one by one until she reached Macy's, at the other end of the mall.

She only spent about twenty minutes in Macy's, then went to the food court, saw her friend, Joan, and then headed upstairs.

After another hour of mindless browsing, she decided to head for home, so she made her way toward the Nordstrom's exit. She pulled out her phone to call Dustyn, then chose to walk instead. No sense in bothering him.

About one hundred yards from the mall, a man wearing a dark hoodie and a black ski mask approached her.

"Hey, bitch."

Megan said, "What did you say?"

He responded, "Hey, bitch. It's about time for you to learn a lesson." He grabbed her and yanked her toward him. Then he dragged her to a remote spot on the hill above the street and kissed her hard while forcing his hand under her dress.

Megan tried to get away, tried to scream for help also, hoping that Dustyn would hear.

I should have called him.

The man tore her panties off then threw her to the ground. She hit with a thud and pain raced through her back.

He then forced himself inside her and assaulted her until he was done. When finished, he removed a hammer from his coat pocket and smashed her jaw. She screamed, and blood splattered on the ground beside her. Then he hit her two more times on the side of the head, drawing more blood but no more screams. She lay still.

~

Megan lay helpless on the blood-soaked frozen ground. No signs of life. Convinced that she was gone, he wiped the handle and head of the hammer clean of prints, cleaned up all he could of anything that might contain DNA, then hurried back to his car before anyone passed by.

~

Ten minutes later, while Dustyn was playing a video game on his iPhone, he heard sirens. It piqued his attention, and he listened to where they were going. Moments later, the sound of the sirens grew closer, and he saw the lights coming toward him.

He panicked, started the car's engine, put it in gear and sped toward the mall.

Don't let it be her.

Dustyn parked by the curb, jumped out and flashed his badge. "Secret Service," he said. "What happened?"

"We don't know what happened," a medical technician said. "Young girl assaulted. Hurt badly."

"Who is it?" Dustyn said.

"I don't know."

"Let me see," Dustyn said and pushed through to get a look.

They were just loading her into the ambulance when Dustyn saw who it was. "Oh my God," he said. "Oh shit! Is she all right? How bad is she hurt?"

I should have stayed with her. Never should have left the mall.

"No idea," the lead tech said. "Check at the hospital." They shoved the gurney into the back of the ambulance, got into the cab and took off, sirens blaring.

Dustyn took out his phone and called Dennis. "We have a problem. Megan has been hurt."

"Hurt how?"

"Assaulted." Dustyn looked at all of the blood on the ground and said, "And it looks pretty bad."

WE HAVE A SUSPECT

Washington, D. C., March 2030

Dennis drove while Langley jotted down questions. Occasionally, he punched the dashboard. "I want to nail this son of a bitch. I mean nail him good."

"Easy, Langley. We'll get him, but we'll do it the right way."

With Langley providing the directions from the sheet of paper Dennis had given him, they arrived at the house about four. It was a small ranch with white clapboard siding and green shutters on the front windows. The porch post leaned to the left and the sidewalk was spider webbed all the way to the front door.

Dennis parked by the curb and got out, unbuckling his holster as he did. Langley's holster was already unbuckled, and he was doing everything he could to keep his hand off the gun's grip, not trusting his emotions.

"Langley, we're just going to invite him down to visit, all right? Nothing aggressive."

"We ought to cuff the son of a bitch and drop him in the Potomac. That's what we *should* do."

"I might agree with you if we knew beyond doubt that he did it, but we don't. For now, he's just a suspect. Try to remember that."

"Suspect hell. He followed her into the mall, all through the mall, then took a ride to intercept her at Nordstrom. We don't need much more than that."

"All we have right now is surveillance of a kid following a girl through the mall. I could probably pull surveillance on any given day and see some kid following a girl as pretty as Megan. At this time, we have nothing to prove he did anything to her. Nothing. Which means that he's a suspect, not a criminal."

Langley walked ahead of Dennis. When he got to the door, he knocked, ignoring the obviously broken doorbell dangling from the jamb on thin wires.

A moment later, a young man wearing a gray hoodie answered. He had dirty-blond hair that draped over his ears and a chiseled face with a sharp nose and a pointed jaw.

"What's up?" he asked when he opened the door.

"We're looking for Vic Todd," Langley said. "Is that you?"

"That's me, but what do you want?"

"I'm Detective Langley and this is Agent Dennis Markum. We have a few questions for you concerning a night in December, before Christmas."

"Ask away, but I have no idea if I can answer. I don't always remember what I did this week, let alone that long ago."

"I think it would benefit you if you did remember," Dennis said. "We're talking about a serious crime."

"Serious crime? You've definitely got the wrong dude, then. I ain't done nothing other than smoke a joint now and then. And the last time I looked, that was not a serious crime."

"Why don't you get some shoes and a coat and come with us," Langley said.

"Go with you? Where?"

"We need to go down to the station so we can ask a few questions."

"Bull. Ask them here. I don't mind answering a few questions, but I'm not going down to any station."

"I'm afraid you'll have to come with us," Langley said.

"Like hell. I know my rights, dude. Unless you arrest me, I don't have to go anywhere."

Langley and Dennis stared at each other but said nothing.

"Well, what's it gonna be?" Vic said. "You askin'? Or am I closing the door?"

Langley turned to Vic, notebook in hand, and said, "Do you know Megan Piersol?"

Vic chuckled. "Is that a trick question? Of course I know Megan Piersol; she's the goddamn president's daughter."

"I mean do you know her personally?"

"Yeah. I know her. We went to school together."

"Did you see her on the night in question at the Pentagon City Mall?"

"I don't know what night's in question. But yeah, I saw her at the mall lots of times. A lot of us used to hang out there. I was at the mall the night she got hurt. She..." Vic stopped talking and stared suspiciously. "Hey, wait a minute. If you think I had anything to do with that, you're nuts."

"Anything to do with what?" Dennis asked.

"I ain't stupid. Megan was attacked there, and now you're asking me about it. No way. No fucking way."

"I'm afraid you're going to have to accompany us downtown," Langley said. "You're under arrest."

"There. You've gone and done it. Now I use the magic word. Lawyer. Hear that. Lawyer. I want you to get me one, and I'm not saying one word until I talk to him or her or whoever the hell they assign."

"So you want a 'pick-and-grab' from the legal aid pile?"

"I don't give a shit what you call them as long as they have a good idea of what to do." Vic held up his hands. "I'm going to get my shoes and coat. Come with me if you like."

On the drive to the station, Dennis looked in the rearview mirror and asked Vic, "What were you doing at the mall that night?"

"Lawyer," Vic said.

"No need for a lawyer to answer a question like that."

"Lawyer. I believe once I ask for a lawyer, the questions must stop. Take note that I requested a lawyer. So stop the questions." Vic pulled an iPhone from his pocket, pressed a button, and said, "Record conversation."

A computerized voice responded. "Voice activation has begun. All parties take note that conversations will now be recorded."

"I assume you heard that," Vic said. "Ask any more questions and they *will* be recorded."

Vic had to wait about two hours at the station, until a woman walked in and introduced herself as Sahrina Jackson, a legal-aide attorney. "Have you said anything?" she asked.

He shook his head. "Not a word."

"Okay, good." Then she turned to Langley and said, "I need time with my client, please."

Langley nodded, then he and Dennis headed for the door.

"And no cameras or audio recording," Sahrina said. "Take note that I'm asking for privacy."

Langley shook his head slowly and sighed. "Why don't you get a real job, bitch?"

"I'll take that as confirmation that you heard me," Sahrina said.

Once Langley and Dennis left, Sahrina sat at the table next to Vic. She was a strikingly beautiful black woman about thirty years old and thin enough to be a model.

"Goddamn, you're hot," Vic said.

"Thank you," Sahrina said. "Now let's get one thing straight. Comments like the one you just made and anything sexist or racist are to be stopped right now. They'll use those against you."

"Wait a minute. I didn't say anything sexist. I said you were hot. And that sure as hell isn't racist."

"I didn't say it was racist. I just wanted to warn you."

"Okay," Vic said. "Now what do you want to know?"

"I've already requested an expedited bail hearing, though considering who the victim is, I doubt if we're going to get it. So you might as well do your best to be comfortable."

"Son of a bitch. This sucks."

"What were you doing at the mall that night?"

"Same thing I do every night I go there—look for chicks."

"I like that. It's honest. But let's try to rephrase it. Instead of saying 'look for chicks', say something like, 'look for girls to date' or 'look for girls to chat with'. It sounds better."

Sahrina wrote a few notes on her legal pad, then said, "And did you see Ms. Piersol that night?"

"Yeah. A bunch of times. She was—"

"No need to elaborate. Give them nothing more than they asked for. A simple, yes would have sufficed."

Vic smiled. "I like you. You're hot *and* good."

Sahrina exhaled deeply. "Vic, what did I say about talk like that?"

"I just said you're hot."

"And there is no need to. I know I'm hot. And I know you think I'm hot. That's enough. End of story."

Vic nodded. "Okay. I won't do it anymore."

"Thank you," Sahrina said.

She spent the next half hour asking more questions and then prepping Vic for the interrogation that was to follow. She planned to be in the room with him but, still, he needed to be ready. "Okay. I think you're all set to go. At least as much as you're going to be. Do you feel prepared?"

"Bring them on," Vic said.

INTERROGATION ROOM #104

Washington, D. C., March 2030

Vic took a bathroom break while Sahrina alerted Langley and Dennis that he was ready to talk. Fifteen minutes later, they walked in.

They sat at the table opposite Vic, yellow-ruled notepads in front of them. "Let's start off with the first question we asked," Langley said. "What were you doing at the mall that night?"

"Looking for girls—or should I say young ladies—to talk to." Vic turned toward Sahrina and smiled. She smiled back.

"And what were you planning on talking about?" Langley asked.

"Nothing. Just talk. Maybe ask if they wanted to go out some night or just hang out, you know, just chill."

"When did you first see Ms. Piersol that night?"

"Look, maybe we can save a lot of time if I just jump to the meat of the story."

"Vic!" Sahrina said.

Vic waved her off. "I'm not saying anything incriminating, because there *is* nothing incriminating." He turned to face Langley. "I saw Megan a lot that night. I saw her at the Guess store, then down by Macy's. Then again on the second floor by Nordstrom. I didn't go into Nordstrom but I saw her about half an hour later on the third floor by Zales."

"And all of this while you were stalking her?"

"Vic sighed. "That's what I'm trying to tell you. I wasn't following Megan. I was following another girl named Joan Davro. She's even hotter than Megan."

Sahrina kicked Vic's leg, and he said, "Yeah, I know. Don't say *hot* but I'm sorry, she *is* hot."

Langley was furiously taking notes. "Joan Davro?"

"That's right," Vic said. "Davro. Megan knows her. She even said hi to her a few times that night; in fact, if you pull up surveillance when Megan went in Zales, you'll see Joan standing outside. You can't miss her. She'll make your dick hard."

"Vic!"

Once again, he brushed her off. "Yeah, I know, but she will. She's *that* hot."

"And you claim you were following this Davro girl?"

"I don't claim it, I was. Ask her. We ended up leaving together."

Langley tapped Dennis on the arm, and said, "Let me get a copy of the surveillance you gave me. Let's verify this story now."

Langley and Dennis left the room, got the surveillance video, then scrolled through the footage, watching Megan enter the mall by Nord-strom, go to Guess and Macy's, back to Nordstrom on the second floor, then detour to the food court, then Zales. "Just like the kid detailed," Dennis said.

"And I'm guessing this is the mysterious Joan Davro," Langley said, pointing to a short blonde-haired girl with a near-perfect figure.

"And he didn't exaggerate about that either," Dennis said. "Excuse me while I adjust my trousers."

"All right, let's keep looking," Langley said.

He continued scrolling through the footage and watched as the girls continued to shop, sometimes together, sometimes not. It was obvious from the interactions that they knew each other, but it was also obvious that they weren't together.

As they were leaving the mall, Megan and Joan turned right toward Nordstrom, or the Nordstrom's exit. Vic headed left toward Macy's.

Langley thought for a moment, then said. "I don't buy it. If Vic was following her, why did he branch off and get a ride with his friend at Macy's when the girls headed to Nordstrom?"

"Good point," Dennis said. "And I can't think of a reason. Let's ask him."

Langley and Dennis walked back to the interrogation room and sat down. Langley said, "I have a question, Vic. Why didn't you follow them to Nordstrom? Why go to Macy's and then hitch a ride?"

Vic's eyes dulled. He looked to the left, then said. "I thought they were too far ahead of me, so I got a ride."

"Bullshit," Dennis said. "You could have walked to Nordstrom faster."

Vic hesitated, then said, "Maybe so, but I didn't, I caught a ride. Then I ran to catch up with Joan, talked a few minutes, then we left together on the metro."

"So why'd you catch a ride when you could have walked faster? And when you didn't need the ride to begin with?"

Vic paused again before answering. He looked to Sahrina and cocked his head.

"Go ahead, Vic," she said. "We're not here for that."

Vic looked at Langley. "I wanted to get my weed. I had a stash in the car, and I wanted to tell Joan I had some. I knew she liked it, and I thought it would put me in good with her."

"Weed. You're telling me you went to get weed to bribe her into going with you?"

Vic nodded. "Believe it or not, yes, that's what I'm telling you. Ask Joan. She may be leery of admitting the truth, but if you tell her what's at stake, she'll fess up."

"Give us the phone number and address," Dennis said.

Vic wrote it on a piece of paper then handed it to Dennis. "Call her. She'll tell you. Tell her I said it was okay."

Langley stood. He pointed to Vic, and then Sahrina. "He stays here until we check this out."

"I understand," she said. "We'll wait, but make it quick. Don't stop for coffee."

Langley called the number Vic had provided, but her mother said she wasn't home. "What is the call regarding?"

As I said, this is Detective Langley. We're working a case involving an attack at the Pentagon City Mall, and we have reason to believe that your daughter may have information that could help."

"Oh my. What kind of attack? When?"

"This was a while ago, ma'am. And it was a brutal physical beating. Do you know where your daughter is or when she'll be home?"

"She's probably at the coffee shop down by DuPont Circle. I tell her not to go there but it does no good. I know she disobeys and does it anyway."

"That's fine, ma'am. We'll find her."

"Shouldn't be too hard finding a girl who looks like that," Dennis said.

"Like a flashlight in the dark," Langley said.

Dennis laughed. "You got that right."

Langley drove toward DuPont Circle while Dennis reviewed his notes. "I can't see this kid lying when he knows we're going to check it out."

"Maybe she's in on it," Langley said.

"I don't buy it. He wouldn't have told us before he had a chance to talk to her if it was a lie. He'd want to make sure he got things straight. Besides, he admitted to having a stash of weed."

"For all that's worth," Langley said. "What's that going to get him—a slap on the hand? Not much more. Considering the punishments they dish out, they might as well make the stuff legal."

T hey arrived at the coffee shop in DuPont Circle less than half an hour later. And as Langley had said, Joan was not difficult to find. She stood out like a lighthouse beacon at midnight.

Langley approached, badge in hand. "I'm Detective Grant Langley, and this is Agent Dennis Markum. We have a few questions for you if you don't mind."

"You have questions for me? You don't even know who I am."

"I presume you're Joan Davro," Langley said. "A Mr. Vic Todd described you to us."

Her face lit up with concern. "Vic? Is he okay? Is anything wrong?"

Langley assured her that nothing was wrong. "We were questioning

Vic about the night Megan Piersol was hurt. He mentioned that you and he were at the mall that night."

"Oh, my God, yes. We were with her probably ten or fifteen minutes before it happened, outside of Nordstrom. I still can't believe it. How is she anyway? Is she any better?"

"Still in a coma," Dennis said. "Can you tell us about what happened the fifteen or so minutes beforehand?" Say from the time you exited the mall."

"Sure. I left the mall about 9:30 or so, and Megan was only a few feet behind me. I stopped and we walked together for a while, just talking. Mostly gossip. Then Vic pulled up in a friend's car. He got out and hollered to Megan to wait up, then when he got to us, we started talking. Within a few minutes, we left Megan and headed out on the subway."

"And you left Megan by herself?"

"Yeah, but it's not like it sounds. I asked her if she wanted to join us and she said no, so I left with Vic."

"What time was this?" Langley asked.

"I can't be positive, but probably about 9:30 or 9:45."

"And Vic went with you on the subway?"

"Yeah. We rode it all the way to Bethesda."

'What time did you leave him?" Dennis asked.

"I didn't leave him. We got off together. He was with me until about midnight, then he went home. I heard about Megan the next day."

"And Vic was with you the whole time?"

"Yeah, he was with me. I just told you. What's this all about? Do you think Vic did something? Do you think he had something to do with

Megan's attack? If so, you're wrong. Vic wouldn't do anything like that. And especially not to Megan. Everybody likes her."

"What do *you* think happened?" Dennis asked. "You and Vic were the last people seen with her, and it was only minutes before she was found."

"I have no idea," Joan said. "Hey, wait a minute. You're not suggesting *I* had something to do with it, are you? Are you nuts? Megan is my friend."

Langley looked at Dennis and shook his head. Dennis put away his notebook, handed a card to Joan, then walked over to order a cup of coffee.

"Ms. Davro, here's my card as well. If you think of anything that might help, call me. I mean anything."

"I will, but I'm telling you, you're on the wrong track with Vic. You better start looking at someone else."

Langley joined Dennis in the line waiting to order. He handed him a few bucks. "Get me an espresso, please."

"Keep your money," Dennis said. "I got this one. You get the next."

"You say that like you think there will be a next," Langley said.

"Oh there's definitely going to be a next," Dennis said. "Based on our talk with Joan, we need to review that surveillance again. We missed something."

ANOTHER LOOK AT SURVEILLANCE

Washington, D. C., March 2030

Dennis arrived with a cup of coffee for himself and an espresso for Langley. He handed the still-steaming cup to Langley. "You ready, Detective? It might prove to be a long day."

"If it's just a long day, I'll be happy," Langley said. "But I'm afraid it might turn into several days."

"Damn shame we had to let Vic go," Dennis said. "I didn't trust him."

"Yeah. I'm with you on that, but trust or not, we had nothing to keep him on. His alibi held."

"Do you believe the girl?" Langley asked.

"I don't know if she's giving us everything, but for the most part, I believed her. I do not think Vic had anything to do with Megan's attack."

"Then we need to go over the surveillance again from start to finish," Langley said. "Something is in those videos that we missed. A clue to who did this and why."

"Then we start at the beginning," Dennis said. "Go to the point where she entered by Nordstrom, then back it up a few minutes. Let's look at what happened before she went inside."

Langley stared at the surveillance video as a few people went in the mall, then he watched as Megan entered. "I don't see anything unusual yet," he said.

"Me neither," Dennis said. "Let's keep going."

They followed Megan's movements all the way down the first level to Macy's, then up the second level to Nordstrom, then to the third level and Zales' jewelers. She walked around the third level for a while, stopping twice to chat with who they now knew as Joan Davro, then continued down the escalator to the food court at the metro level.

After eating at Subway, she went back to wandering the mall aimlessly, ending up walking toward the Nordstrom's exit with Joan. "I don't see anything," Langley said.

"Keep watching," Dennis said. "We might see something yet."

Langley and Dennis kept their eyes glued to the screen but nothing of interest showed up. Finally, after watching Megan exit Nordstrom, Dennis said, "That's it. She'll be in a blind spot in a few feet, and the rest of the video will show nothing. I've seen it enough times to know."

"But we've got no video of anyone coming out right after her. So who did this? And where did they come from? You think they came up off of Hayes Street?"

"They could have," Dennis said. "But whoever did it must have known where the blind spots were, or else they got damn lucky."

"My money is on him knowing about the blind spot," Langley said.

"Let's look at this again," Dennis said. "She wouldn't have been going to the metro by exiting at Nordstrom. She would have just accessed it via the escalator from inside. So what was she doing down here?"

"The only logical assumption is Hayes Street," Langley said.

"Son of a bitch," Dennis said. "I just thought of something. If she was heading toward Hayes Street, someone must have been planning to pick her up. Assuming that's the case, why didn't that someone inquire about her whereabouts when she didn't show up?"

"I like it except for one thing," Langley said. "She had her car in the parking lot. So why would she have someone pick her up?"

Dennis nodded. "Yeah. Doesn't make sense. If she had a car, why would she be going to meet someone on Hayes Street? It was late for someone to be just coming to the mall."

Langley tapped his pen on the back of his hand. "But not too late for a rendezvous."

Dennis looked puzzled. "Explain."

"Suppose she was like most teenagers, and she wanted to hook up with her boyfriend before going home. She calls him and tells him to pick her up so Dustyn doesn't see, then sneaks off with him and does the dirty deed."

Dennis frowned. "I don't like your crudeness, but I have to admit, you may be right. If she did do that, there should be a record of a phone call either coming in or going out."

Langley tapped the technician on the shoulder. "Pull up the phone records for incoming and outgoing calls on Megan's phone that night."

Five minutes later, Dennis and Langley were searching through the list. It didn't take long to find what they were looking for. About half an hour before the attack, there was an outgoing call from Megan's cell number.

"And you know whose number that is?" Dennis asked.

Langley shrugged.

"It's Justin McCabe's. The one who swore he was home all night studying."

"This doesn't prove he wasn't," Langley said. "All it proves is that he received a phone call. We'll have to see where he was when he got it."

"My guess is, Megan called him, and told him to come get her so they could sneak away while Dustyn thought she was still in the mall."

"And then something happened," Langley said. "But what?"

"I don't know what set it off, but it had to be quick. She was attacked within moments of leaving the mall. And whoever did it must have left in a car or on foot. If he took the metro we'd have spotted him on surveillance."

"And you looked?" Langley asked.

"Of course we looked. We checked metro surveillance six times at least. And we ran all cards against known sex offenders and criminals, as well as friends of Megan's. Nothing."

"Then why didn't you pick up on Vic? Joan said they rode the metro that night."

"I don't know," Dennis said. "Let's call Vic and find out."

few minutes later Vic answered his cell.

"Yeah?"

"Vic, it's Agent Markum. You said you rode the metro home, but we didn't see you on surveillance."

There was a pause, then Vic said, "Check a little later. Joan and I stopped for a few joints and a little something else. We didn't catch the metro for another fifty or sixty minutes."

"All right, but we're checking so you better be telling the truth."

"Man, I don't like you guys, but I ain't lying about something like this. I liked Megan."

Ten minutes later, Dennis and Langley confirmed Vic's story on the surveillance videos. Then Langley said, "I think it's time we talked to Megan's friends again. All of them. This is looking more and more like a planned, well-orchestrated attack rather than the random mugging we thought it was."

"Then we should start with her boyfriend," Dennis said. "Even if he has an explanation for the call, he'd know who else to talk to."

"And we can count on him?"

"Definitely. He's Senator McCabe's son, and he adores Megan."

"I wonder why he wasn't with her that night?" Langley said.

"I don't remember why—he told us, but we'll ask again," Dennis said. "Come on. I've got the address in my phone."

"Where did Megan go to school?" Langley asked.

"A private school, out by Bethesda, not far from the Bradley Manor-Longwood section. Why?"

Langley whistled. "The ghetto, huh?"

"Yeah, the ghetto." Dennis laughed. "In that part of town, anything less than a million-dollar house is deemed ghetto."

"Back on target," Langley said. "If we assume that someone was going to meet Megan, and that whoever was going to meet her, knew her, we'll make a guess that they went to the same school and lived somewhere close to most of her friends, in Bethesda. If that's the case," Langley said, "the shortest route to the Pentagon City Mall is across the Francis Scott Key Bridge."

"You're right," Dennis said. "So we check the surveillance on that night from around 10:00 to 11:00 and see if anything pops up. Don't forget, we've got surveillance almost everywhere now, especially on major roads or bridges coming and going."

Langley smiled. "Some things are for the better. At least for us."

Dennis made a special request for surveillance video of the bridge.

The videos arrived the next morning just as Dennis and Langley were finishing coffee.

Dennis drained his coffee, then tossed the empty cup into the trash. "Might as well get to work," he said. "We've got plenty to do."

It was a grueling operation, and after six hours of staring at videos, all they had to show for it was eye strain.

"We're getting nowhere with this," Langley said. "We don't even know who we're looking for. I've passed a hundred kids, and any one of them could have been one of Megan's friends."

"Then we need to know what her friends look like," Dennis said. "We'll talk to Justin. Maybe he has pictures; in fact, with the proliferation of smart phones and their cameras, I'm sure he has pictures."

"Tell me about it," Langley said. "My niece inherited her father's old iPhone, and within days she had hundreds of pictures."

"Then let's go see McCabe," Langley said.

"I know where he lives," Dennis said. "Like I told you, we have the senator's address."

Dennis provided directions while Langley drove. It wasn't long before they pulled in front of McCabe's house. "Is this it?" Langley asked. "It looks more like a hotel."

"It might be bigger than a hotel," Dennis said. "At least bigger than the ones I've stayed in."

They rang the doorbell and within seconds a servant answered, as if he'd been waiting for them to ring.

"May I help you?" he said.

Dennis displayed his badge. "Agent Dennis Markum," he said. "And this is Detective Langley. We need to speak with Justin."

"May I inquire as to why?"

"You can inquire," Dennis said. "But I won't tell you. Just let Justin know that we need to talk."

The servant frowned, then spun on his heels and left. "I'll be back momentarily."

Just when Langley was beginning to think the servant had tricked them, a young man bounded down the steps wearing a smile.

"Yes?" he said. "Morgan said you wanted to see me?"

"I'm Agent Markum," Dennis said. "And this is Detective Langley. We're here regarding Megan Piersol."

"Megan? Oh, God. Is she—"

"Nothing has changed," Dennis said. "We're still investigating the incident that put her in the hospital."

"Really? That happened so long ago, I thought it was dead. I'm glad to see you're still working on it."

"Don't worry, sir. We intend to find out who did this. It might take a while, but we'll get him."

Justin flashed a smile. "Come into the kitchen where we can talk more comfortably. Would you like something to drink or eat?"

"No, thanks," Dennis said.

"Water for me," Langley said.

As they walked toward the kitchen, Justin said, "You'll have to excuse Morgan. He's leery of strangers."

"I hadn't noticed," Langley said, barely containing his sarcasm.

"That's nice of you to say, Detective, but I'm certain you *did* notice. You're a detective, and Morgan is not good at concealing his emotions."

Justin got himself and Langley a glass of water, then he sat at the table and invited Langley and Markum to do the same. "What can I help you with?"

"We'd like a list of Megan's friends," Langley said. "Especially any of them who were envious or at odds with her."

Justin laughed. "I don't know how well you knew Megan, Detective, but I don't know of anyone who was at odds with her. She is a wonderful person. That's why I love her so much. She never says an unkind word and never says anything bad against anybody."

"Never?" Langley said.

Justin nodded. "Never. And the best part is, if she hears someone else talk about a person, like most of us do from time to time, she'll blindly defend them while reminding you that there might be other factors at play. She is truly a gem of a person."

"And you don't know anyone who might have wanted to hurt her?"

"No one," Justin said. "The only person even close to combative was a guy named Vic Todd, but I can't believe even Vic would do something like that. Whoever did that to her was an animal."

Langley looked at Dennis and raised his brows. "Vic Todd? What can you tell us about him?"

"Not much. He's not one of us," Justin said. "I mean, he's not from around here, but he's not a bad guy. I used to be friends with him."

"Used to be?"

"Yeah, we kind of fell apart when he tried to pull a move on Megan. It pissed me off because he knew she and I were dating."

"What happened?" Dennis asked.

"He grabbed her in the hall, dragged her into an alcove and tried to kiss her. I told her to press charges, but like I said, she's too nice."

"And it ended there?" Langley asked.

"Yeah. It never went anywhere after that. But that ended our friendship also." Justin stopped to sip on his water. "I have an old picture of Vic if you want it."

"We don't need his," Dennis said, "but if you have any pictures of Megan's other friends that you could share with us, that would be great."

Justin beamed. "Sure. Hang on and I'll get them. They're on my phone."

He got up from the table and returned a moment later holding a new iPhone. "If you have an iPhone, turn on Air Drop and I'll send them to you."

Langley opened the settings for his phone and did as instructed. Within moments, he received a couple of dozen pictures. "These were all her friends?"

"Nowhere near all of them, but they probably represent her best friends. If you need more I could probably get them."

Dennis shook his head. "This is good for now, but thanks. By the way, where were you on the night Megan was attacked?"

"Here," Justin said. "We had a test the next day and I had to study."

"And Megan didn't?"

He shook his head. "She never studies. And she aces all of the tests, too. I don't know how, but she does. I used to tease her that she only aced them because the teachers knew she was the president's daughter." Justin grabbed a napkin and wiped away tears. "Now, I wish I hadn't said that."

"I wouldn't worry about it," Dennis said.

"When did you hear about the incident?" Langley asked.

"I got a call from her father around 11:00. I was in my room when he called, then I rushed to the hospital. Been there almost every night since."

"Did you talk to Megan that night?" Langley asked.

He nodded. "She called about 9:00 or so. We only chatted about a minute then she said she'd be going home soon and she'd call when she got in." Justin started tearing up again. "When her dad called around 11:00, I thought it was her."

After a few more questions, Langley and Dennis left. Langley drove slowly back to the office. It wasn't as if he had a choice, considering the traffic. "This traffic is a bitch," Langley said.

"Tell me about it," Dennis said. "Drives me crazy."

"At first, I was suspicious of the boy," Langley said. "But not now. He seemed pretty broken up. And he came right out and mentioned the call."

"We need to look at that surveillance again, now that we have pictures to compare with. If somebody matches, we've got a suspect," Langley said.

They made an array of the photos situated on the desk between them, then they zoomed in on every car that appeared to have a teenage driver—or, for that matter—a driver under thirty. After five more hours, they still had nothing.

"All right," Langley said. "Maybe we've missed them. These images aren't the clearest. Or maybe the person who attacked her wasn't in the photo array."

"Or maybe whoever did this is smarter than us and didn't take the Francis Scott Key Bridge? He took a different route to thwart us."

"Or maybe he's stupider than we give him credit for and took a different route," Langley said. "Either way it thwarts us."

"Let's assume for a minute that we don't know which route he took. What else have we got?"

"Phones," Langley said.

"What?

"Maybe whoever did it called somebody or got a call during our window of opportunity."

"It's a long shot," Dennis said.

"If you've got anything better, let's jump on it. If not..."

Dennis sighed. "Okay. Give me half the names. We'll have to get the numbers from Justin, assuming he'll give them. If not, it'll take a lot longer, but we could go the route of the phone company."

"I'm sure Justin will give them to us," Langley said. "He seemed to want this cleared up."

IT'S MY FAULT

Washington, D. C., March 2030

Langley was on his way home when he passed a group of teenagers hanging out on the corner by the park. He brought the car to a screeching halt, rolled down his window, and almost called out. Almost.

He had been about to make a fool of himself again. About to shout his son's name to a total stranger. Fortunately he'd caught himself this time. Realized that the average-looking, long-haired kid on the corner was just that—a kid on the corner and not Eric. When was he going to get over this? Eric had been dead for years.

Langley drove along in silence, feeling like pounding his head against the steering wheel. Then his cell phone rang. "Hello?"

"Langley, it's Dennis. I just got a call from the man. Megan is awake. It's in spurts, but she talked."

Langley checked his rearview mirror and when he saw that the lanes were clear behind him, he made an illegal U-turn. "On my way," he said. "It'll take me fifteen minutes tops."

"Meet you there," Dennis said.

Two agents were in the hall, drinking coffee and talking. They came to full alert when Langley approached, but he quickly put them at ease. "Easy fellas. It's me, Grant Langley. I'm going to slowly open my coat so one of you can grab my gun, okay?"

The agent they called *Fish* nodded, then said, "I've got you, Langley. I don't plan on shooting you yet."

"Good to know," Langley said, then stood still while they frisked him.

"Sorry for the trouble," Fish said. "But we need to do it."

"Understandable," Langley said, "and it's no trouble."

He started to enter the room, and then he raised his brow and looked at Fish. "All right to go in?"

Fish said. "We're giving him private time. But you can see if he's busy."

Langley slowly opened the door and took a step inside. The president was sitting on the edge of Megan's bed, holding her hand.

"I miss you, Megan. We all do. Your mother called from California today. She misses you, too. She said she especially misses the talks you two had on Sundays."

The president patted the back of her hand, then kissed it. "I wish you'd hurry up and come back to us. I don't know how much more I can take. Besides, I blame myself. I listened to you and had Dennis and his men back off a little, and now look what's happened. I should have had them watching over you. Dustyn should have been with you that night."

The president leaned forward, kissed her on the forehead, then folded his hands to pray. "God, if you're listening, please hear me out. I know I haven't been your best disciple, but Megan is a good girl, and she needs you. The doctors don't seem to be doing any good, so she needs some other kind of help. I'm counting on you, God. Please help her? Please?"

Langley felt like a piece of shit, standing at the doorway, eavesdropping on a man as he prayed. Earlier, Langley had been wallowing in self-pity, now he was with the president—a man Langley hadn't even voted for, didn't even like from a political standpoint—and he saw that the president was walking in the same shoes as he had been, experiencing the same things, praying to the same God. And for what? It did his son no good. It hadn't helped Eric.

Vivid images returned of he and Rhonda spending countless nights in the waiting room consoling each other or holding Eric's lifeless hands as he lay in a coma, unable to respond. And all the while they said prayers to...who knows whom and asked for help that never came.

Langley shifted weight, then cleared his throat to let the president know that he was in the room.

Startled, the president spun around. "Detective, I didn't know you were here. Have you been standing there long?"

"Long enough, sir. And I apologize. I didn't know..."

Ellis brushed his hand in the air. "No matter. I'm through with worrying about little things." He gestured to Megan, lying in the bed. "As you can see, there are more important issues."

Ellis used his sleeve to wipe tears from his eyes, then he let out a small chuckle and said, "I guess that's not very presidential, is it?"

Langley looked at the tears in the president's eyes, then he remembered his own tears from what seemed like yesterday. "No, sir. It's not presidential, but it's not supposed to be. It's fatherly, and since that's your daughter lying in that bed, it's understandable. Your reaction is what it's supposed to be."

The president nodded. "Thank you, Detective. That was very kind." Then he gestured to a chair. "Have a seat, please."

Langley sat, then took out his notebook. "Dennis said Megan was awake. Has she said anything?"

The president shook his head. "Barely. A couple of times, she called Justin's name. Nothing else."

Langley smiled. "Teenagers have a one-track mind, sir. I wouldn't let it worry you."

"You have kids, Detective?"

His smile disappeared, then Langley clenched his jaw. The muscles in his face tightened. "I did, sir. My son died years ago, murdered."

The president stood and placed his arm on Langley's shoulder. "Oh my God. I'm sorry. I didn't know."

"That's all right, sir. No way you could have known. And I'm sorry for being so sensitive. I just...haven't been able to deal with it."

"I completely understand. And please forgive my asking, but how old was he when that happened?"

"He was sixteen. About the same age as Megan. He went out with friends and never came back. It broke his mother's heart. She's never been the same. *We've* never been the same."

The president wrapped his arms around Langley to console him. "Detective, I'm so sorry. I never should have brought that up. It was selfish, and I apologize."

"Nonsense," Langley said. "It's long past time I should be able to discuss it. The fault is mine. I should be the one thanking you for asking."

"Did you catch the person who did it?"

Langley bit his upper lip. "We thought we had, sir. He was even convicted and sent to prison. Three years later, we found out we had the wrong man behind bars, but before we could effect the other man's release he was killed—stabbed to death."

"Oh my God. And the real killer?"

"Remained free for five more years, then someone killed him."

"It's a tough world out there," the president said. "At least justice was done in the end."

Langley nodded. "There is that, although it didn't do anything to bring Eric back."

"Of course not," the president said. "And like I said, I'm sorry for bringing this up. I do want you to do one thing for me, though."

"Anything, sir."

"Don't say 'anything' until you know what it is."

"Okay, what is it?"

"I want you to promise me that you'll do everything to bring whoever did this to justice."

"You can count on it," Langley said.

"I don't think you understand—when I say *anything*, I mean *anything*. No matter what."

"I understand perfectly, sir. And my answer is the same, 'You can count on it'. Remember, I lost a son, and this case brings back those memories. Megan reminds me of him."

The president lowered his head. "Thank you, Detective. It makes me feel better to get that off my chest."

Langley looked at the president, started to say something, then stopped.

"What is it, Detective? You looked as if you were going to say something. Speak up if you were. You're with friends."

"What I was going to say was that I didn't vote for you when you ran; I didn't like your politics. Now I think I should have. I will next time."

"Thank you," the president said. "I appreciate honesty, but I'd rather that you get the guy who did this to Megan."

"I will, sir."

He stood and started to leave, then looked back. "And sir, if she does wake and I'm not here, ask her if she knows anything about who did this. We could use something to go on."

"I will, but so far all she's said is her boyfriend's name. Nothing else."

"Okay, sir. Thank you again."

Langley opened the door, walked into the hall, and paced. He thought about the similarities between Megan's condition and what his son's had been. It was eerie—almost too much to handle. Maybe he should ask to be taken off the case.

Megan was in much the same situation as Eric had been. And some asshole had done almost the same thing. Somebody had attacked her brutally. Almost killed her, probably would kill her. And now that person deserved to die, not be put in prison.

Langley wanted nothing more than to make that person die, which was one more reason why he should not be on the case. He wasn't equipped mentally to handle this. Not yet.

Not yet? If not now, when? Am I going to beg off every teenage case forever?

"Everything go okay?"

The attempt at conversation snapped Langley out of it. "I'm sorry. What?"

Fish looked at him strangely. "I asked if everything went okay."

Langley nodded slowly. "Yeah. Fine. She didn't say anything, though. Just mumbled the kid's name."

"That's all she ever does," Fish said. "Of course that's all she ever did."

Dennis came up the hall at a half-jog pace. "Sorry I'm late. There was a damn accident that held me up forever."

"Don't worry about it," Langley said. "You didn't miss anything."

"She didn't say anything?"

Langley shook his head. "Nothing of interest. Looks like it's going to be up to us, so we better get our asses in gear."

"Mine has been in gear for a long time," Dennis said. "I think you're the one who's been coasting."

Langley laughed and punched Dennis in the arm. "Asshole."

Fish handed him his gun back, then Langley and Dennis turned around and headed for the exit.

"Where to now?" Dennis asked.

"I don't know about you, but I'm going home to eat. We'll start fresh tomorrow."

A PROBLEM WITH THE TRIAL

Washington, D.C., December 2029

Ginesh got to the office at his usual time, but to his surprise, Nancy was already there. "Nancy, what are you doing here? Did you spend the night?"

Nancy laughed. "No, I didn't spend the night, but I wanted to get in early and discuss something."

Ginesh looked around, saw nobody, then said, "Speak freely. It's just us."

"And I need it to stay between us."

"It will. You have my word."

She pulled alongside Ginesh's chair, leaned close, then whispered, "I got a call from Martha last night."

Ginesh looked puzzled. "Martha?"

"From Spring Meadows, remember?"

Ginesh nodded. "Oh yeah, now I remember. She was the one giving you all of that sass."

"Last night she called to tell me that we had been right, that the patients have been fighting regularly, and that Connor had to take them off the meds to stop it."

"Really? How many?"

"I don't know the numbers, but apparently it's been a lot. The key is that Connors knew, or better stated, he knows. And he didn't say anything, even when we went to Spring Meadows and told him about the problem with the rats."

"Maybe he didn't want to say anything?" Ginesh said. "Maybe he's in on it?"

"You phrased that as if it were a question," Nancy said. "I don't think there's any doubt. He's in on it in a big way."

"If that's the case," Ginesh said. "What do we do? Tell Barney?"

"I can't imagine Barney being in on it."

"Somebody from the company had to be," Ginesh said. "According to Vic, the database online and the security access had to have been designed with the highest approval."

"My guess is Ratcliff," Nancy said. "And McCabe. I told you, I've never trusted McCabe."

"So who do we confide in? We better choose carefully, or we'll be looking for new jobs. And you know my situation with Raji. We can't afford to look for new jobs."

"It makes no difference," Nancy said. "We're the ones who did this, so we're the ones responsible. We've got to decide."

"If you put it that way," Ginesh said, "I'd go with Barney. I don't trust Keith any more than I do McCabe."

"Barney it is," Nancy said. "I'll call for an appointment."

Ginesh shook his head. "Maybe we should wait until he comes here. That way we don't make it seem so urgent."

"But it is urgent."

"He'll be here today or tomorrow," Ginesh said. "He stops by at least once a week."

"Ginesh, we *have* to tell him. It's him or someone else."

"We'll tell him," Ginesh said. "But let's make it seem as if it were an afterthought. I don't want it to seem as if we're concerned."

"Why not? We are concerned."

"I understand, but if possible, I want to safeguard our stock position."

"Ginesh, we've worked with each other for years, and I love you dearly, but screw your stock. We're talking about people's lives. Which is more important?"

Ginesh lowered his head. "Okay. Enough embarrassment. We'll tell him."

Nancy called Barney's office and requested an appointment. Barney's admin said, "Let me check his calendar." A moment later, she got back on the line. "Mr. Franklin doesn't have any openings but he is scheduled to come by your lab late this afternoon. Is that soon enough?"

"This afternoon? That would be great. Thanks."

Barney showed up around 3:00. He inspected the lab then sat down next to Ginesh. "My admin told me you two wanted to talk. About what?"

"Nothing in particular," Ginesh said.

"Bullshit," Nancy said. "We've got problems with the drug. Ginesh is just afraid to tell you."

Barney sat up straighter. "Problems? What kind?"

"First we had problems with the rats; they started fighting among themselves. One bit Ginesh, then we found one dead."

"That's terrible," Barney said, "But I'm not pulling the plug based on the reactions of a few rats. Not with what's at stake."

"I know that," Nancy said. "But people at Spring Meadows have been having the same reactions."

"Who said so?"

Nancy thought for a moment about what Martha said, about keeping it quiet. "It doesn't matter who said so. It's happening. Isn't that enough to know?"

"Connor didn't tell us anything." Barney said.

Nancy nodded. "I believe Mr. Connor may be attempting to cover this up. I wouldn't take his word as fact for what's going on."

"But you think something is going on?"

"I *know* it," Nancy said. "It's way beyond thinking it."

"All right. Good. I'll look into this," Barney said. "In the meantime, tell no one. We don't want this getting out. Can I count on you to be quiet?" Barney asked. Then he looked at Ginesh and Nancy.

"You can count on me," Ginesh said.

"Good." He turned to Nancy. "And you?"

Nancy nodded. "Me too. But only if you promise you'll do something."

"You have my word on that," Barney said. "I'll get right on it."

Nancy waited for Barney to leave, then she turned to Ginesh. "I don't know about you, but I feel good. Good and clean."

"And I feel poorer," Ginesh said. "One way or another, I'm sure that our stock position is not going to be worth much anymore."

"I'm not worried about the stock," Nancy said. "At least we did what was right."

"You're not worried because you don't have a kid," Ginesh said. "It makes a difference."

"It shouldn't," Nancy said.

"Maybe it shouldn't," Ginesh said, "but it does."

Barney closed the door behind him, then almost ran to his car. Once inside, he sped off and rushed to Keith Ratcliff's office. He had to wait about ten minutes for Keith to finish up a meeting with the CFO, but then he was shown in.

"What's up, Barney? You look excited."

"We've got problems, Keith. Big problems."

Keith grew concerned. "What kind of problems?"

"The kind where there is something wrong with NeuroScan, and Nancy is getting ready to blow the whistle."

Keith leaned to his left side, shifting weight to his elbow. "We can't let that happen, Barney. Too much is riding on that stock. Margaret already bought a new car."

"And my wife put a down payment on a house in Germantown. Without the stock, we'll never afford it."

"Then let's make sure nothing happens," Keith said. "Neither one of us can afford to have things derailed."

"Okay," Barney said. "I'll see what I can do."

~

Keith waited a few seconds, allowing Barney enough time to get out of earshot, then dialed McCabe.

"Hello?"

"McCabe, this is Keith. One of the scientists is planning on causing trouble."

"What kind of trouble?"

"She's found some problems with the drug—adverse effects that would interfere with long-term use, which is what we need to make the visors work."

"Is there any way around it? Any way to stop these reactions?"

"Hell, I don't know," Keith said. "I just found out about them a few minutes ago. Regardless, we can't afford the bad publicity."

McCabe remained silent for a moment. Afterward, he said, "Then we'll have to make sure there is no bad publicity. Which scientist is causing the problem?"

"Nancy. She's the one with such high standards."

"I'll have a talk with her," McCabe said. "It's time she understood what will happen if things get out of hand."

SEX WITH A STRANGER

Washington, D.C., December 2029

Vic hadn't liked the reaction he'd gotten from Ginesh, and he felt his new livelihood threatened. If someone pulled the plug on the visors now, his income would plummet, go from sky high to below sea level in one swift movement.

He had to do something fast, and it had to be drastic. Thrills sold well, but they were dangerous, and, besides, they weren't the best. He imagined sex would be better. He wasn't sure, but he presumed that girls might want to see sex memories more than guys.

Despite the fact that girls had long ago achieved equal rights, girls still had to fight the reputation thing, and guys had the reverse situation. If a girl slept with three or four guys, she was considered a slut; if a guy did it, he was a stud. A slightly different connotation.

The big difference, though, was that Vic was sure the girls wanted to do it as much as the guys. If they could do that through visors, and do it safely and with no threat of injuring their reputation, there would be no problem. It would be risk-free, disease-free, pregnancy-free, and reputation-free sex. The only possible way a girl could be found out is if she told someone herself.

Vic was so convinced this would work that he ran it by Joan for her analysis. She listened, at first appearing slightly jealous, then said, "Yeah, it would definitely work. "Girls want sex as badly as boys, but we have issues to deal with. Take those away and it's all systems go."

"And you think they'd pay fifty bucks for it?"

Joan laughed. "My friends pay hundreds of dollars for a purse or a pair of shoes. Fifty dollars for sex is nothing."

"Then let's get started," Vic said. "We could have five memories out there by the weekend."

"Whoa! What are you talking about? I'm not doing this."

"Why not? Reputation? Earn enough money and reputation doesn't matter. Besides, people figure we're screwing already. This will just confirm it."

"But what if my father sees it?" Joan said.

"There's only one way for your father to see it," Vic said, "and that's if he buys a sex memory. If he does, question him about it."

"Suppose he hears it from a friend?"

"Is he going to admit his friend bought a sex memory of a teenage girl? If he does, just strike back and tell him. 'Dad, I'm almost eighteen. If I want to have sex, I will.'"

Vic pulled her close and hugged. "Trust me, it won't be a problem."

Joan sighed. "It better not be a problem. When do you want to start?"

"The sooner the better," Vic said. "How about now?"

"Right now? Right here?"

"No better time or place," Vic said. "Let's start with plain vanilla sex. Some minor foreplay followed by the missionary position."

"Kind of dull, isn't it?" Joan said.

"It's dull, but it will sell to the beginner crowd. Guys who are still virgins—and there are more of them than you think—and girls in the same situation. They'll both flock to it. Once word spreads about how hot you are, you'll become the new pin-up girl for the whole country."

"And the girls?"

"The girls will all want to be like you. Look like you. Have your figure. And...do other things like you."

Joan reached down and lifted her sweater up over her head, leaving only a bra showing. She smiled, stood on her tiptoes and kissed him. "Why don't you help me off with these clothes?" she said in a sultry voice.

Vic checked to make sure his visors were turned on and within range, then he said, "Gladly." And he undid the zipper on her pants.

After performing what Vic termed plain-vanilla sex, they moved on to oral sex, demonstrating the sixty-nine position, and then individual oral performances by Vic and Joan, each complete with full-blown orgasms. And in each case, graphic images were available with the memory purchase as photographic stills.The one thing Joan insisted on was not having a clear image of herself, so all of the pictures of her face were blurry; however, her body was almost high definition.

"As long as we can see your figure," Vic said. "I don't care about your face."

"What now?" Joan asked.

"*What now?* We'll finish this tomorrow," Vic said. "You wiped my ass out. I don't want to look like a wimp."

Joan, naked as can be, wiggled up to Vic and wrapped her arms around him. She kissed him on the lips and whispered, "What's that old saying? If the shoe fits?"

"Screw you," Vic said.

"I'm game," Joan said. "Let's go."

Vic kissed her back hard, and his hands roamed over her ass cheeks, but although is mind was willing his body wasn't. "I can't," he said. "It'll have to be tomorrow."

Joan kissed him again, then said, "I hope you take your vitamins tomorrow. I don't want to be left abandoned."

The next night, Vic lay down on the bed and Joan climbed atop him. She started riding him cowgirl style as if they were old hands at it. Suddenly, she felt something poke at her backside. When she spun around, a naked man was standing there prepared to penetrate her. "What the hell?" she hollered.

Vic smiled, reached behind her head and pulled her forward. "I wouldn't worry if I were you. You'll love the way it feels and it will make us tons of money."

"I don't want tons of money," Joan said. "I don't need it."

"But I do," Vic said, and he pulled her forward to kiss. The man behind her shoved into her. She screeched but soon she began to moan. Before the guys were done with her, she was screaming for them to do other things.

This will be perfect, Vic thought. *The girls will love it and so will the guys.*

At the end of the session, after the other guy had left, Joan turned to Vic. She was furious. "Don't ever do anything like that again."

"Why not? You liked it, didn't you?"

"Whether I liked it, is not the issue. I didn't want it; that's what matters. So don't do it again."

"Calm down," Vic said. "No harm done."

"Maybe it's no harm for you," Joan said, "but word will get out about who the girl is in the video, and I don't want people to know it's me doing something like that."

By the end of four days, sales had skyrocketed. If they continued at this rate, the memory would be selling about $50,000 per month. Vic was ecstatic.

"Did you hear that, baby? Fifty grand a month for screwing. What do you think of that?"

"Fifty grand? At that rate, I guess I'm not so particular. Do whatever you want, just tell me first."

Vic threw her down on the bed and unbuckled her pants. "Good. Because I have some other ideas."

MURDER FOR FUN AND PROFIT

Washington, D. C., March 2030

Cyrus kicked the beer can out of his way, tossed the empty wine bottle in the trash, then sat on the sofa, where he dumped the ashtray—complete with a mountain of crushed butts—into the trash bag.

He stared out the window at the snow falling, cursing the day for what it was. He hated snow. Life was shit, just like the day, and he had to find a way to change that.

But how?

He thought he might have had something when the Memory Visors came out, so he waited until he was prepped, then put up a few memories for sale, memories of highs, of hiding from the cops, and other minor infractions. Nothing worked. Buyers flocked to the more dangerous or more thrilling memories.

He decided that he'd try something new. *Tonight's the night.*

After dinner, Cyrus dressed in jeans, a dark-colored shirt, a black hoodie, and a pair of Nikes. In the dark it would be tough to identify him, even up close.

He got out his needle, injected himself, then locked the door behind him as he left.

It's time for some fun.

As Cyrus walked down the street, the excitement built. Nobody was going to have a better thrill than this. Nobody.

He rode the metro to the worst part of town, got off, and continued walking, head hung low. Before long, someone approached from the rear. He heard their footsteps, a dull thud on the pavement behind him.

As the stranger got closer, Cyrus spun to face him.

"What's up, dude? What're you doing down here?"

"I don't see that it's any of your business," Cyrus said.

"None of my business? That's no way to talk to a friend. We are friends, right? You wouldn't come to *my* neighborhood if we weren't friends, would you?" The man slowly stepped forward as he spoke. His hands were inside the pocket of his jacket. As he continued moving forward, his smile broadened and he was joined by another young man.

Cyrus watched carefully. He shook his head. "No, I wouldn't do that," he said, then pulled out a gun and shot both men twice in the chest.

Blood splattered everywhere. They fell as if they'd been hit with a sledge hammer. And through it all, the sound of the gunshots echoed in the streets. A few porch lights went on, but only a few. Most remained dark, unlit.

Cyrus took off running. It would not be good to be found next to two bodies.

He'd only gone a few blocks when he heard the sirens. Once the cops saw what took place and got reports from the few neighbors who were brave enough to say anything, they'd be searching all over for him. He had to get off the streets quickly.

Instead of returning via the metro, where cameras were prevalent, he opted to walk home. He'd already made the mistake of riding the metro on the way there, and besides, the walk would do him good. Help to clear his mind.

It took about forty minutes to get home, but once he got there, he felt safe. He dropped a few tabs of acid then settled in to listen to music, old time R&B. It always put him in a reflective mood.

As he pondered his situation, he thought about what he'd done and whether he should monetize it. It's why he did it, but would others get as much of a thrill? Or would he be exposing himself for possible arrest?

As the acid kicked in and logic turned to dreams, he decided he'd do it. He'd sell the murder memory.

Now committed to a course of action, he took the visors from his pocket and put them on, then found the label marked *Sales* and pressed it to begin the process.

Before long, he had uploaded his memory. All that remained now was to see if it sold. Considering it was the only murder or even the only killing for sale, it should fly off the virtual shelves.

Three days passed before Cyrus checked his sales. When he did, he was shocked. In that short amount of time, he had sold almost $200,000 worth of memories. Now, he was excited. His venture had been worthwhile.

Cyrus went on a spending spree with his newfound wealth, but he was already thinking of what to do for an encore. He bought a new Audi, which he'd always wanted, shopped for new clothes, and ordered a refrigerator and microwave, which were due to be delivered in days.

He ate dinner, dropped some more acid, and tried to think of ideas. After about twenty minutes of nonsense, he hit on one he thought would work. He'd put up a memory for sale of a first degree murder, not manslaughter. As he thought of the details, he had another idea. He wouldn't *sell* the memory, he'd *auction* it. He would start an auction for people who wanted him to murder someone. Whoever won the bid could choose anyone they wanted to be killed, or it could be a random person.

He took time to create an ad, then put it on the site.

Murder for Hire

I'll kill anyone for a price.
Place your bid.
One bid only. No second chances.

All Cyrus could do now was wait. He lay back, lit a joint to accompany his acid-high, and turned on some music appropriate for the situation. He closed his eyes and sang along with the lyrics to an old Beatles' song—*Lucy in the Sky with Diamonds*.

Cyrus didn't have to wait too long. Somewhere around midnight, he received an alert that bids were recorded. He went online with his visors to check them and thought he would fall off the couch.

There were four bids. One for a specific person. One for a specific place. And two were random. The bid for the specific person was for $1,000,000. Cyrus could barely think straight. His money problems were solved.

He contacted the bidder and accepted, after agreeing on transfer details. The bidder had only one requirement—that Cyrus repeat a phrase provided by the bidder before he killed the man. And that had to be recorded on the visors.

Cyrus extracted the name and address of the target, then made plans to scout the area the next day. It was on University Avenue, by Glen Echo Park.

In the morning, Cyrus climbed into his new Audi and drove to the site. He parked about a block away and waited for the man—now known to him as Sinclair Rush—to exit the house, then Cyrus made note of his morning routine.

Sinclair opened the front door and picked up a newspaper from the porch floor. It was unusual as most people no longer had newspapers delivered. Most either read the news digitally or read the paper at a coffee shop or restaurant or at work. Once he picked up the paper, he disappeared for half an hour or so, then exited through the back door, climbed in his car and drove off.

Cyrus watched him do this three days in a row, then, on the fourth day, he arrived early, tossed the paper onto the sidewalk leading to the porch, and hid behind some shrubbery next to a short stone wall that surrounded the property.

Ten minutes later, Sinclair appeared. He scoured the porch for the paper, then must have seen it on the walk. He descended the four steps and walked to where the paper was. That was what Cyrus had been waiting for. He dashed from behind the shrubs, gun in hand, and came up behind Sinclair.

When Sinclair turned, he stopped, staring at the gun, now pointed at his face. "Wha's this?" he asked. "You want money?"

"Not quite, well, not from you anyway."

Cyrus looked him in the eyes and said, "I was told to tell you that 'You shouldn't have done that to Linda.'"

"What?"

"That was the message 'You shouldn't have done that to Linda.' That's all he said."

"That's all who said?"

"I guess somebody who liked Linda," Cyrus said, then he pulled the trigger twice. One bullet hit Sinclair in the face by the nose, and the other hit his eye.

Afterward, Cyrus ran and got into his car, which he had put fake plates on, then sped away.

THE CITY HAS GONE CRAZY

Washington, D. C., March 2030

Langley snatched the phone from it's cradle. "Hello," he said impatiently.

"Bad mood, Langley?" Dennis asked.

"Sorry about that, but this has been a shitty morning already. The goddamn city has gone crazy. Four murders and it's not even 10:00. Who knows what it will be by tonight?"

"Four murders? What's the normal?"

"About three per week, so this is out of control and then some. And we're not talking gang shootings or drug deals or muggings. For the most part, these are upstanding citizens who were gunned down for what appears to be no reason."

"Always a reason," Dennis said. "But good luck finding it."

"I guess you want to go over Justin's statements regarding Megan."

"If we can. We need to get ahead of this."

"I'll see what I can do, but right now I've got to work on these murders. You know how it goes."

Dennis exhaled a slow, deep breath. "I've got to get to work on this case with Megan. I'll call if I need anything."

"Sounds good," Langley said. "And sorry about not helping but..."

"No worry," Dennis said. "Catch those bad guys, then we'll get this one. See you later."

Langley finished his coffee, gathered his files, then headed out. He was supposed to have a partner today, but the guy got sick. No matter, he'd go it alone. He drove to Glen Echo first, following up on the original crime scene unit's investigation. Not that he thought they missed anything, but he wanted to see the scene for himself.

He parked on University, across from Rush's house and stared at the surroundings.

Why? He thought. *Why him and why here?*

There must have been a better place to kill someone. By all accounts, Rush drove to work every day using the same route. If someone wanted to kill him, they could have done it more safely plenty of other places.

And why kill Rush to begin with? His financials showed nothing unusual. He had no record. By all appearances, he looked clean.

So why kill him?

Langley questioned the neighbors, found two who said they may have seen a foreign car speeding away, but neither one could identify the make or model, or even swear to the color. In other words, no help. None of the other neighbors saw anything, so less than nothing as far as help goes.

On the way back to the station, Langley's cell rang. "Hello?"

"Langley, this is Dennis. You been hearing anything about these visors that are out there?"

"In what way?"

"I mean in a criminal way. Ever since they came out, I've been catching wind of them as the reason why crime is up so high."

"How so?"

"Drugs, sex, and today I heard rumors of murder."

"Are you shitting me? Like what? How?"

"Memories. You know they store memories, right?"

"Yeah."

"I'm hearing stories of people buying other people's memories, like buying a heroin addict's memory of gettin' high. That kind of thing."

"Okay, I understand the drugs, and I don't even know if I'm against it, but the murder baffles me."

"It's the thrill, man. Kill somebody, feel the adrenalin rush, then sell the experience. You know how many people must be lining up to feel that way? From what I hear on the street, it's a lot."

"You mean people are paying to get the feeling of killing someone?"

"I know how it sounds, but that's exactly what I mean. And it's bound to get worse."

"How so?" Langley asked.

"You're not going to stop people from making themselves feel good. If the visors are what does it, and especially if they're legal, then we're shit out of luck."

"Yeah, I got that," Langley said. "Okay, thanks. Let's keep each other posted."

Langley thought about what Dennis said about the thrill effect. *What if these murders are tied in somehow?*

He called in and got the name of the primaries on the other murders, then he got their phone numbers. Marcello Dixon was the first. He'd caught the two cases in the projects. Samantha Reynolds got the mailman murder. Langley called Dixon, and he picked up right away.

"Dixon," he said.

"Dixon, this is Langley. I'm working the Sinclair Rush case out in Glen Echo. I wondered if we could get together and go over a few things. There might be some connection to your cases."

"Name the place," Dixon said. "I'll be done by six."

"Then how about seven o'clock by Union Station. I want to get Reynolds in on this, too."

"You got it," Dixon said. "Call me back and say exactly where."

Next, Langley called Reynolds and told her the same thing. Then he texted Dixon and suggested they meet inside of Union Station at seven.

While waiting, Langley tried to gather all the information he could on the visors. He had the department spring for a pair, but the person sent to buy them was denied access.

"What do you mean, *denied access?*" Langley asked.

"When you buy these things, you have to supply DNA. I gave mine, then it pulled up a screen that said *denied access—reason:* law enforcement. When I asked for an explanation, the lady working the counter said they won't sell to anyone associated with law enforcement, including attorneys or judges."

"Makes you wonder what they're hiding, if they won't let cops buy a pair."

"Not just buy a pair either. I've inquired since trying to purchase them, and no one but the buyer can wear them, or make them work. If they try, they get the *denied access* message."

"Son of a bitch. Okay, thanks." Langley said.

B y ten past seven they had all arrived. Langley suggested they get some coffee and chat to discuss the cases.

"I didn't come here for a therapy session," Reynolds said. "Let's hear what you want."

"Tell me about your case," Langley said.

"Not much to tell," Reynolds said. "A postal worker doing his job was shot and killed."

"Where?"

"While he was on his normal route, in the city. And before you go blaming the neighborhood, know that this was the same route he'd had for twelve years. All the people knew him and, apparently, liked him."

Langley turned. "What about you?"

Dixon looked at both of them, then said, "Two kids, seventeen years old. They were walking the neighborhood when somebody shot them. No reason. I'm still investigating, but so far it doesn't look like they were doing anything wrong."

"Any surveillance on either of them?"

Reynolds and Dixon both shook their heads.

"What about yours?" Dixon said.

"Guy going to get his morning paper off the sidewalk. Someone walks up and shoots him. Same thing. No reason."

"You think it's the same lunatic?" Reynolds asked.

"It might not have to be. But it might be a number of lunatics."

"How's that?" Dixon asked. "And why now? What spurred them on?"

Langley took a moment, then he said, "Maybe it's those visors?"

"What?"

"The visors, the new Memory Visors."

"Why would that be the cause?" Reynolds asked.

"From what I've been told, people are doing bad things, illegal things, then selling the memories. Some are reasonably innocent, like smoking a joint, but from there it gets more brazen. Maybe this is the ultimate?"

Dixon shook his head. "Can't believe it. Who the hell is going to kill someone so they can make a few bucks?"

"Are you joking?" Reynolds asked. "Last month I had a guy shot for fifteen dollars. Fifteen!"

"Happens all the time," Langley said. "And I'd venture to bet something like this would be in the thousands. Think about it. Every one of these killings could have been done elsewhere if they just wanted the people dead. Why kill them out in the open? Unless someone wanted the thrill of it."

"Makes sense," Reynolds said. "Think of how they were all killed. My mailman was on his job, in broad daylight. Dixon's kids were walking the neighborhood. And your guy was getting his paper, again in broad daylight. Any one of them *could* have been shot elsewhere."

Dixon nodded. "Maybe it's some kind of challenge or game. Kill someone in the open with potential witnesses around."

"We need to shut this place down," Reynolds said.

"Not going to be so easy," Langley said. "I did some digging before we met. This is not some mom-and-pop operation. It's a billion-dollar corporation. That means they're going to protect it with everything they've got, and for a company that size, it means a lot of lawyers; in fact, I tried to buy a pair to see what's inside, and the company wouldn't let me. Supposedly, they won't let anybody who is with the police buy a pair, and it's all tied to DNA."

"Gotta' be a way," Reynolds said. "I'll get working on it."

"Me too," Dixon said. "But for now, I've got to go. My wife is expecting me."

Langley stood. "All right. Let's keep each other up to speed on progress on the cases, as well as investigation into the visors."

"You got it," Reynolds said, and reached to shake hands.

"Same here," Dixon said.

On the drive from Union Station, Langley thought about nothing but the visors.

How can I get in? There has to be a way.

MEMORY LANE

Washington, D. C., March 2030

Langley drove home slowly, but resisted all temptation to stop and talk to teenagers, no matter how much they seemed to look like Eric. This happened every day—he'd see a group of kids and think one of them was his.

But Eric was dead, so logic told him they couldn't *be* Eric. Still, it was difficult to live with. Difficult to be reminded every day of what he had lost. What could have been.

Langley reached over, turned the radio up louder, and did his best to focus on the road ahead of him. He looked at the cars, covered in brown slushy snow mixed with the salt that had been spread on the streets to make driving safer, and he noticed how unsightly the street gutters were, filled with litter that was too big to fit down the sewers.

This negativity was not healthy, he knew, but it did serve a purpose. It kept him from thinking about Eric, and it worked. Since it took his mind from thinking of Eric, it had to be good. At least better than the alternative. With that resolved, he looked around to see what else was wrong with his fair city.

Langley beeped his horn at an older man who was jaywalking—dangerous considering the icy conditions of the streets—then he made a vow that whoever did this to Megan wouldn't get away. He *would* get justice for the Piersol family, no matter what it took, just like he had promised the president.

It took another twenty minutes to get home. He parked in the drive-way, went up the sidewalk, and stepped through the front doorway. The sound of dishes clanging together echoed from the kitchen. Langley ignored it, went to the bedroom, and sat on the side of the queen-sized mattress.

He stared at the blank wall while images of him and his son playing with building blocks and having a catch in the front yard rushed through him. He saw it as if it happened yesterday. Eric, with hair that always needed cutting, and a smile on his face that wouldn't quit.

"Grant! Grant, is that you? I thought I heard something."

A moment later, the bedroom door opened and Rhonda stood in the doorway staring at him. "Why didn't you answer me? You had me scared. I knew I heard something, but when you didn't answer it made we worry."

Langley kept staring at the blank wall.

"Grant. Grant, answer me. Are you all right?"

Finally, Langley broke his trance-like state and turned to Rhonda. "I'm okay. I was just thinking."

"Just thinking my ass. I saw the signs, Grant. The drawn-out expression on your face; the blank stare in your eyes. You've got to stop this. It has *got* to stop."

"I know," he said. "I know it has to stop. I'm trying, but I don't know how." Tears flowed uncontrollably. His head sagged. "Rhonda, I think I'm going crazy. I might need help. I keep seeing him in the streets. At the park. Everywhere. The other day, I even stopped and rolled down the window to call him."

Rhonda rushed to him and put her arms around his shoulders. He leaned his head on her. "It's all right," she said. "Things will be all right. We'll work this out together."

Langley cried harder. "I see him every day, hanging out on a corner or waiting in line to get on the metro. I *know* it's not him, and yet, I see him."

Rhonda patted his back. "I know. It happens to me, too. It's not our fault."

Langley's head raised. He stared at her. "Maybe it's not *your* fault, but it's mine. I could have stopped it."

"Nonsense. We've been over this before. There's nothing you could have done."

Langley raised his voice. "Nothing I could have done? I spend all day on the streets helping other people, but when my son needed me, I was nowhere. I let him die."

"You did nothing of the kind. If you had, I wouldn't be here with you. I loved Eric, too, you know. He was my son as much as yours."

"Yeah, but I should have stopped him that night. He asked to go out and I said okay. In my gut I didn't like it. I should have said so."

"And you think he would have listened? You remember Eric. He was strong-willed. He would have fought with you until you said it was okay."

Langley let the tears come out harder. He shook his head, and the harder the tears flowed the harder he shook his head. "Maybe if I'd have gone out and looked for him. Maybe if I'd have stopped him somehow. Kept him in and played one of those asinine video games. If I'd have done that, he wouldn't be dead, and I wouldn't be sitting here thinking about it."

"Stop it, Grant. There's nothing you could have done."

"When he didn't come home on time, I should have gone looking. Maybe I'd have found him before something happened."

"You wouldn't have. You remember the report. It said he was shot at 9:30. That was far before his curfew."

"You've got an answer for everything, don't you?"

Rhonda stroked his hair. "No, not everything. I'm trying to be logical. If a person looks hard enough they can find a reason to fault themselves for anything. But this wasn't your fault. You have *got* to accept that."

"Rhonda, don't you think I've tried? I try every day, but all I come up with is that it was my fault. *Mine.*"

Rhonda leaned down and hugged him. "You can't think like that, Grant. We've been through this before. It must have been God's will for him—"

"God's will! Are you crazy? If it was God's will, screw Him. How could any God be decent if He took our son away? Snatched him from our arms in the prime of life."

"Grant, you can't talk like that."

"I can, and I will; in fact, I am. And I'm going to continue to talk that way."

"Grant..."

Langley stood and walked, slowly pacing the floor and shaking his head. "Yes, I said his name. His name was Eric. And even though I hadn't said it but a few times before tonight, I said it earlier and I'm saying it now. I'm sorry, Eric. I'm sorry for failing you. I wish that I could go back in time and do it over again."

Rhonda placed her arms over his shoulders and leaned against his back. "Don't, Grant. Stop blaming yourself. It does no good to blame anyone. He's gone, and no amount of blame or regret or anything will bring him back. We have to live with that. Somehow, we have to."

Langley broke down. He turned and hugged Rhonda and then he squeezed her tightly. "I should have done something, baby. I should have helped."

She patted his back and whispered in his ear. "It's all right, Grant. It's all right. We've still got each other."

He held her tightly. "Do we? Sometimes I wonder."

She broke the embrace and grabbed him by the hand. "Come and eat. I have tomato basil soup and we have a little bucatini left that I can heat up."

Langley swiped his sleeve across his eyes, just like he'd seen the president do earlier. "Soup sounds good," he said. "Thanks. And thanks for being patient."

"No need to thank me," Rhonda said. "I'm here forever."

A LARGE SELECTION

Washington, D. C., March 2030

Christopher walked into McCabe's office and quickly took a seat. "You called me, sir?"

"I need to see what's going on with the visors and the database."

"We've already got some new ideas based on suggestions from users."

"What kinds of ideas? And more importantly, will they make us any money?"

"I think one of them could be huge. I've tentatively named it the names database. Of course, you'll want to rename it, but that's okay for a working project."

"What is it and what does it do?" McCabe asked.

Christopher pulled a manila folder from his briefcase and spread the contents out on the desk. "This is going to be dynamite for the sex category, but it could apply to any."

"Go on."

"Example: suppose you see an ad on TV of a woman selling Audis and you say to yourself, *Man I'd love to fuck her.* The next question is 'Why not do it'?

"But the problem is how do you do it? With this enhancement, it's no problem. A person would go to the names database—or whatever you decide to call it—type in 'Audi ad + sexy woman', and any other information they might have, then the database will produce her name if possible. And chances are it's more than possible—it's probable."

"I'm liking it so far," McCabe said.

"Then go back to the main database, choose the category, say 'sex' and type in her name. The database will show you all sex memories for sale featuring that woman. When you get a hit, you buy it."

"Damn, Christopher, I like that idea."

"The same holds true for anything. If you want to know what it feels like to be stung by a wasp, type it in. It will produce results listing different part of the body, such as, stung on eyelid, stung on finger, on nose, on lips, on thigh…

"We've refined the database so that anyone can find almost anything with little or no effort. And *that* should push sales of memories through the roof."

"We still need people to think of what they want or they won't know what to look for."

"Don't worry. I may have a solution for that also. When a person first enters the database area, we have ads running that provide examples of what a person might be interested in."

"What do you mean?"

"Show a picture of a dentist working on somebody followed by a voice saying 'Need a bridge put in? Or a root canal done? See what it feels like first.' Then you'd have a built-in link they could click to buy it. Or buy any one of many."

"We could do that for anything, I'm guessing."

"Anything at all. How many people have a fear of getting a colonoscopy or of getting a stent put in?"

"Damn, this really could be big."

"And that's just the medical. Think of the thrills section. How does it feel to go 120 mph? Or ask people if they've ever been driving fast down the road and hit a patch of ice? Then tell them now you can do it safely, without hitting a bridge or another car or a tree. Then provide the link."

"Keep going. I'm all ears," McCabe said.

"Ever do a high-dive into a pool? Jump from a second-story window? Parachute from a plane? Scuba dive with sharks or barracudas? Or catch a cobra or a rattlesnake? With Memory Visors, you can do it all from the safety of your home."

"Sounds good," McCabe said.

Christopher smiled. "Hold on to your seat. We're not done yet. Imagine this."

"I'm ready," McCabe said.

"You can do all of this and more when you *subscribe* to the thrill section of memories. Each month you'll get a new thrill to experience. And it's not random. You choose from hundreds and select the one you want. It only costs twenty-nine dollars per month. Or whatever you want to charge."

"Oh my God, that's fantastic. It's a way to guarantee money for the memories."

"We're still not done," Christopher said. "The newest development is the 'request a memory' section. It's a new twist, to go along with the search names database."

"How does it work? What does it do?"

"Right now, the sellers of memories can opt to remain anonymous, which is the safest way, or they can provide names so that others can search for them *by name* to see what else they have for sale. It's like looking for other movies by the same actor or other books by the same author or other songs by the same musician."

"What makes this different? We already have something similar."

"Now they won't need a name. We'll have the name in our records, so the seller can remain anonymous and a buyer can still search what else that seller has for sale by clicking a link that might say 'More memories by same person.'"

McCabe clapped his hands. "Christopher, this is more than I expected. Good job. Let's get it refined and fine-tuned, then get it out there. I want it live in two weeks."

"You can count on it, sir."

WHO CALLED WHOM

Washington, D. C., March 2030

"How do you want to work this?" Langley asked.

Dennis looked at the pile of paperwork in front of him. "First we need to get the phone numbers. Give me the names, and I'll call Justin."

Langley gave Dennis the names of all the kids; there were twenty-six. "I sorted them alphabetically so that if he has their numbers in his phone contact list, which I'm sure he does, then he'll have easy access."

"Good," Dennis said. "Now let's hope he's cooperative."

Dennis dialed Justin's number and waited for him to answer. "Justin, this is Dennis Markum. We met earlier."

"Yes. I remember," Justin said. "Did the pictures help?"

"We're not sure yet. But I do need one more favor. If you could give us the phone numbers of Megan's friends, that would save a lot of time."

"What do you need the phone numbers for?"

"I need to ask a few questions. Why? Is it a problem?"

"I don't know. Pictures are one thing, but phone numbers? Most of these are cell phones. I don't know if I should give them out without an okay."

Dennis exhaled a deep frustrating sigh. "Justin. I'm with the Secret Service. I work for the president. I'm *not* going to be making spam calls to these kids."

Justin laughed. "No timeshare condo sales?"

"None at all," Dennis said.

"I still don't know if I'm comfortable giving them to you."

"Justin, you want to help Megan, right? If so, you'll do this. It might help."

Justin sighed, then said, "Okay, let's do it, but don't tell them that you got the numbers from me. It'll be my ass."

"You got it," Dennis said. "How do you want to work it? Do you want me to give you the names alphabetically?"

"That'll work. Shoot."

Dennis read the names to Justin, and almost as quickly as Dennis said their name, Justin provided a number. When they reached Samartha Vellana, Dennis said, "That's it. That's all of them."

"Okay," Justin said. "Let me know if you need anything else."

"We shouldn't. This should be good. And thanks for your cooperation."

Dennis hung up and turned to Langley with the list in hand. "Got them all," he said. "Justin came through for us."

Langley looked at the numbers, then said. "I presume these are cell phones?"

"That's what Justin said—well, he said most of them were."

Good, I'll make a copy of the list, and we can split the numbers up."

"But split them up to do what?" Dennis said.

"First, we see if any calls were either received or made from these numbers between 8:30 and 11:00 the night in question. If so, we then get the phone carrier to get us a location. If it's on any of the routes between Bethesda and Pentagon City Mall, we then check surveillance at *all* locations and see if we can spot them."

"I like it," Dennis said. "I like it a lot. Let's get moving. But we need to get a warrant."

"We don't have time for a warrant," Langley said. "I know guys at Verizon and AT&T. Between the two of them, that should cover most of the phones. If a few of them use another carrier, we'll have to wing it."

They worked several hours and found that seven of the twenty-six people had received calls during the time period. Three were with Verizon, two with AT&T, one Sprint, and one T-Mobile.

"I'll take Verizon and Sprint," Dennis said. "You get T-Mobile and AT&T."

"Here's another one with AT&T," Langley said. "Never mind. It's Justin."

"Take it anyway," Dennis said. "You've got one less than me."

"Are we going to need a warrant or a court order for this?"

"Not necessary," Dennis said. "We can get the location data with an administrative subpoena."

Dennis and Langley got to work. After several more hours, they had what they needed. Of the eight possibilities, four were in Bethesda around ten o'clock, one was in Frederick, and one in Baltimore. That left only two numbers, both of which were near the Francis Scott Key Bridge at ten-fifteen and eleven o'clock.

"Which two are we talking about?" Langley asked.

"Bridgette Mercer and ... Justin," Dennis said.

"Justin? I thought he was home all night studying for a test?"

"That's what he said. I guess we need to look into this further," Dennis said. "Boyfriend or not. This makes him a suspect."

"Besides, I don't see Bridgette doing something like this. First of all, she'd have had to have an accomplice to do the rape, and besides, I don't see a girl doing this to another girl."

"Me neither," Dennis said. "We'll check it out, but I doubt if it will go anywhere."

"What time was that call to Justin? It was an incoming, right?"

Dennis looked at the sheet. "Yes, an incoming, and it was right at 11:00. That must have been the call from the president about Megan's condition."

"So why would Justin tell us he was home, then give us the phone numbers that would hang him?"

"I don't know. But to be sure, let's go back over the bridge surveillance and see if we can spot him."

Forty-five minutes later, Langley called out. "Got him."

Dennis stopped what he was doing and came to stand beside Langley. "Where?"

Langley pointed to a car just passing under the cameras. "Right there," he said.

When Dennis looked closely, it was plain to see who it was. A glance might have missed him, but close scrutiny revealed Justin as the driver. No one else was with him.

"Looks like McCabe has some explaining to do," Dennis said.

"And a *lot* of explaining at that," Langley said.

"You want to go out there now?" Dennis said. "Or should we wait until tomorrow?"

"No time like the present," Langley said. "You drive."

"Hang on," Dennis said. "We might need a warrant before proceeding. This kid will have the best lawyer money can buy."

"Then file for one, and we'll go see him tomorrow."

Dennis nodded. "I think that would be better."

The next day, using a sympathetic judge and the president's influence, they obtained a warrant, then drove to McCabe's house.

Dennis made his way to Bethesda in reasonable time, and after parking outside of McCabe's house, they got out and knocked on the door. Morgan answered in his stuffy, unfriendly manner and said he'd fetch Justin.

Dennis shifted weight from one foot to another while waiting, and Langley leaned against the brick wall. After a few moments, Justin showed up.

"What's up? Did the information I gave you guys help?"

"It might have," Langley said. It certainly raised some questions."

"What kind of questions?" Justin asked.

"Like why you said you were home when we have you on surveillance cameras going over the Francis Scott Key Bridge?"

Justin laughed. "You must be mistaken. I was in my room."

"Not going to cut it," Langley said. "We have you dead to rights. The image is as clear as can be."

Just then McCabe senior walked in from the kitchen. "Is something wrong, Justin?" Then he looked at Langley and Dennis, and asked, "Who are you?"

"Detective Grant Langley," he said, showing his badge. "And this is Agent Dennis Markum."

"Agent? What are you doing here? What do you want with my son?"

"We have a few questions for him," Langley said. "If it's—"

"No, it's not all right. No matter what you were going to ask. My son will only speak through his attorney. He won't say another word." Then McCabe turned to Justin and said. "That'll be all, Justin. I'll see you in the kitchen."

"We just had a few questions regarding his whereabouts on the night of his girlfriend's assault."

McCabe stepped close and whispered. "I don't care what questions you had. I'm not going to stand by while you railroad him into something he didn't do. You can call tomorrow and speak to his attorney. I'll have him engaged before noon."

"If that's the way you want to play it, Senator. We'll be back tomorrow."

On the way back to the car, Dennis said. "We better put a car on the house in case he tries leaving. With the money these people have, no telling where he might go."

Langley pulled his phone out and punched a button. "I'm on it. We'll have to wait until somebody arrives, though."

"No problem. I've got nowhere to go."

A half an hour later a patrol car pulled alongside them. The officer on the passenger side rolled his window down. "This the house?" he asked, gesturing to McCabe's.

"That's the one," Langley said. "Make sure the kid doesn't leave. The Senator can or the servant can leave, but not the kid."

"You got it," the officer said. "See you later."

Dennis started the car and drove off at a slow pace. "We need to get our ducks in a row," he said. "McCabe isn't going to let his baby boy go down easy."

"But he *is* going down. You know, now that I think about this. In hindsight, maybe Megan calling his name when she woke those few times was *not* her calling *for* him, but her telling us it was Justin who did it."

"Son of a bitch," Dennis said. "You might have something there."

"In that case, head back to the station. We'll work on our stories."

"What stories are we supposed to work on?" Dennis asked.

"The way I see it, McCabe's lawyer will do everything possible to push on the fact that we didn't have a warrant. So that's what we need to work on."

"Then we better get creative," Dennis said. "Because we *didn't* have one."

WHAT CAME FIRST—THE BRIDGE OR THE PHONE?

Washington, D. C., April 2030

Langley was parking his car at the station when his phone rang.

"Langley, it's Dennis. We might have a problem"""

Langley laughed. "When don't we have a problem. I'm used to it."

"Yeah, but this could be a big problem. The DA asked to see us. It seems like McCabe's attorney requested a pretrial hearing on the legality of the phone-record search. If the judge throws that out, we're screwed. If we don't have the phone records, we don't have the footage of Justin crossing the bridge—and if that happens, we've got nothing."

It didn't take Langley long to respond. "Then we'll have to make sure the judge doesn't throw out the phone-record search."

"And how the hell are you going to do that?"

"We'll do it. Trust me. Meet me at that café in DuPont Circle and we'll discuss."

"I can be there in twenty minutes," Dennis said.

"I'll be waiting," said Langley.

Twenty minutes later, Dennis parked and went inside to meet Langley. A coffee was waiting for him. "Hope it's not too cold," Langley said. "It's been sitting here for a few."

"I'm fine," Dennis said. "I'm one of those assholes who can even drink cold coffee."

Langley shivered. "Tell me what's up."

"The DA said Justin's lawyer is screaming bloody murder that we pressured him into okaying his phone-record search and into providing the other kids' names."

"And they're buying that shit?" Langley asked.

Dennis cocked his head. "Guess. If you're a judge in D.C. and you have to believe either a cop or a senator's son, who would you pick?"

"Okay, let's look at it a different way. Legally, what is the problem?"

"Legally, they're probably right. We should have gotten a warrant before getting the phone records from the phone company or the names from Justin."

"Okay, I have an idea," Langley said. "We might have to stretch the truth, but if we do, I think it will work."

"I'm listening," Dennis said.

Three days later, Langley and Dennis met the Assistant DA, Raul Moritz, at the pretrial hearing. Justin's lawyer was waiting when they arrived, and the judge showed up a few minutes later. Langley leaned toward Dennis and whispered, "I guess it's okay for judges to be late."

Dennis smiled, and said, "Always. I think it's considered fashionable."

Justin's lawyer stood, nodded to Moritz, and faced the judge. "Your Honor, I'm Richard Young representing the defendant. I move to dismiss any charges brought against my client or any charges intended to be brought against him as a result of the phone-record search you have before you."

"And why is that?" the judge asked.

"The search was obtained without a proper warrant, and my client, the son of distinguished Senator Richard McCabe, was pressured into giving the police his permission as well as the names and phone numbers of numerous friends."

"How so?"

"My client said he was uncomfortable giving out the numbers, but Agent Markum pressured him into doing it."

The judge looked over at Markum. "Is that right?"

Dennis nodded. "It is, Your Honor. But we never forced him. I simply mentioned that he'd be helping his girlfriend—who, I might add, is the president's daughter—find justice."

"Is that right, Counselor?" the judge asked Young.

"That's not the point, Your Honor. It doesn't matter who the person is or what it's about. The point is that Agent Markum should never have asked for the phone numbers nor obtained the records without permission."

"And how do the phone records affect the case?"

"Without the phone records, they would have no way of proving where my client was or at what time."

Langley stood. "Your Honor, if I may?"

"You should let your attorney speak, Detective."

"I understand, Your Honor, but since this is a pretrial hearing, and since so much is riding on the outcome, including justice for Megan, who is still in a coma, I wanted to make sure you understand."

"Go ahead, then, if it's all right with Mr. Moritz."

"Fine by me," Moritz said.

Langley straightened his tie, and said, "While it's true that Agent Markum asked Justin for the phone numbers, and while it's true that we obtained those numbers without a warrant, the incriminating part of the evidence had already been found. So if you want to throw out the phone records, do so, but we would have gotten them eventually as a normal course of investigation. It is a case of inevitable discovery, Your Honor."

Young almost leaped from his seat. "Nonsense! They got the bridge surveillance based on the phone records."

"Not true, Your Honor. We had pulled bridge surveillance as part of the normal investigation. We presumed that whoever did that heinous act to Megan must have known her. This was based on the brutality of the crime. And since we presumed the person who did this knew her, we presumed that person probably lived in, or near, Bethesda. If that were the case, we further presumed that the person would have taken the most direct route from Bethesda to the mall, which would take him over the Francis Scott Key Bridge. It was because of *that* logic, that Agent Markum and I requested the bridge surveillance. After close examination, we identified Justin McCabe driving over the bridge during the time in question—a time, I might add, when Justin told us he had been at home, studying."

"And the surveillance was obtained when?"

"Two days prior to the phone records, Your Honor. The phone records were only to back up the information we already had. We had video of Justin going over the bridge shortly before 11:00 pm, and we had a statement from the president that he had called and spoken to Justin at approximately that same time. It was standard police investigation to take the next logical step and obtain the phone records. At best, Justin could have saved himself a day or two by us waiting for a warrant. As I said, it was *inevitable*."

"And you'll swear to this?"

"Better than that, Your Honor." Langley approached the bench, holding a slip of paper. "Here is the receipt for the bridge surveillance. And as you can see, it is dated two days prior to Agent Markum talking to Justin."

Young stood again. He had gotten to his feet almost before Langley sat down. "Your Honor, this is nonsense. The only issue here is whether they had a warrant? and the answer is *no*."

The judge thought for a moment, then said, "I beg to differ, Mr. Young. I agree with Detective Langley that discovery of the phone records was inevitable, and based on this receipt, which shows the delivery date of the surveillance videos, I am allowing use of all of it."

Young made a few more motions and a few more objections, but it was over. They were going to get the evidence entered, and Langley felt sure it would convict Justin.

On the way out of the courtroom, Dennis put his arm on Langley's shoulder. "You did pretty good back there, Langley."

He smiled. "I think it went well."

Dennis looked around to ensure they were alone, then said, "And you didn't even have to lie much."

Langley turned his head. "Do you think he's guilty?"

"I *know* he's guilty."

"Then I don't mind the lie. I'm tired of seeing scumbag rich kids get off when they should be in prison."

"I'm with you, Langley. All the way."

"Then let's put the cuffs on the kid. I don't want him running free for one more night."

"I still don't understand why the kid would have done it," Dennis said. "We need to have motive to get a smooth conviction; otherwise, people are going to believe whatever crazy story he comes up with. Even the president says they loved each other."

"Then we need to dig deeper," Langley said. "Beneath that sweet-kid image, there's a psychopath hiding somewhere."

THE SITUATION WORSENS

Washington, D. C., April 2030

L angley was at his desk when the call came in—a dead scientist found at NeuroScan's laboratory, stabbed to death.

"NeurScan? Isn't that the company that makes the visors?" Langley asked the guy sitting next to him.

"No, but they make the drug that people have to take to use the visors."

"Hey, Reilly, you got anything pressing?"

"No."

"Want to come with me? I'm going to check it out."

Reilly reached to the side and grabbed his coat. He stood and began putting it on. "Let's go. As long as you stop for coffee."

"I'll drive," Langley said. "Meet me in the parking lot."

They stopped for coffee, and twenty minutes later they pulled in front of the entrance to the lab, parking just behind an ambulance. "Looks like the crime scene crew is already here," Langley said, gesturing to another car ahead.

Once inside, Langley took over. He introduced himself and Reilly then asked everyone to introduce themselves and to state their relationship to the deceased.

Barney Franklin shook hands with Langley, then said, "Her name was Nancy Hornby. She's worked at the lab for almost ten years."

"Who found the body?" Langley asked.

"I did," Ginesh said, stepping forward. "I'm sorry for eavesdropping but I presumed you'd want to talk to me."

"And you are...?"

"Ginesh, Nancy's lab partner. We've worked together for years. We were close."

"You have any idea who would want to hurt her?" Langley asked.

Ginesh shook his head. "I have no idea. She was a good person."

"Aren't they all," Langley said. "You never hear anyone say a bad thing about the dead."

"Langley, you want to come over here?" Reilly asked.

Langley walked over slowly, then knelt next to the body. "What have you got?"

"According to the crime scene guys, she's been dead about three hours. That puts TOD at about 7:30 this morning."

"Cause?"

Reilly gestured to a pair of scissors that were now inside of an evidence bag. "Looks like the scissors. And that other guy, the one you were talking to, said they were always on the desk next to hers."

Langley looked to the side. "So it could have been an argument gone wrong? Something like that?"

"Maybe," Langley said. "Or it could have been someone who knew the scissors were there and used them. Any prints?"

"Not according to Sammy. He's not through dusting, but nothing obvious."

Langley walked over to Sammy. "Anything else on the murder weapon?"

"Nothing yet on the weapon, but from the initial looks of the wounds whoever stabbed her was about six feet tall and stabbed her in a downward motion."

"How many times was she stabbed?"

"Twice near the heart and once in the neck. Whoever did this wanted her dead for sure. I'm not sure which was first."

"Okay, thanks," Langley said. Then he and Reilly walked off. "Who had access to the lab besides Nancy and Ginesh?"

"According to Franklin, he did, and a guy named Keith Ratcliff, the CEO, and two other technicians, plus—of course, the janitorial crew."

"Then we know what to do," Langley said. "We start there and clear those people first."

"Or not."

"Yeah," Langley said. "Or not. Because the chances are, one of them did it."

"Could be somebody she let in, too."

"There's always that, but it would be cutting it close."

Reilly hollered to Sammy. "Make sure to dust for prints on the door handle and the windows, just in case. And don't forget DNA on the body and surrounding areas if you haven't done it yet."

"You want me to do the chimney, too?" Sammy asked. "This isn't my first case."

"Screw you," Reilly shot back. "Just get your shit done."

Langley and Reilly spent almost two hours going over the scene and asking questions. They interrogated the techs and the janitorial crew and talked to Franklin and Ginesh again. "We need to see Ratcliff," Langley said. "He's the only one we haven't talked to."

They were about halfway down the hall, when Ginesh came out of the men's room. He looked both ways quickly, then grabbed Langley by the arm and pulled him toward the bathroom.

"We need to talk," he said.

Langley tugged on Reilly's sleeve and said, "Come on. You need to hear if it's that important."

Once inside the bathroom, Langley asked Ginesh, "What's going on?"

"You asked earlier if anyone might want to hurt her."

"Yeah?"

"There are several people, but I couldn't say back then."

Langley took out a small notebook from his shirt pocket. "Who are you thinking of?"

"Barney Franklin is one of them, which is why I couldn't talk in front of him."

"One of them? There are more?" Reilly asked.

"Definitely. Keith Ratcliff is another. And Senator McCabe."

Langley's eyes lit up. "McCabe? Why would *he* want to hurt her? What did she have to do with McCabe?"

"He and Ratcliff control NeuroScan and the visors. If something were to happen, they stand to lose tens of millions, maybe more."

"What? McCabe? Are you shitting me?"

Ginesh shook his head. "No, and this isn't speculation. Nancy had proof that NeuroScan was causing problems with long-term use. Adverse effects, the kind that we are required to report."

"Let me guess," Langley said. "Nothing was reported."

"Not only has nothing been reported, we just told Barney about it yesterday. And I'm certain Barney would have told Keith."

"Has McCabe ever been here? At the lab?"

"Many times. At one time, his son and his son's friend were participating in clinical trials here. That was when they were friends, though. Oh, and Senator McCabe has a key, too."

Langley looked back at Reilly. "And Barney forgot to mention McCabe."

"Pretty convenient," Reilly said.

"I think it's time we found out where McCabe was this morning."

"Ratcliff, too," Reilly said.

"Yeah, both of them," Langley said. Then he turned to question Ginesh again. "You said when Vic and Justin were friends? Did they end up arguing?"

"More than that," Ginesh said. "I don't know what caused it, but whatever it was, seemed serious. Justin wouldn't even drive him home. I had to give Vic money for fares on the metro."

"And what was wrong with the drug? What problems was it causing?"

"Violence," Ginesh said. "At least we think so. The rats have shown signs of it and so have the elderly patients from Spring Meadows."

"What kind of violence?" Langley asked.

"Unexplained violence. And unprecedented. One of the rats killed his cage partner."

"Okay, thanks," Langley said, then he and Dennis left. "This could go a long way to explaining the rash of violent crime we've been having."

"As well as provide motive," Dennis said.

Langley drove to McCabe's office, and within minutes he and Reilly were shown in. Langley pulled out his badge. "I'm Detective Grant Langley and this is Detective Nelson Reilly. We have a few questions for you."

"By all means, sit," McCabe said. "What is it you want to know? I presume this is about my son."

"Actually, it's not," Langley said. "Although I am familiar with that case. As it turns out, I'm working that also."

"Case? You make it sound so formal. What is this about?"

"Where were you this morning, Senator?"

"Could you please be more specific?"

Langley laughed. "Now, you see there. That was the answer a guilty man might give. Most people would just say where they'd been and let us ask for specifics."

"Count me as someone who has had too many interactions with the law, Detective. I don't fully trust you."

"I see. Okay, let me be more specific. Where were you between 7:00 and 8:00 this morning? And, being the suspicious type, I guess you know we'll need alibi witnesses."

"I'll let my assistant know. If you give me a card for her, I'll have her call you and fill in the details."

Reilly laughed. "I'll bet you will. Tell me, though. Is it so difficult for you to remember where you were this morning? I can tell you every-place I was."

"Good for you, Detective. I applaud your memory skills. Mine, however, are not so refined. I rely on my assistant. It comes from decades of doing something useful—relying on others, I mean."

Langley reached to the side and put his hand on Reilly's forearm. He suspected Reilly was about to do something foolish. "Thank you, Senator. We appreciate your time. And we'll check with your assistant."

McCabe smiled. "She'll be in touch."

"Let me correct myself, then. We'll wait to hear from your assistant."

Langley then led Reilly out of the room.

As they walked to the car, Langley said. "Go home and cool off, Reilly. I'm going to check out something on another case."

"I'm all right," Reilly said.

"Like hell, you are. You're fuming, and I can't blame you. But still go cool off. It will do you good."

WHAT'S THE MOTIVE?

Washington, D. C., April 2030

Dennis drove south on the freeway. Langley sat quietly in the passenger seat. "Like I said, Langley, we need a motive. If we're going to get a conviction for a spoiled brat like McCabe, we have to give the jurors a reason why he did it. Especially a crime this severe."

"The visors."

"We can't use speculation as a motive. They don't even know for sure if there is a problem."

Dennis got no answer, so he prodded. "Langley. Langley, you listening to me?"

Langley shook his head vigorously, as if coming out of a trance. "Sorry, Dennis., I was thinking about this other case, the one where the scientist got killed. I really should be working that, trying to close it up."

"You should be working this, too."

"This isn't even my case. I'm helping you. I should have dumped it long ago."

"Yeah, but you didn't. And it's something you started with, so you should finish it."

"It gets to the point where you wonder *what* is worth it. You see all of these spoiled rich kids get off and say *What's the use?* I guess you never felt that way in your job."

"I don't have to experience it to know the feeling. Even ordinary citizens can feel it. People are tired of it. They want it to stop. Let's give them a reason to make it stop."

"Okay, you got it," Langley said. "Let's go talk to Vic. He might know something. Remember what Ginesh said, that he and McCabe used to be friends."

"He also said that they had a falling out," Dennis said.

"All the more reason to talk to him. He might actually say something."

"You remember his address?" Dennis asked.

"Take a left at the next light. It's not far from here."

Ten minutes later, they were sitting in front of Vic's house. There were no cars in the driveway, but lights were on in the house. "Might as well give it a try," Langley said, and he got out of the car and walked toward the house.

Vic answered the door after one set of knocks. "Detectives, I didn't expect to see you back here."

"We had a few questions," Dennis said. "Mostly about Justin McCabe."

Vic swung the door wide. "I don't know if I can help or not. Justin and I aren't close anymore."

"That's what we're here about," Langley said. "I understand there was a time when you were friends, that you participated in some clinical trials together."

"Yeah, we did, but that was a while back. Seems like forever ago."

"What happened between you two?" Langley asked.

"Megan," Vic said. "He got jealous because I thought she was hot, which she is."

"What do you mean by that? Nobody gets jealous because someone thinks a person is hot."

"Tell Justin that," Vic said. "In all fairness, I didn't just think it, I said it. I told him how hot she was, and that I'd like to...you know, do her."

Dennis shifted uncomfortably in his chair.

"See, there I go again, pissing people off. I don't mean it. I didn't mean it with Justin, I was just being crude. I thought Megan was into me, but I guess she wasn't. I tried kissing her in the hall one day, but she wouldn't have anything of it. Somebody told Justin, though, and he got pissed. I tried telling him that nothing happened, but he wouldn't listen. I haven't spoken to him since. Anyway, who can blame a guy for trying. Like I said, she's a fox."

"So Justin got jealous?" Langley asked.

"More than jealous," Vic said. "The dude wouldn't talk to me anymore. It's been a while, too, and he still doesn't talk."

"Anything else you can tell me? Either about Justin or Megan?"

Vic shook his head. "I haven't even seen Megan since the night she was attacked. And Justin doesn't act like he's in mourning or anything. He goes to visit her, but he acts the same as always otherwise. I'd think something would be different. I'm not a sympathetic person, but I think I'd show something."

Langley nodded. "Okay, thanks, Vic. You've been helpful."

"Any time, dude. Hey, don't I get some kind of get-out-of-jail-free card or something?"

Langley laughed. "I wouldn't dare," he said, then handed Vic his card.

"But the next time you get in trouble, call me and I'll see what I can do. No promises, though."

Vic smiled. "Expect a call. I'm sure I'll need it sooner or later."

"My guess is sooner," Langley said. He stood to leave. "And thanks again."

Langley and Dennis were on the way back to the station when Langley said, "You were there, Dennis. You wanted motive, now you have it. The oldest motive in the book—jealousy."

"And *that's* one that people can understand. Everyone's felt jealous at one time or another. Jealous enough to want to do something about it. Usually nothing is done; people have more control than that. But some people let jealousy rage out of control. That's when shit like this happens. That's what we'll have to prove."

"Shouldn't be hard now," Langley said. "With the bridge surveillance, phone records, and now this motive, I think young McCabe is as good as hanged. Especially if we can get even the possibility of violence introduced as a result of the drug—and we may be able to since Justin was taking it."

"Let's hope so," Dennis said. "I'd like to close this problem out. The president has been waiting a long time, and besides, this isn't my line of work."

"It doesn't show. You're doing a great job, if I must say so, and you know it pains me to say so."

"Screw you, Langley." Dennis looked to the side and coughed. "What now? Assuming we have enough to convict Justin, it's now time to get his old man. I'm convinced he either killed the scientist or had something to do with it."

"Me too," Langley said, "but this really isn't your case. It falls squarely in my lap."

"I know that, but I can help if you want me to."

Langley looked sideways to where Dennis sat, then said, "Okay, deal. I've got a partner, but you can join in. I plan on getting McCabe down to the lab tomorrow if we can. Let's talk by mid-morning and I'll let you know."

"Deal," Dennis said. "Good luck."

RATS HAVE MEMORIES, TOO

Washington, D. C., April 2030

Dennis checked in just before ten o'clock. "Anything?" he asked.

"McCabe is meeting us at the lab at one. Reilly is going with me, so meet me there, or show up here by 12:30 and we'll ride together."

"I don't know how the day is going to go, but I'll see you by 1:00, one way or the other," Dennis said.

Dennis showed up by 12:15. They shot the shit a few minutes, then headed off to the lab. Dennis rode in the back seat; Reilly up front with Langley.

"You got a plan for this?" Dennis asked.

"Tie him to the visors first to provide a motive, then prove he had accessibility to the crime scene, then try to nail him. Solving a crime like this usually involves catching a person in a lie, and people like McCabe don't know how to do much else."

"Ain't that the truth," Reilly said.

True to his word, McCabe met them at 1:00, and he had his assistant call Langley about 2:00. She filled him in on the morning schedule. The time slot that Langley was most interested in—the 7:00 to 8:00 one—was supposedly spent with Keith Ratcliff, who happened to be the number-two suspect.

"That's pretty damn convenient," Reilly said.

"And I bet there weren't any witnesses aside from them,," Langley said.

McCabe was talking to Barney Franklin on the side, when Chaz, the rat began chittering incessantly.

"For God's sake, will somebody kill that damn thing," McCabe said. "It's driving me crazy."

"I'll take care of him," Ginesh said, and moved the rat to a cage near the back of the room.

While Ginesh was making the transfer, Langley walked up to him and whispered, "Are you sure McCabe had something to do with this operation?"

Ginesh looked to make sure he wasn't being scrutinized, then said, "Senator McCabe had *everything* to do with this. He orchestrated the whole thing, but he said he didn't want his name associated with it."

"What about the stock?" Langley asked.

"I assume it's in someone else's name, but I don't know for sure."

Langley made notes, patted Ginesh on the shoulder, called research at the station and told them what to work on, then rejoined McCabe and Franklin.

"Gentlemen," Langley said. "Why don't we look at some video?"

"Porn movies?" McCabe asked.

"Not quite," Reilly said. *But I'll bet you wish they were.*

Langley started the surveillance video that he'd gotten from the outside camera. It was set for shortly after 7:00 that morning.

About 7:20, a man wearing a dark-brown hooded jacket approached from the south side, holding his head low. It looked as if he knew about the cameras, as his face was not visible at all.

"He's hiding from us," Langley said. "He knows where the camera is." When he said this, he looked to McCabe to see if it drew any reactions, but none showed.

A moment later, the man reached up and covered the camera lens with a small towel or blanket. The picture went blank, although the audio was still working.

Langley listened closely. "What's that noise?"

"It's the alarm indicating the outside door was just entered," Ginesh said. "It should only last a few seconds."

Sure enough, about ten seconds later, the alarm shut off.

"Does the lab have video inside?" Langley asked.

Ginesh shook his head. "Nothing inside the lab, just the exterior. We used to have surveillance installed, but Mr. Ratcliff removed it before the clinical trial started."

"This isn't showing anything," McCabe said. "It's a waste of time."

"Not quite," Langley said. "We now know what time the killer came here, assuming whoever came in was the killer."

A few minutes later, the man in the hooded jacket left. He was as surreptitious leaving as he was entering. No way to recognize him. He even took whatever he had used to cover the lens with him.

"How tall does he look to you?" Langley asked.

"About six feet or so, maybe more. Why?" Reilly said.

"Remember, Sammy said the attacker was probably that tall. Look at the outside wall, and mark his height by using the joints in the concrete blocks. We'll get a better idea of how tall he was that way."

There was more chittering from the back of the room where Chaz was. McCabe picked up a pencil and threw it at him. "My God, shut that thing up."

"I'll get him," Ginesh said. "He probably wants his food. It's past feeding time."

Just then, Langley's phone rang. "Hello?"

"Detective, it's Reyna in research at the station."

Langley was confused. "Yeah?"

"Are you alone?"

Langley looked around, then began walking away so he would be able to talk freely. "I am now, why?"

"I've been working on tracking the owners of that company you sent us the name of. There was nothing obvious—at first."

"At first?"

"Yeah, but when I looked further, there was a woman who received a lot of calls from a burner cell. We couldn't do anything to trace the burner, but that same burner called other numbers that were frequently dialed by Senator McCabe."

Langley thought for a moment. "No proof, but convincing nonetheless."

"That's what I thought," Reyna said.

"Okay, thanks. And text me the woman's name and number as well as the number of the burner phone."

"Will do."

A few moments later, after rejoining the group, Langley's phone sounded, indicating an incoming text. "Excuse me, gentlemen," Langley said.

He looked at the text, which was from Reyna, then immediately dialed the number Reyna had sent him for the burner phone.

Seconds later, the sound of a ringing phone could be heard in McCabe's pocket.

"Aren't you going to answer that?" Langley asked.

"No need to," McCabe said. "Probably a salesman."

"I don't think so," Langley said. He disconnected the line, then said. "Let's see if it rings again." And he hit redial. McCabe's phone rang again.

Langley nodded his head to Reilly, who pulled out his cuffs and put them on McCabe.

"What the hell are you doing? Do you know who I am?"

"Of course I do, Senator. And pretty soon, the whole world will. You'll be famous as the senator who was convicted of murder."

"You're nuts. I want to call my lawyer."

A sound emanating from Nancy's previous desk came from behind them.

"What's that?" Langley asked.

"It's the memory alarm," Ginesh said. "But there shouldn't be anything." He walked to Nancy's computer, stared at the screen, then said, "Detective, you should see this."

Langley went to stand beside him, and stared, spellbound. On the screen was a video of Senator McCabe, dressed in the same dark-brown jacket as the intruder, and he was apparently arguing with Nancy.

"Can you adjust the volume?" Langley asked. "And how are we seeing this?"

"I'm presuming it's coming from Chaz, the rat. He was the only one here, and this is his monitor." Ginesh hit a few keys, and then McCabe and Nancy could be heard.

McCabe was poking his finger at her and shouting, "You'll shut up, because if you don't it will cost you millions. Worse, it will cost me hundreds of millions. And nobody, I mean *nobody* is taking that away from me."

"Some things are worth more than money," Nancy said.

"Maybe they are," McCabe said. "But the lives of a few old stroke patients aren't. They've got nothing to live for."

"I beg to differ," Nancy said, "And no matter what you say, I'm reporting this. It's not just the clinical trial patients; it's anyone who takes that drug at that dosage for a long enough period of time. Or at least we think so."

"See, that's what I mean, you don't even know. Why don't you leave it alone until we know more?"

"Because it's probable. We need to pause the trial and do a new, clean trial, one done properly, with good supervision. Not some guy up at Spring Meadows."

"It's not going to happen," McCabe said. "I've got too much invested in this."

"I'm afraid it *is* going to happen, Senator. I'm going to the authorities tomorrow, and it won't be to your FDA buddy."

McCabe picked up the scissors from the desk and jammed them into Nancy's neck. She screamed and blood spurted all over. Next, he lifted his hand and stabbed her in the chest, twice.

"This is nonsense," McCabe said. "That's garbage. I didn't do that."

"Where is this coming from?" Langley asked for clarification.

Ginesh smiled. "Like I said, it must be coming from Chaz. It has to be."

Langley laughed. "How's that for justice, Senator? Given up by a true rat."

"You can't use images from a rat. They're not reliable," Langley said. "Besides, the whole visor thing is not reliable."

"That's not what you said."

"What are you talking about?" McCabe asked.

"When you addressed Congress, you said the visors could be used for eyewitness testimony. 'Nothing was better,' you said. 'Someone might forget what a person who committed a crime looked like, or they might mistake the make and model of a car or the license plate, but a computerized memory won't. It's invaluable. Priceless.'"

"That's nonsense," McCabe said.

"Sorry, Senator. Those are your words."

"Wait a minute," Ginesh said. "Look at monitor seven."

"What?" Langley asked.

"Monitor seven," Ginesh said. "Nancy was tagged to monitor seven. Instead of using our visors for playback, Senator McCabe's man tagged us to specific monitors so that we each could see the other's memories, which we couldn't have done if we left them on the visors. So the monitor would have the same memory as the one we just saw from Chaz, and it is irrefutable. Senator McCabe's man tied it to our DNA, just like the visors."

Ginesh and Langley walked over to the desk where monitor seven sat. Ginesh hit a key on the keyboard to wake it from sleep. In a flash, a message appeared on the screen.

You have a video waiting.

Ginesh hit *play* and the video started. It showed the same thing as the one from Chaz, only from a different angle.

"It's like a deathbed confession," Langley said, then he turned to Reilly. "Take him away, Detective. Lock his ass up with his son."

"You'll pay for this," McCabe said. "I'll get you. You must have a vendetta."

"Yeah, I've heard it all before, Senator. But I'd save my breath if I were you. You're going to need it to defend yourself at trial."

TIME TO FORGET

Washington, D. C., April 2030

Two days later, on his way home, Langley got a call. It was Dennis.

"Langley, you got your radio on?"

"No, why?"

"Turn it on to any news channel. You'll be thrilled."

Langley tuned in to WTOP, and listened.

The president has convinced Congress that NeuroScan, the drug required to operate the controversial visors for replaying memory and dreams, is a danger, and they have voted to shut down any further shipments of the drug. This happened after a scandal involving the head of the FDA, the lead psychiatrist at a local nursing home, and Senator Richard McCabe—who is under investigation for the murder of one of NeuroScan's scientists—uncovered evidence that long-term use of NeuroScan is dangerous.

Now, take a moment to listen to the president as he addresses Congress.

"I'm appalled that Senator McCabe was involved in all of this, but the evidence is overwhelming. What's more appalling is how the senator used the Constitution in his fervent defense of the company that we now know he was intimately involved with. He repeatedly referred to the company's *rights* when he talked about them in their defense.

"It's obvious now that McCabe was never defending the company's right to sell the product, just his right to make money. It's time people realized that the Constitution was written several hundred years ago. It was written by intelligent men, yes, but men who had no idea— could have had no idea—what today's technology would be like. They could not have anticipated events like this occurring. Think about that the next time someone tries using the Constitution as a basis for their rights.

"Isn't it time to stop the nonsense and the insanity, and attempt to restore the country to what it was before this whole visor thing started? I'm ready. Are you?"

The news returned to the announcer, who continued coverage on his own.

There is further evidence which shows that Senator McCabe and others involved with NeuroScan, including the CEO, knew of the danger but attempted to cover it up for reasons having to do with stock value.

In more shocking news, the president's daughter, Megan Piersol, who had been brutally attacked weeks before Christmas, has awakened from her coma and is talking. She has apparently named Justin McCabe, who was her former boyfriend, as her attacker. According to her, jealousy was the motive.

On the international front, a terrorist attack was prevented in Munich today, when...

Langley smiled. Maybe God *did* take a hand in what went on in this world. Maybe He did look out for the good guys. He brought Megan back.

Langley parked in his usual spot, got out, and walked to the door. He went inside, quietly. Rhonda was in the kitchen doing dishes. "Rhonda, I'm home."

She dried her hands on a dish towel, then turned and walked toward him.

"We finished up the case," he said. "And the president's daughter is awake."

"I heard," she said, and smiled. "It's all over the news. And the president and Congress shut down that company that makes the visors."

"And the one making the drugs," he said. "By the way, you got anything planned for tonight?"

She shook her head. "Nothing. I didn't know if you'd be working. I didn't even take anything out for dinner, but we could order pizza."

Grant took hold of her shoulders and pulled her to him. "I was thinking the same thing. We'd order pizza, then maybe pack up the things in Eric's room and put them in the attic. This weekend we can repaint it, and convert it to an arts-and-crafts room for you. You always wanted one."

"Tears formed in Rhonda's eyes. "Are you serious? Really?"

Grant kissed her. "Yeah. I'm serious. It's long overdue."

She wrapped her arms around him and squeezed. "Oh, my God, I love you. It's good to have you back."

"You'll never lose me again," Grant said.

ACKNOWLEDGMENTS

It is with great honor that I give eternal gratitude to my wife and all four of my grandkids—Giuseppe (Joey), Dante, Adalina, and Carmine. They give me the inspiration to keep going.

Special thanks to beta readers Jeanne Haskin, Rose Hutchinson, Paul Campbell, and Rick Carter-Squire. You found the mistakes I missed.

ABOUT THE AUTHOR

Giacomo Giammatteo is the author of gritty crime dramas about murder, mystery, and family. He also writes non-fiction books including the No Mistakes Careers series, No Mistakes Publishing, No Mistakes Grammar, and No Mistakes Writing.

When Giacomo isn't writing, he's helping his wife take care of the animals on their sanctuary. At last count they had forty-five animals—eleven dogs, a horse, six cats, and twenty-six pigs.

Oh, and one crazy—and very large—wild boar, who takes walks with Giacomo every day and happens to also be his best buddy.

nomistakespublishing.com
gg@giacomog.com

Old Wounds

Promises Kept, the Story of Number Two

OTHER BOOKS COMING SOON

You can always see the current and coming-soon books on my website.

Fiction

A Promise of Vengeance (Fantasy)

My first fantasy, and the first book in a four-book series—the Rules of Vengeance. (Three are already written and the fourth is being outlined.)

Murder Is Invisible (going through editing)

Frankie and Nicky are back.

Premeditated, Redemption IV

A Hard Life, the Story of Tip Denton

Non-Fiction

No Mistakes Grammar, Volume III, More Misused Words. (being proofread)

Whiskers and Bear—Volume I of the Life on the Farm Series (sent to editor)

No Mistakes Publishing, How to Self-Publish a Book

No Mistakes Writing, How to Write a Bestseller

Children's Books

No Mistakes Grammar for Kids, Volume I—Much and Many (Sent to editor)

No Mistakes Grammar for Kids, Volume II—Lie and Lay (Sent to editor)

No Mistakes Grammar for Kids, Volume III—Then and Than (Sent to editor)

Shinobi Goes to School—Life on the Farm for kids. (working on illustrations)

Get on the mailing list and you'll be sure to be notified of release dates and sales.

<u>Mailing list</u>

And don't forget to leave a review!